About the Author

Martin Butler is a freelance writer and editor focused on academia. This is his first novel. During the 1960s, his mother and grandmother were stalwart Hertfordshire women's institute members. Martin's childhood memories of WI fêtes and mystery tours lovingly inform the novel's characters and the world they inhabit, as do his real-life adventures: surviving dynamite-throwing protesters in South America, skydiving out of a bullet-ridden plane in Africa and being submerged in a Pacific Ocean sinkhole. He lives in Vancouver, Canada, and is married to a fearless adventurer.

The Queens of Kaboom

Martin Butler

The Queens of Kaboom

Vanguard Press

VANGUARD PAPERBACK

© Copyright 2025
Martin Butler

The right of Martin Butler to be identified as author of
this work has been asserted by him in accordance with the
Copyright, Designs and Patents Act 1988.

All Rights Reserved

No reproduction, copy or transmission of this publication
may be made without written permission.
No paragraph of this publication may be reproduced,
copied or transmitted save with the written permission of the publisher, or in
accordance with the provisions
of the Copyright Act 1956 (as amended).

Any person who commits any unauthorised act in relation to this publication
may be liable to criminal prosecution and civil claims for damages.

A CIP catalogue record for this title is available from the British Library.

ISBN 978-1-83671-025-7

This is a work of fiction. Names, characters, businesses, places, events and
incidents are either the products of the author's imagination or used in a
fictitious manner. Any resemblance to actual persons, living or dead, or actual
events is purely coincidental.

Vanguard Press is an imprint of
Pegasus Elliot Mackenzie Publishers Ltd.
www.pegasuspublishers.com

First Published in 2025

Vanguard Press
Sheraton House Castle Park
Cambridge England

Printed & Bound in Great Britain

Dedication

For Jennifer, the original Dynamite McQueen.

Acknowledgements

To Jennifer Butler, your support and encouragement throughout the writing and editing process gave me the confidence to finish the book and share it with the outside world. To Sue Sutherland and Liz Roberts, thank you for reviewing early drafts and providing fantastic feedback. To Iolanda Millar, your knowledge of the publishing industry and advice was invaluable. To Pegasus Publishers, thank you for taking a chance on a new author.

The Queen's Gambit

The queen smoothed out her skirt, waiting for the prime minister to enter, bow and sit opposite.

"Thank you for coming, Prime Minister. I do so enjoy our discussions."

"Good afternoon, ma'am," said the prime minister as the afternoon tea tray was placed between them. With genuine affection, he smiled at the young woman, over fifty years his junior, to whom he had been reporting on a weekly basis since her ascension to the throne in 1952, barely three years prior.

"I am delighted to see you twice this week. Did you enjoy the film?"

"Pardon, Your Majesty. I mean, ma'am?" said the prime minister, stymied by this unusual opening to his weekly audience with the Crown.

"The Royal Command Performance, Prime Minister, of *Dynamite McQueen and the Queens of Kaboom*. Not my cup of tea, but my husband and sister seemed to enjoy it."

"My apologies, ma'am. I was called away on urgent business before I could take my seat."

"I am sorry to hear that, Prime Minister. I presume you are referring to the recent security breaches from which our nation has been suffering."

"Yes, ma'am, you are quite correct. Although I was unsuccessful in viewing what I am sure is a paragon of British film-making at its best, I could not escape being buttonholed by the director requesting my permission to crash a double-decker bus into 10 Downing Street for the next Dynamite McQueen adventure."

"Ah, yes, Mrs Currie of the Eighth Wonder Film Company. Quite the force of nature, isn't she? She also took the opportunity to request permission to fly an aeroplane into Buckingham Palace! I refused, of course. We cannot have the great British public entertained by symbols of the establishment being brought to their knees, can we? However, I do appreciate her vigour. It cannot be easy being the female director of the most successful film series in British history. I do believe their box office takings could eliminate the national debt."

"Maybe we should nationalise them," said the prime minister, suppressing a laugh. "Nevertheless, I did give Mrs Currie permission to crash a bus into any building on Fleet Street housing certain national newspapers."

"Oh, Prime Minister, I do enjoy your sense of humour. Now, shall we get on? What pressing matters of government do you have for me this week?"

Once he had finished, the prime minister waited expectantly for the queen's insightful questions. An inexperienced head of state she might be but her depth of historical knowledge, insight into current affairs and capacity for sage counsel in someone so young constantly surprised him.

"Now, before you leave, Prime Minister, I have my

own question related to the security of the country."

The prime minister sat up a little straighter, sensing a slight edge in the queen's voice.

"Please go on, ma'am."

"Prime Minister, I think you remain unaware that near the end of the war, we met in person."

"I do not think so, ma'am. I would have remembered."

"I would like you to take your mind back to 1945. Do you remember the radical *Fleur de Lys Crime Syndicate* and the role it played in supporting Germany's last-ditch attempt to invade our shores?"

The prime minister's cup rattled in its saucer and he failed to notice his teaspoon dropping to the carpet. "Ma'am, may I ask how you know this piece of classified information?"

"If you remember, Prime Minister, the intelligence services were not quite functioning as they ought during the early days of the war, so the Women's Intelligence Service was launched to plug gaps and shore up weaknesses."

The prime minister nodded slowly, wondering where the queen was taking him.

"And do you remember that the Women's Intelligence Service uncovered a plot to overthrow the government led by a clandestine faction of syndicate members and fascist subversives based at Cuffley Manor in the Hertfordshire village of Maiden Combust? Specifically, do you remember the night the group was captured?"

"Indeed, ma'am, I do remember that night in excruciating detail. But I am curious, how you know about what was a top-secret operation?"

"In addition to being a driver for the Auxiliary Territorial Service during the war, I also drove for Women's Intelligence. I cannot claim that my contribution was significant, but I was present that night and did my job."

"You were present! That is a turn up for the books! And one that can never be written."

"And I am sure your role that night was a first for you as well?"

"It was indeed. I was the bait used to catch a very big fish."

"Our meeting was brief, Prime Minister. I drove you to the rendezvous point."

"My apologies, ma'am. I had no idea my driver that night was you." The prime minister was flooded with anxiety. For many years, he had obsessed about how close the country had come to 'all hell breaking loose' as his mother was wont to say, quoting 'Paradise Lost'.

"I think you were rightly preoccupied with the matters at hand and part of my job was to maintain my anonymity. Much good eventually came out of that dark night, of course. We would not be here now if things had turned out differently. We repelled the Germans. Lord Cuffley survived to father twin sons, and the MacGuffins were moved to your constituency of Woodford and had three daughters."

"And may the Cuffley and MacGuffin families never meet again," said the prime minister ruefully.

The queen leaned forward, picked up the prime

minister's teaspoon and refilled their cups. "I do need to raise the important subject of our current intelligence services and how they continue to suffer from the same weaknesses today as they did during the war."

The prime minister nodded slowly, wondering what was coming next.

The queen took a sip of tea and continued, "I have it on good authority that the litany of recent security breaches, the prospect of further economic austerity, increasing levels of labour unrest and this ghastly, unrelentingly winter weather provide the perfect conditions for the British fascist movement to emerge from the shadows and regain popularity."

The prime minister deliberated carefully before he spoke somewhat nervously, "May I ask, ma'am, on whose authority you are referring?"

"Yours, Prime Minister. Yours."

"And may I ask how you came to be party to this confidential information, ma'am?"

"I have my sources, Prime Minister, all in due course. What I would like to discuss is what we can do immediately to address the woeful incapacity of the intelligence services to meet the nation's security needs, particularly their inability to conduct surveillance and gather, analyse and share information with the speed the situation requires. The boys are not sharing their toys, Prime Minister. Would you agree?"

"Well, merging twenty intelligence units into MI-5 and MI-6 has helped, but I admit challenges remain. It is an extremely complex situation, and I have our best men on to it, I assure you."

"You only having your best men on it is why I am going to make a proposal."

"Ma'am?"

"I would like your government to resurrect WI-5, the Women's Intelligence Service, to perform the same function now as during the war. Fast, accurate information gathering, analysis and dissemination."

The prime minister frowned slightly. "The contribution WI-5 made to the war effort certainly helped turn the tide."

"Not only that, Prime Minister, and not to put too fine a point on it, they saved your bacon. Especially on that fateful night in 1945."

"Indeed," said the prime minister, feeling there was more to come.

"I know you are a pragmatic man, Prime Minister. You have proof that the injection of the Women's Intelligence Service and, may I say, women's intelligence in general into the security services provided unparalleled value. You may be interested to know that WI-5 did not completely cease operations when the war ended, despite being formally disbanded, rather heedlessly if I may say so. Personnel have stayed in place, ready for action with their skills woefully underutilised. What they lack are the necessary resources, and by resources, I mean money. When you return here next week, I would be most obliged if you would bring me written confirmation of the Treasury's approval to relaunch WI-5 with the requested funds."

The queen opened her handbag, removed a sheet of parchment paper and handed it to the prime minister.

"I hope my request has been clearly expressed."

The prime minister was a little unsure as to whether this was a question or a declaration. "Very much so, ma'am. I can certainly see the need and, as you say, we do have proof that the model works." He paused and added hesitantly, "May I ask if you would be so good as to enlighten me regarding the WI-5 personnel who have remained in place since the end of the war?"

The queen removed a second sheet of paper from her handbag. "I suggest, Prime Minister, that you contact these women immediately."

Mrs Morag Fyfe.
Mrs Joan Spatchcock.
Mrs Blessing Otukile.
Dynamite McQueen.

The prime minister reviewed the four names, his eyes widening with each, and took a deep breath as the events of that terrifying night in 1945 played in his head in full technicolour. He would never forget the enemy being disarmed by a phalanx of high kicks, the terrifying loud rumble of the Showgirl Squadron's final approach and how scared he had been flying through the air. "Of course, I remember Mrs Fyfe, Mrs Spatchcock and Mrs Otukile for the part they played in 1945. But surely you cannot be suggesting I talk to the fictional heroine of a British adventure film!"

"Prime Minister, of course not. Dynamite McQueen is the codename for WI-5's most special agent. It is what the Americans call an 'in-joke'. If I revealed her real name, I would be obliged have you hung, drawn and quartered. Do not look alarmed, it is just my attempt at gallows humour. I suggest you talk to Mrs Fyfe first. She has remained at London headquarters and will put you in touch with the others. And also, please talk to your wife, Prime Minister. Lady Churchill is a stalwart supporter of her local women's institute. She will fill you in."

"My wife! The Women's Institute!"

"Yes, your wife, Prime Minister. You must have been aware that WI-5 and the WI were deeply intertwined during the war. My joining the WI in 1943 led directly to recruitment by WI-5, and many women's institutes throughout the country still have a Cloak and Dagger Committee acting as cover for WI-5 operatives, conducting on-the-ground surveillance."

The prime minister's mind fizzed alarmingly. What had been going on right under his nose?

***

Two months later, WI-5 was relaunched by Winston Churchill as his last act as prime minister before retiring. And eleven years later, in 1966, with the eyes of the world on England's hosting of the World Cup at Wembley, the MacGuffin sisters met the Cuffley brothers, the Showgirl Squadron took to the skies once again, and all hell broke loose.

1966 and All That

In her Ridgeway Council Estate flat on the outskirts of Hertford, a mile from Cuffley Manor across fields, a rabbit warren and the town dump, Regina MacGuffin [twenty-one, meticulous, favourite film: documentaries] wrestled with opening a packet of custard creams while Ashwariya Raj [twenty-three, fearless, favourite film: *Hell Drivers*] let out a deep sigh.

"Is there any way someone in our line of work can avoid sabotaging a serious relationship? GloGlo thinks I am holding something back, which of course I am, having signed the Official Secrets Act. I know she's your sister and all but I would really appreciate your advice." Ash sat back reflecting how her life had changed since meeting Gloria MacGuffin [twenty-two, enterprising, favourite film: *Those Magnificent Men In Their Flying Machines*].

Reggie pushed the open packet across the table. "It is a cross we have to bear, Ash."

Ash looked crestfallen, as she sipped from her mug and reached for a biscuit. "Unless we can figure something out, my relationship with GloGlo is doomed. You know, this problem would disappear if WI-5 just recruited GloGlo. My goodness, that is not such a bad idea." Surprising herself, Ash instantly brightened.

"Well," said Reggie, "to recruit GloGlo, WI-5 would

require a compelling reason to take to the skies again. Remember, Joan was a high flyer twenty years ago? She would be all for relaunching the Showgirl Squadron, as it was derogatorily known by MI-5."

"So, there is hope," said Ash as she glanced at the clock. "Shouldn't Joan and Blessing be here by now? How did they get to headquarters? Minx, bus or train?"

Reggie swallowed her biscuit. "I know they didn't fly, though I wouldn't put it past Joan to land her Tiger Moth in central London."

A squeal of tyres signalled the Hillman Minx coming to a halt outside the maisonette. Reggie opened her front door and waved down at the new arrivals. Joan Spatchcock, President of the Maiden Combust Women's Institute and its WI-5 Cloak and Dagger Committee, waved back. She had called the emergency meeting that morning. Joan was intensely aware that Reggie and Ashwariya were champing at the bit for a change of pace from their regular forensic accounting (Reggie) and driving (Ash) activities, and both she and Blessing were ready to let WI-5's next generation take on a greater role.

"Such cold weather for May, and the Minx's heating wasn't functioning as well as it ought so we are frozen to the marrow," boomed Blessing, as she fumbled in the depths of her shopping bag for a Tupperware box. "These little treats should defrost us all from within."

"Hold on, ladies," said Joan. "Before my vice-president of snacking brings out her latest batch of homemade goodies, I would like to let you know that at last Madge has selected us for a special mission."

Reggie and Ash put their mugs down in unison. Joan and Blessing had their complete attention.

Joan continued, "Blessing, if you reveal your goodies, I will reveal the mission."

Blessing removed the tupperware lid with a flourish. "*Ta dah!* Let us celebrate the exciting news with my mutton rissoles. I have Innocent coming over with his new boyfriend this weekend. I want to put on a bit of a show, so Morag and I made a test batch last night. My darling boy has been playing his cards close to his chest, so I know something is up. This one could be a keeper. I have had everything crossed for the past three weeks and have been biting my tongue."

"Which I know for you is a superhuman feat," said Joan to her old friend, archly but not unkindly, while she placed a thermos on the table and nibbled on a rissole. "Tuck in, everyone, and we will begin. My goodness, Bless, Innocent will absolutely be glowing at both ends after one of these! Anyhow, your lovely boy deserves every happiness. Is his new young man another medical professional?"

"Oh, I don't think so, Joan. Hertford County Hospital has been quite picked over by now." Blessing giggled.

"And how about your upstanding daughter, Vanessa? Things going well with the Hertfordshire Constabulary? I would love to recruit her if only you would be a *soupçon* more supportive."

Blessing refused to be goaded and changed the subject. "Now, Joan, pour us all a slug of Horlicksuccino to calm down the kick of the rissoles and warm us from within."

"And to warm us from without are four stones from the aerodrome kitchen garden heated in Reggie's oven," declared Ashwariya, lifting them wrapped in tea towels onto the table.

"Right," said Joan, as she picked up a stone and put it on her lap. "Now that we can be confident of not starving or freezing, let's discuss the mission. We are about to play a pivotal part in WI-5's highest priority for 1966 – to take down the *Fleur de Lys Crime Syndicate* once and for all. This is all due to Blessing's amazing brain and Reggie's investigations into whether any financial connection remains between the Cuffley family and the *Fleur de Lys Crime Syndicate*."

Blessing grinned and Reggie looked appropriately bashful as Joan continued. "We know the syndicate's leader died last year and it is in the midst of electing a new one from its seven-member inner circle. Whichever member commits the most audacious crime during the year secures the leadership. Therefore, we expect multiple syndicate attacks throughout the year. We were in London to not only enable Blessing to perfect her rissoles but also to delve into WI-5's files and identify the most likely targets. Over to you, Bless."

Blessing's demeanour changed instantly from motherly frivolity to utter seriousness. "I uncovered multiple links between the syndicate and all major accidents and disasters occurring on British soil over the past ten years, from 1956 to now, especially those which involved significant loss of life. I deliberately cast my net wide to include aeroplane crashes, shipping and train accidents, industrial explosions, mine collapses – you know the sort of thing. Morag used the British Library to source official accident reports, local newspapers and relevant bus, train, airline and ferry timetables – anything that runs to a schedule. My hypothesis was that each disaster resulted from a series of unknown, interconnected events which would form a pattern if anyone bothered to look. A pattern that could lead us to the syndicate. If you study the knitting, you can always reverse-engineer the pattern."

"Well, Bingo Buffalo to that! Sorry, do carry on, Bless," said Joan, catching herself interrupting.

Blessing smiled. "The multiple connections we found all rested on the Eighth Wonder Film Company being reported by entertainment industry trade papers to be scouting or filming within fifteen miles from where more than two thirds of the disasters and near-disasters took place. We confirmed this by overlaying the flight plans from the film company's two aeroplanes, a large Brabazon Skyfreighter cargo plane for moving sets and equipment and the smaller Brabazon Speedbird passenger plane for transporting cast and crew."

Reggie caught Ashwariya's eye, raised an eyebrow and smiled at the mention of aeroplanes. Blessing drained her mug and clasped her hands with authority.

"Wembley Stadium during the World Cup Final in two months' time is the most likely target, as over one hundred thousand people and the royal family will be in attendance along with the world's media and millions watching on the telly. Morag and Reggie suspect the box office receipts from the Dynamite McQueen films have been financing the *Fleur de Lys Crime Syndicate* for years. She also thinks the syndicate has been using the film company's aeroplanes to move people, money and weapons around. As Wembley Stadium is barely fifteen miles away from Ravenwood Film Studios, the likelihood the syndicate will use the Eighth Wonder Film Company as cover for an attack on the World Cup Final is high."

"Brilliant work, Blessing. Over to you, Reggie, for what you have uncovered within the Cuffley Manor and aerodrome accounts," said Joan, refilling her mug. Reggie looked at each of her colleagues in turn.

"We all know the current Lord Cuffley's grandfather was an infamous fascist who played a central role in the creation of the syndicate in the 1930s. Since late last year, I have been working at Cuffley Manor, ostensibly to sort out their books after the sudden death of the current Lord Cuffley's father, last November. In delving into whether any financial connection remains between the Cuffley family and the syndicate, I have not found a sausage. The aerodrome accounts are a mess, but nothing you would not expect from a family-run business where the older generation has recently died off, leaving the younger generation completely unprepared to take over. Also, not only are they dealing with all the grief and running the estate without their dad, solicitors have contacted the new Lord Cuffley and his brother with a claim on their estate from someone purporting to be old Lord Cuffley's illegitimate son and their older half-brother. Not only does this obvious conman want the estate, he wants the title too. For now, the boys' solicitor has sent the claimant a cease-and-desist letter, as without proof he does not want the boys to be more troubled than they already are. However, although I cannot find a direct financial link between the syndicate and the Cuffley family, I have found an indirect one. Six months ago, soon after the unexpected death of the old Lord Cuffley, the Eighth Wonder Film Company contacted the newly orphaned Cuffley brothers. The company wants to explore using Cuffley Manor, grounds and aerodrome as a location for filming the latest Dynamite McQueen adventure, *Dynamite McQueen and the Hanging Gardens of Babylon*. Recently, I have been helping the boys conduct negotiations, and they signed on the dotted line yesterday. Eighth Wonder is currently shooting at Ravenwood Studios and will move to Cuffley Manor in August, paying thousands of pounds for the privilege. We already have had a visit from the production manager and set designers measuring up the rooms and gardens. As Joan says, we suspect that box office proceeds from the films fund the syndicate, and with them filming at Cuffley Manor, we have our link."

"Thank you, Reggie," said Joan. "The film company not arriving at the manor until after July 30th's World Cup Final does tend to eliminate Cuffley Manor as a base from which they will attack the World Cup. Therefore, we need to infiltrate the syndicate as soon as possible to spy on its plans. Morag suspects syndicate members have been holding secret meetings at Ravenwood Studios' Dynamite McQueen soundstage. If we could install listening devices around the soundstage before the next syndicate meeting, we will be able to eavesdrop. We suggest exploiting Reggie's legitimate connection to the film company by having her arrange for the Maiden Combust Women's Institute to go on a mystery tour of Ravenwood Studios. The Dynamite McQueen soundstage is Ravenwood's largest by far. It towers above the lot, over one hundred and fifty feet in the air. On its roof is an enormous hoarding featuring the face of Dynamite McQueen, which will be perfect for hiding the antenna and transmitter equipment. Reggie, please set up the visit with the film company, and oversee mission operations and logistics with me. Blessing, you will be in charge of communications and costuming. Ashwariya, you will be in charge of ground transportation and equipment. Reggie or Ashwariya, I think Blessing and I are getting a bit too long in the tooth to be climbing ladders. We will need one of you to install the antenna and transmitter equipment on the soundstage roof. Who is volunteering?"

Knowing that Ashwariya was afraid of heights, Reggie volunteered. "As long as you show me how to handle the equipment, I can scramble up a ladder," said Reggie, wondering what she was letting herself in for.

Ash looked at her gratefully. "Do not worry, Reg, I will show you what to do. The antenna and transmitter are simple to set up."

"Excellent," said Joan. "Does anyone have any more questions?"

"Does it matter if I cannot stomach football?" asked Reggie, smiling broadly with a glint in her eye.

Ash and Blessing chuckled. Sensing everyone might need a moment to reflect upon what they had just heard, Joan made a suggestion. "Ladies, how about we adjourn to the warm embrace of the Aviatrix Arms for a round of B-52 Bombers, and cheese and onion crisps? My treat. Then we can hash out the details of our plan. By the way, this has to be kept just between the four of us. There have been more leaks at headquarters and one of our buses was attacked in central London. Morag thinks WI-5 has a mole, and so with her encouragement, we are going rogue."

Showgirl Squadron Scramble

Three weeks later, on a bright June afternoon, Reggie stood in front of her hall mirror, evaluating. Blessing had done a sterling job coming up with outfits designed to communicate the benign activities of the Maiden Combust Women's Institute on an outing. Sea-foam green blouse, A-line crimplene mini-skirt, Marks and Spark's cardie, salad-cream-coloured coat, cat glasses, high-denier tights, capacious handbag and a shopping bag.

A grey boiler suit lay on the carpet like a discarded snakeskin. Standing beside it was Blessing, pulling off the full Margaret Rutherford in her hounds-tooth tweed three-piece, pince-nez and carrying a leather briefcase.

They both turned, as Joan appeared on the stairs, resplendent in a peacock-blue, satin character turban, poncho and go-go boots, jauntily waving her communications compact. "Do not worry, Reg, we will be with you every step of the way."

After packing a safety helmet, radio transmitter, booster antenna and the boiler suit into Reggie's shopping bag, they headed outside. Ashwariya's pride and joy had just pulled up, displaying a Bluebell Coaches Mystery Tour sign on its windscreen. Ashwariya, magnificent in her mauve driver's uniform with gold epaulettes, had arrived on the dot, having already picked up twenty unsuspecting Maiden Combust WI members dressed in florals and jewel tones.

Ashwariya's eyes widened as she gave Joan's outfit, Blessing's ensemble and Reggie's getup a horrified once over. Reggie handed Ash her shopping bag and slid her handbag under the driver's seat, meeting her eyes in the rear-view mirror and exchanging a knowing look. Ashwariya stowed Reggie's shopping bag in the rear luggage compartment.

Blessing turned on her unnecessary microphone to a raucous surge of feedback, adjusted her pince-nez and peered out at the sea of polyester. "Ladies, I know it is not much of a mystery tour when you all know today's destination is not the Ridgeway Council Estate, lovely though it is, but Ravenwood Studios. And, specifically, the studio where *Dynamite McQueen and the Hanging Gardens of Babylon*, the latest in the long line of those famous adventure films, is being filmed as we speak. I cannot guarantee we are going to see any film stars, but we will experience first-hand how a major motion picture gets made, and maybe one us will get discovered."

A ripple of excitement spread throughout the coach. "Nobby, the production manager, is expecting us in an hour, so depending on traffic we should have time when we arrive for a reviving cuppa. Does everybody have their thermoses? I have brought enough goat pasties and custard apple turnovers for all of us."

***

Less than an hour later, Ashwariya brought Bluebell, the coach, to a stop outside Ravenwood Studios' mock-tudor main gate where she opened the door to allow Blessing to glare at the approaching security guard, indicating she wasn't to be messed with. "Good afternoon, young man. I have the ladies of the Maiden Combust Women's Institute here to tour the Dynamite McQueen soundstage. They do have an appointment and I have been asked to instruct you to telephone a Mr Anubis Abdelmahmoud who, I have it on good authority, goes by the name of Nobby."

Five minutes later, Nobby bounded on to the coach. "Hello, everyone, I am so happy we could do this. We should probably get moving sharpish, as I can only let you in for an hour. If you are quiet, there might be a chance you can stay a bit longer. However, if our director, Mrs Currie, hears any noise whatsoever, she will have my guts for garters, and you will have to leave."

Once everyone had disembarked in front of the Dynamite McQueen soundstage, Ashwariya parked Bluebell next to a fire escape leading up to the roof and pretended to relax by putting her feet on the dashboard.

Nobby led the ladies through the soundstage's huge front doors and they all stopped and gasped in awe at the over one hundred feet high *Hanging Gardens of Babylon* set, exact copies of Cuffley Manor's dining room, statuary garden and the front undercarriage and nose cone of a Brabazon Skyfreighter.

"Ladies, can I trust you to wander about by yourselves? Do not touch anything as paint might still be wet. You are in luck as Mrs Currie has just now scheduled a surprise dance rehearsal on the Babylon set. I need to see if all is going according to plan. Can I leave you alone for five minutes?"

Once Nobby had disappeared, Joan, Reggie and Blessing sprang into action. After a quick reconnoitre, Joan nodded at the dining room set as the focus for their activities. Blessing was on her knees, ostensibly admiring the dovetailing of the woodwork, but secretly affixing listening devices underneath the tables and chairs to enable any conversation occurring in their vicinity to be transmitted to the soon-to-be-installed rooftop receiver-transmitter which would then communicate with a second receiver and tape machine in a bread van parked in neighbouring Black Park. Reggie kept a lookout for Nobby, ready to distract him should he return before they finished. Blessing surreptitiously took photographs with her brooch camera, and Joan took video recordings of the whole panorama using a cine camera hidden in her turban.

Suddenly, a tiny, highly irritated woman in a purple leotard confronted the ladies. "Who are you and what are you doing on my set? Actually, I don't want to know. Get out! I have a rehearsal to organise and I cannot do it with a mothers' meeting happening. And Phoebe! Where are you? I need my emergency bourbons and a Tizer on the rocks."

Luckily, at that moment, Nobby ran in, waving his clipboard. "I am so sorry, Vesta, I was just trying to find you. These are the ladies of the Maiden Combust Women's Institute. Let me introduce you to Regina MacGuffin who is our liaison person at Cuffley Manor, where we will be filming in August. You know, the stately home of Lord Cuffley."

"Oh, why didn't you say? Lady MacGuffin, my name is Mrs Vesta Currie, director and choreographer, for my sins, of the Dynamite McQueen films. Please call me Vesta, perhaps Dame Vesta one day! Do you know Lord Cuffley personally? I think we must have met socially. Maybe Glyndebourne or Henley Regatta? No, I tell a lie, it was Ascot."

Reggie hoped Joan was capturing all this with her cine camera. "Mrs Currie, Vesta, the current Lord Cuffley is barely nineteen years old and not yet a mainstay of the summer season social circuit. I think you must mean his father, the previous Lord Cuffley, who unfortunately passed away late last year. May we stay for your rehearsal if we are quiet?" Reggie ostentatiously glared at the other WI members to keep quiet.

"Of course," said Vesta, "anything for a personal friend of Lord Cuffley. Oh, there you are Phoebe. Corral the dancers for act two, scene forty-six. Lights, we need lights."

A wan young woman with a clipboard sidled up to Vesta with a glass of fizzy red liquid and a packet of biscuits. Nobby signalled for all the WI ladies to quietly follow him to the side of the stage with the best view of the set's staircase. The ladies each took a folding chair, dug out their thermoses and sat in a row, agape in anticipation and tittering animatedly as male and female dancers arrived in costume and congregated in a circle around a hectoring Vesta.

Joan gave Reggie the nod, indicating Ashwariya was ready for her so Reggie used the commotion of the rehearsal to sneak out and return to the coach. After a long pause while Vesta and the dancers fidgeted and waited, the lights came on and the WI ladies collectively gasped as the set, bathed in light, came alive and two figures, dazzling in head-to-toe glitter, appeared at the top of the staircase.

A chunk of goat pasty fell out of Blessing's mouth as she realised they were in the presence of Yazmine Navarra, the actress playing Dynamite McQueen, accompanied by her male co-star Fontaine de Havilland, playing Dynamite's nemesis, Hesketh Van Hydethorpe. Vesta scampered up to the actors and held their hands in hers, while the dancers took their positions on the staircase. The WI ladies craned their necks but could not hear anything more than murmuring until Fontaine loudly communicated his contempt.

"Vesta, I thought you said this was going to be a closed set for *She's the Bee's Knees*. I cannot possibly work with all these old crones in attendance." Vesta muttered a few words, and, duly pacified, Fontaine sulkily took his place on the stairs next to Dynamite who looked like she was used to waiting for his tantrums to subside. The WI ladies remained agog and collectively jumped, spilling their tea in unison as the overture to *She's the Bee's Knees* blared out and Dynamite McQueen sang.

Women have changed!
And men have received a shock,
Darning their own socks,

Winding their own clocks.

In days of yore,
A flash of ankle,
Was sure to make the fellas rankle,
And decree,
She's the bee's knees.

Modern women who,
Used to need saving,
Now demand that men go caving
Into their needs,
'Cause they're the bee's knees.

And then the dancing began which almost caused the ladies to clap. Blessing nudged Joan as the dancers performed their high kicks in unison and whispered, "Well, this brings it all back. Just like Showgirl Squadron's heyday." Joan smiled back, eyes glittering.

Dynamite, Fontaine and the dancers were in the midst of some complex choreography weaving up and down the staircase when the music stopped abruptly.

"What is going on, Nobby? What happened to my music? I cannot work like this." said Vesta furiously. Pushing a half-eaten goat pasty, which Blessing had pressed on him, into his pocket, Nobby ran over to Vesta. They exchanged a few words and Nobby motioned for the WI ladies to leave, mouthing at Joan that some unexpected visitors were about to arrive.

"It must be more film stars making an entrance,"

exclaimed Blessing. "Why don't we hang about outside and have a cup of tea by the coach just to see who turns up? Bring your chairs, ladies." Joan nodded and pretended to check her appearance in the compact while communicating with Reggie about what was happening and to meet them at the rear of the coach.

Nobby turned back to talk further with Vesta who encouraged Dynamite, Fontaine and the dancers to exit the soundstage. "More to the point, how can I work like this?" yelled Fontaine. "First, it's the Old Mother Hubbard fan club over there, and now my rehearsal has been cancelled."

Nobby looked at them all, shrugging. "Sorry everyone, there is nothing I can do. It has come from upstairs, apparently some emergency meeting of the executive."

Joan led the WI ladies out the front doors of the soundstage and around to the side by the coach. They set up their chairs in front of the coach where they all had a good view of the road leading to the soundstage and the entrance doors. Blessing encouraged them to unscrew their thermoses and make themselves at home. At the rear of the coach, Joan, Blessing, Ashwariya and Reggie – the latter having changed into her boiler suit, helmet and plimsolls – revised their plan.

"You know it might be the syndicate's inner circle arriving for an emergency meeting," said Joan. "Reggie, you had better hurry and climb up to fix the antenna and radio transmitter to the roof so we can listen in. Something must be kicking off, as usually they hold their meetings after the cast and crew have finished for the day."

Suddenly, a guard appeared from the rear of the soundstage and came up to the women, grabbing Reggie's shopping bag of equipment. Joan reacted swiftly with a high kick to his jaw with a well-aimed go-go boot which knocked him out and sent him sprawling to the ground.

"Still got it I see, Joan," said Blessing smiling, while Ashwariya and Reggie looked both aghast and impressed.

"Once a high-kicking showgirl, always a high-kicking showgirl," said Joan proudly. "Ash, do you have some rope we can use to tie this idiotic young man up and hide him in the bushes behind Bluebell?" Ash nodded and ferreted about in the recesses of the luggage compartment. "Now, Reggie, get up the ladder and onto the roof sharpish. We need the antenna and receiver in place before we leave. We will stall down here to give you enough time to set up the equipment and clamber back down unseen."

Reggie put her own compact and Blessing's proffered turnover into her pocket, grabbed the shopping bag and scrambled up the fire escape to affix the antenna and radio transmitter to the rooftop hoarding on which the thirty feet high face of Dynamite McQueen, with one eye closed, looking along the length of a crossbow, was ready to fire a lit stick of dynamite at an invisible enemy in the sky. Looking at the base of the hoarding, Reggie came to an abrupt stop and opened her compact.

"Calling, Joan. Over."

"What is it, Reg? Surely you cannot be done already? Over."

"Joan, behind the hoarding there is a pile of real dynamite connected to a fuse and timer. What should I do?

Over."

"Descend immediately. Over," hissed Joan, utterly alarmed.

Suddenly, the tour group was surrounded by a phalanx of armed security guards who motioned for them to get on their coach. Joan looked at Blessing and shook her head. There were too many guards for them to disarm. Reggie heard the commotion, peeked over the side of the roof and watched the ladies clamber aboard and the coach slowly drive off.

"Reggie…" ordered Joan from inside the coach, "hide quickly. Armed guards are scaling the fire escape. Over."

Reggie surveyed the roof and realised her only option was to hide behind the hoarding next to the dynamite. She inserted herself between the scaffold and the explosives as the guards arrived at the top of the fire escape and over the parapet. After a couple of minutes of silence, she peeked and saw the guards standing along the roof edge, facing away from her. She drew back quickly. "Joan, I am safe. They haven't spotted me, yet. Over."

"Reg, can you see a timer? Over."

Reggie craned her neck. "All the wires end in a Melting Moments biscuit tin which has been nailed onto the roof. The bomb is timed to detonate in ninety minutes."

"Hold on while we call for reinforcements. Don't worry, we will get you down. Operation Showgirl Squadron Scramble is underway."

Joan told Reggie to calm her mind by thinking about anything other than the situation she was in, such as the summer fête that the women's institute was organizing at

Cuffley Manor. *Fat chance of that,* thought Reggie who was high enough such that from her hiding place she could watch the coach leave the studios and come to a stop in a copse of trees at the edge of Black Park. Furrowing her brow, she peeked around the side of the hoarding, hoping she would be able to descend freely, but the guards remained in position, busy with their walkie-talkies.

Reggie squatted down next to the pile of dynamite and faced away from it, trying to take Joan's instructions to heart. She reflected on how her accountancy training should not have led her to be stuck on the roof of a film studio about to get blown up or shot at. Surely, her daredevil era had ended years before when malfunctioning equipment during a tandem parachute jump at after-school air cadets had caused her to break her leg and lose her bottle. Accounting was meant to be the opposite of dangerous, and yet here she was, thrust into the line of fire. If only Ashwariya had not been afraid of heights. She could have installed the equipment while they were all inside watching the rehearsal.

Ten minutes passed before Reggie's compact reverberated and Joan informed her that they had parked next to the bread van on the edge of Black Park and could see a fleet of seven chauffeur-driven Rolls-Royce limousines, each likely containing a member of the syndicate's inner circle, entering through the main gate of the studios, heading towards the Dynamite McQueen soundstage. Reggie's mind pirouetted with possibilities. Not only was it WI-5 that had not known about the dynamite but also evidently the syndicate. They were all caught in a deadly trap.

Joan's voice broke through Reggie's thoughts. "You now have eighty minutes before the dynamite explodes. While we brainstorm how to get you out of there, stay put and remain calm. We cannot risk you being seen if you attempt to install the equipment. Saving you is our highest priority. Place your trust in us, and focus your mind elsewhere. The WI summer fête is looming and we have not yet started planning. Think about that. Over."

Maybe Joan was right. Thinking about the summer fête would be a distraction, thought Reggie as she tried to detach herself from the danger she faced and mull over the details of the fête. All the food for the afternoon teas the WI served on the day would need to be organised as Mrs Gascoyne, Cuffley Manor's cook and housekeeper, who usually took care of all the baking, was out of commission with her dicky heart. Reggie's sister Gloria, GloGlo for short, was in charge of the fête's flying display which was one less thing to worry about. Reggie had been watching vintage Tiger Moth biplanes practice manoeuvres, including some horrifying wing-walking that involved GloGlo flying low over Cuffley Manor upside down with Reggie's good-natured Canadian lump of a boyfriend, Beaver, having the time of his life strapped to the top wing, grabbing a Union Jack from the flagpole on the manor's roof. Reggie's stomach lurched as she thought she might never see Beaver again. *Well, I didn't see that coming,* she thought to herself.

Huddling with Joan and Ashwariya at the front of the coach, Blessing took charge. "Okay, ladies, Reggie is stuck a hundred and fifty feet in the air, on the roof of the soundstage which will explode in seventy-five minutes. She cannot escape, as the roof is surrounded by machine-gun wielding guards. How do we get her out of there?"

Joan peered through her binoculars at the huge face of Dynamite McQueen aiming her crossbow loaded with a lit stick of dynamite into the sky. "I do have an idea; however, the fewer eyes that see us do what I am proposing, the better. Ash, how about you drive the WI ladies back to Maiden Combust in Bluebell as if everything is normal? You can tell them Reggie, Blessing and I are going to have dinner with the producers. Gloria is the lynchpin of my plan, as she has been practicing hard for the summer fête flying display, honing her skills flying upside down and buzzing her tiny flag target. I suggest she could snatch Reggie from the roof in the same way. The wing-walking frame is already installed on Gloria's Tiger Moth." Blessing and Ashwariya went silent for a minute before nodding at each other slowly.

Joan warmed to her own idea as her eyes glittered. "Girls, I do think this could work. We would need to get Gloria to fly the Tiger Moth to the closest airfield ("That would be Iver Heath," chimed in Ashwariya.) where Blessing and I will meet her in the bread van. Reggie is much heavier than a flag so we are going to need two wing-walkers to grab her. Blessing and I will do the grabbing. Gloria will need to bring harnesses for both of us and Reggie. We would need Reggie to climb to the top of Dynamite McQueen's crossbow and stand facing the sunset holding her elbows out like chicken wings, hands on her waist. What do you all think? We only have seventy minutes to make it happen, and we need to give Gloria enough time to fly to Iver Heath, pick us up and save the day."

Ashwariya nodded wholeheartedly realising this would mean GloGlo would be recruited immediately into WI-5, bypassing all normal processes. Her emphatic nods were returned by Joan and Blessing who clapped her hands to signify the game was afoot.

***

Using the bread van's telephone, Ashwariya contacted GloGlo to explain she was being drafted into a covert operation to rescue her sister and she needed to drop everything, grab three wing-walking harnesses and fly immediately to Iver Heath airfield to pick up Joan and Blessing. Hearing a different timbre to Ashwariya's voice, GloGlo understood a curtain was being pulled back on a heretofore unforeseen world. She trusted the urgency of Ash's message and was ready for any opportunity to save her sister.

Ashwariya drove the rest of the WI ladies home, elated, her mind torn between the horror of Reggie stuck on a roof about to explode and the joy of GloGlo being recruited to WI-5. For the first time, she could share her whole truth with GloGlo. They could have a future after all, but only if Reggie did not die!

***

An hour later, Reggie had climbed up the three storeys of scaffolding which supported the enormous plywood and neon sign promoting the latest Dynamite McQueen adventure. Still hidden behind Dynamite's grinning visage, Reggie could look down on the disorderly patchwork quilt of corrugated iron and brick formed by Ravenwood Studios' soundstages. She looked up at the enormous hoarding supporting a crossbow and stick of dynamite brandished at the sky and shuddered at the task ahead. When Joan had explained the plan, Reggie had burst into tears at the thought of the danger GloGlo, Blessing and Joan would be facing and the horror of what she had to do to survive a terrifying death. Could this be the end of the Showgirl Squadron before they had even been relaunched? Would her youngest sister, Loveday, be left as an only child? Would her parents, Alfie and Delice, have to bury two daughters? What had she been thinking? Tears dampened the collar of her boiler suit. *Come on, Reggie, pull yourself together.* Reggie heard her mother's voice. She shook her head, blinked slowly and gathered her forces. There may not be much of a chance but there was hope. Focus on the hope.

It was almost evening. The sun's warmth was waning and the wind was starting to wuther. Here she was, waiting to be rescued like a silly damsel in distress. Thank goodness she was wearing her boiler suit and helmet, otherwise she would be freezing, and hurrah for goat pasties. Reggie checked her watch. Fifteen minutes to *kaboom!* Where were they? Why wasn't her compact buzzing with an update on the Tiger Moth's arrival? Didn't they realise she needed their reassurance to maintain her composure? Reggie's heart sank as she realised that she had only experienced this level of fear once before during parachute training at air cadets when she was eighteen. Reverberating in her brain was the memory, *I should not be doing this. Never again do I want to do this.* And yet, here she was.

Startled out of her vortex of fear, Reggie jumped as the neon lights outlining Dynamite McQueen's cupid's bow lips and the stick of dynamite fizzed and flickered into life. She breathed deeply and scanned the full circumference of the horizon. To the east, murky pollution shrouded London and its crenelated skyline of dark grey tower blocks. GloGlo, if she was coming, would be flying from the east to see her silhouetted against the setting sun. There was not much time remaining. She had to keep positive. No news was good news.

Looking down, she could see the guards had remained in position around the roof's edge, still facing away from her. Reggie steadied herself as she moved up the scaffolding, remaining hidden, protected by the hoarding from the guards and the wind. However, without being spotted, she now needed to caterpillar on her stomach twenty feet along the four-foot-wide crossbow and stick of dynamite. Hopefully any guard turning to look would be dazzled sufficiently by the neon lights not to notice her shimmying skyward, and be distracted by the sound of the breeze not to register the loud rumble of the Tiger Moth's engine. Ten minutes to *kaboom!* Reggie's stomach lurched as her compact buzzed in her breast pocket. About time! GloGlo, Joan and Blessing were five minutes away. Time to shimmy into position.

Reggie gingerly stood up at the end of the neon-lit dynamite stick, pointing into the sky one hundred and fifty feet from the ground, and shakily whispered into her compact, "In position. Over."

From the Tiger Moth's cockpit, GloGlo replied, "Very good, Reggie, we can already see you silhouetted against the setting sun. One more minute and we will pluck you from the heavens. When Blessing and Joan grab you, kick your knees up to your chest and hold them there until they have harnessed you to themselves and the wing-walking frame. Over."

The voice of her sister helped Reggie calm her body, as she shivered from fear. As instructed, she stood straight and tall in the breeze which was fading as the sun set. With fists on her waist and elbows stuck out, she stared intently towards the setting sun, willing the guards not to look up.

***

Flying over the edge of Black Park, GloGlo aimed for the highest point of the Ravenwood Studios' lot, targeting the tiny, dark figure standing on the end of the stick of dynamite, framed by the glow of neon lights. She expertly rolled the Tiger Moth upside down and lined up Joan and Blessing so the harness they held between them would wrap around Reggie's torso and buttocks. GloGlo, squinting at Reggie's silhouette getting larger and larger, slowed the Tiger Moth a touch, and aimed straight for her. As the engine roar grew louder, Reggie concentrated on holding her position and shut her eyes.

An upside-down Blessing and Joan slammed into her, and all breath left Reggie's body as she brought her knees up into a ball and pain enveloped her. Blessing held Reggie in her strong grip while Joan clipped on her harness and secured the buckles.

GloGlo waited for Blessing's signal indicating Reggie was securely attached before righting the biplane, and as suddenly as they arrived, they were gone. The guards, unsure what had just happened, investigated behind the hoarding, discovered the dynamite and leapt down the fire escape.

Then the soundstage roof exploded.

Reggie, numb with fear, scalding pain overwhelming her shoulders and torso, was buffeted by the noise, heat and sound waves from the explosion, causing her to lose hearing for the remainder of the flight home. Once her breath returned, she burst into sobs. Had the wing-walking frame not kept her upright, she would have fallen to her knees. All she wanted was… actually, for the first time in her life, Reggie did not know what she wanted.

Family Plot

One month later, Reggie watched her youngest sister Loveday take a bite of some ancient haslet which until two minutes ago had been mouldering away forgotten in the back of their parents' fridge.

Loveday MacGuffin [nineteen, unproven, favourite film: *A Taste of Honey*] picked up the crumbs from her Danger Man pyjama top, stared at the kettle, willing it to boil, and then examined the remaining haslet slices in her hand. "Best before doesn't mean bad after," she said as she threw another slice in her mouth. Reggie waited for her youngest sister to come back to Earth, shivering in the early morning cool of the kitchen. It was well into July but the full force of summer seemed to have deserted them.

Loveday silently handed Reggie her open notebook. A wobbly line was drawn down the middle of the page, the left-hand column topped by a plus sign, the right-hand by a minus. Underneath the plus were: *well-stocked kitchen, fridge never empty, washing gets done, low rent, love London, lots of work in London*. Underneath the minus sign were: *no job, no money, living with Mum and Dad, reaching end of tether, cannot afford to move out*. Lopsidedly pursing her lips, Reggie compared both columns and surmised that although Loveday could cope in the short term with living at home, something had to give over the long, especially in light of Loveday's latest drama.

"So, what happened exactly?" asked Reggie, who had not made much headway grasping what had led Loveday to lose another cooking job.

Loveday rolled her eyes and took a deep breath. "I was hired to cater a reception for a pre-wedding party at a house in Balham on Friday. They were providing all the wait staff and ingredients, I only needed to compose the hors d'oeuvres and put them on trays. However, when I arrived, the house was empty, apart from a tearful bride who told me the wedding was off and apologised for forgetting to tell me. She had all the champagne ready to go, so we cracked a bottle and then another one. We both got a bit legless. She didn't want to talk about the wedding, so she asked all the ins and outs of my life and about you all. Then the ex-groom arrived and threw me out."

"Because you and the bride had moved upstairs by this point and fallen asleep in their *supposedly* marital bed?"

"Well, yes, but nothing happened, so I came home."

Reggie tried to look supportive as she rubbed her still sore shoulders and listened to the early Sunday morning soundtrack of the two-up two-down where she and her sisters had been born. The ripple and crackle of the boiler coming to life, the familiar floorboard and plumbing creaks as the house warmed up, the slow rolling burble of the kettle approaching the boil, the rhythmic, metallic creak of the mattress springs under her parents, the odd siren and horn toot from the main road and next door up and at it early in their usual muffled rar-rar-rar way.

Loveday theatrically raised one eyebrow as she looked down. The blue eyes of Patrick McGoohan gazed up from her pyjamas, not at all concerned by their close proximity to haslet crumbs raining down. "What are you looking at, Drake, John Drake? Want to make something of it?"

The kettle finally rattled on the belling. Loveday stuffed the last of the haslet into her mouth, licked her lips and fingers and quickly pushed her chair away from the kitchen table, as it would only be a few seconds before the kettle's banshee whistling would drown out all the noises of the house and the rest of London. Time to get going on her dad's birthday breakfast and then get her life in gear.

Reggie smiled at Loveday, aware that as the only MacGuffin sister still living at home, she carried a heavier burden. Loveday had taken Alfie [forty-seven, quite-happy-as-I-am-thank-you-very-much, favourite film: *Dynamite McQueen and the Queens of Kaboom*] on a father-daughter morning jaunt to Borough Market for him to pick out his favourite birthday breakfast ingredients and select whatever Sunday lunch beef joint (bone in, marbled with fat, plus an extra fat blanket to gift wrap it in the oven) took his fancy with the classic Alfie query, "What are our budgetary constraints, my little scrawnbag of a chook?" Alfie was very happy eating all the market's free samples he could lay his hands on before a midday pint of pale ale and two bacon butties with extra butter, tomato sauce and an onion bhaji on the side at the 'Dog and Partridge' on Borough High Street. They were home in time for Alfie to have a nap before watching the Saturday afternoon sports and the build-up to the evening's England vs Mexico World Cup match. In time for a pre-match nosh on chips, curry sauce and battered sausages, Reggie and GloGlo arrived on the train from, in Loveday's mind, dull-as-ditch-water, dot-on-the-map, nothing-ever-happens, Hertfordshire (yawn). Then a post-match family trip to the local pub for a pint of McMullen's (Alfie), a ratafia (Delice), a half of bitter shandy (Reggie), a pint of Guinness (GloGlo) and four B-52 bombers (Loveday). After the pub, Alfie played his favourite records, and the furniture was moved back to enable them all to dance around the room, each taking turns to swing dance with Alfie as they had done throughout their childhoods. Alfie was in a happy place.

Once the kettle had boiled, Loveday dragged herself into second gear and mouthed, "Let's talk later." at Reggie while they put the tea on, organised the food for breakfast, put the oven on and laid the table. At five and twenty to eight, she stomped loudly upstairs to her parents' bedroom with a pot of tea under an ancient, chunky, hand-knitted tea-cosy, two warmed mugs, a small jug of milk, and a plate of chocolate digestives and Iced Gems. The teapot had slopped onto the tray and made some of the biscuits soggy, but otherwise it was a remarkably drama-free example of Loveday taking care of business while their parents remained in bed. Having heard Loveday trundle up the stairs, GloGlo guiltily roused herself from their childhood bedroom and appeared in the kitchen ready to help.

By half past eight, Delice [forty-nine, prescient, favourite film: *À Bout De Souffle*] and Alfie were enjoying their second cuppa in bed, reading the Sunday Times for news (Delice), the Sunday Express for scandal (Alfie) and perusing the Radio Times for what film Alfie could fall asleep in front of on a Sunday afternoon. Not only was *Summer Holiday* on but also one of his favourite Dynamite McQueen films. Which one to choose? As if they didn't all know.

Alfie's stomach rumbled. He was champing at the bit to sink his teeth into a huge English breakfast, so he threw on his baggy old jeans and his new gift-from-Delice paisley shirt, the colour of mint jelly, and headed downstairs barefoot. Although he was relieved there was no burning smell emanating from the kitchen, he could hear Loveday, GloGlo and Reggie chatting, catching snatches of their conversation through the closed door. He doubled back upstairs and rolled his eyes. "As per usual, Loveday is distracted, gabbing with her sisters rather than focusing on the food. I heard her tell GloGlo that she needs to find a new job… again."

Delice looked up from the financial pages. "How long shall we let this continue?"

In the opinion of her much-put-upon-but-perfectly-reasonable-in-their-minds parents, Loveday had been faffing around the London job market for long enough. Alfie could tell Delice was gathering steam for a birthday-be-damned confrontation, so he let out a deep sigh as he settled into a particularly insightful Nigel Dempster feature on Princess Margaret Rose's footwear. The article also reported on the suspected hijacking of a bus in the West End, the deaths of six people found in the ruins of the Ravenwood Studios fire, the theft of the World Cup trophy and whether the fire and theft were the work of the renowned criminal and explosives expert, Suzette Crepaldi, known in the press as Crêpes Suzette, Marquise of Disguise and Queen of Kaboom, as her incendiary devices were famous for flattening buildings like pancakes. Alfie spluttered in mock outrage, "I cannot believe that the *Sunday Express* is associating my beloved *Queens of Kaboom* to a hardened criminal. They are on some very dodgy ground. I might have to write a strongly worded letter."

Delice raised her eyebrows at Alfie in amusement and kept on reading.

"And in regard to Loveday, let's not say anything until after breakfast," requested Alfie.

Delice looked over the top of her reading glasses. "I think Reggie and GloGlo might be on our side this time. Even they are getting fed up with the whiplash from her lack of traction and talent for havoc. If only we could harness Loveday's energy for good rather than the chaos she leaves in her wake. And, Alfie, look! You have already gotten a stain on your new shirt."

Alfie looked sheepish and examined his chest. "I do have an idea that might kick Loveday into gear." He explained how his employers at the Victoria and Albert Museum were finding it hard to keep staff at the bottom of the ladder – portering not being considered an exciting career.

"Alfie, you know I worry about Loveday following in your footsteps at the museum and causing headaches for us all. I don't worry too much about GloGlo, she is so happy just tinkering with planes at the aerodrome. I really think we can stop fretting about both our daughters being at Cuffley Manor. And Reggie seems to be finding her niche in bookkeeping, of all things, just when I was hoping her childhood daredevil streak might have come to something exciting. It would be nice if one of my daughters took after me. But Loveday! If she starts at the museum, it absolutely must be in a low-on-the-ladder position with no potential for distraction or drama. Do you understand me?"

Alfie nodded. "I wouldn't have it any other way. She will just be a porter. Rest assured, I will keep her shielded from anything remotely exciting. How about I ask tomorrow if they would be interested in hiring Loveday as a porter to start Tuesday?"

And so, the collective decision was made. Delice stepped out of Alfie's favourite nightie and threw on her it-may-be-Alfie's-birthday-but-I-still-mean-business slacks and twisted her hair into her usual, stylish despot-librarian bun, while Alfie put the newspapers, dirty mugs, empty teapot, milk jug and uneaten biscuits back on the tray and tiptoed behind Delice downstairs. Today would be the day the Loveday MacGuffin parental unit cum relationship-swat-team cum Loveday-disaster-clean-up-crew put their feet down firmly, no holds barred.

***

Loveday was now in full steam in the kitchen. "Happy Birthday, Dad! Morning, Mum, food is on the way."

Alfie hugged his daughters in turn. "Hello, my little knickerbocker glories. Loveday, thanks for all this action in the kitchen this morning after your long day of looking after me yesterday. I did enjoy it. And GloGlo and Reggie, I really appreciate you staying overnight. It's such a treat to have us all together." He fawned over the treats starting to emerge from the belling, exclaiming when he discovered his favourite double-baked, individual Yorkshire puddings made with eggs, cheese, and Guinness puffing up in the oven and a warming drawer full of sausages.

Unable to contain herself, Delice took the bull by the horns. "Now, Loveday, let us put Dad's birthday breakfast to one side for one moment (Alfie looked briefly aghast). We need to have a chat. Are we to understand that you have lost another job?"

Reggie and GloGlo exchanged furtive glances and busied themselves staring at Sunday lunch timings in Delice's ancient cookery book (Reggie) and taking an unexpected interest in Princess Margaret's shoe collection in the *Sunday Express* (GloGlo). Alfie attempted to look grave without smirking at his lightning-in-a-bottle-oh-my-goodness-she-is-her-high-voltage-mother-thirty-years-ago-look-out-world daughter.

Loveday sent Delice her best death-by-scowl stare. "Don't worry, Mum. I already have some irons in the fire." Although she registered her mother was spoiling for a fight, she also registered the breakfast Yorkshires required removal from the oven to avoid going nuclear. Similar to Loveday's own burgeoning mood. She handed out plates of food to her sisters and father and slammed down a plate in front of her mother.

Delice surveyed her food with undisguised horror. "Loveday, you burnt the sausages. Alfie, what exactly did she learn at cooking school?" Giving his wife some side-eye, Alfie tucked in, silently waiting for his wife and daughter to finish locking horns. Loveday harrumphed onto the only free kitchen chair, fiercely biting a chunk off a sausage.

Delice went in for the kill. "Loveday, what is murdering us is seeing you wasting your time stuck in this house cooking heart attacks on a plate, while every cooking job you do ends in some sort of disaster which is always somebody else's fault. With your verve, energy and intelligence, we think you could run the world, but you need to gain some traction, persevere, stick at things and learn from your mistakes. To that end, we are going to find you a non-cooking job, helping out at the V&A, and start charging you the going rate for rent. You can probably go anywhere in the world to cook but you haven't. Why are you sticking around here? The world is so much bigger than London."

"First of all, Mum, I couldn't possibly put up with the repetitive jobs you and Dad do. I don't even know what you actually do, but I know it's a bunch of boring meetings and paperwork. You and Alfie are not going to stick me in the windowless bowels of the V&A. I am starting to nod off just by saying the words *Victoria and Albert*. It's the nineteen sixties, Mum, not the eighteen sixties. Nothing ever happens behind the scenes at the museum. Dad often works late and on weekends, and comes home exhausted. What's it all about, Alfie? Then you, Mum, spend your time complaining about your work with the British Legion."

Alfie, who had been diligently making his way through the gloriously greasy, tomato-sauce-covered midden on his plate, swallowed whole a cheesy, guinnessy Yorkshire pudding he had filled with baked beans. "Actually, Loveday, firstly, don't Alfie me, I am still Dad to you. Lovely Yorkshires by the way."

Delice could not contain herself. "Loveday, you are causing chaos everywhere you go. Eventually, this is all going to come crashing down."

Loveday glared at her mother. "I'm a bit like Dynamite McQueen, as I like a sense of adventure and a hint of danger. Look, I am nearly twenty and allowed to still be figuring things out so back off... please."

Elbows on the table, Reggie rested her chin in her hand and waited for Loveday's storm to pass. Delice, also, did not take the bait. "Loveday, all this stops right now. Your father is going to find you something at the museum where he can keep an eye on you."

Alfie spluttered, swallowing a sausage after forgetting to chew. "Loveday, the museum is not what you think it is."

Loveday harrumphed once again. "Stuck in a frigid old museum is not where a vibrant, young woman of today should be focusing her energies. Your generation is so miserable, always revelling in the past, going on about the good old days of war and rationing."

Alfie grabbed a slice of bread, liberally spread it with butter, put two sausages on top with a big shake of tomato sauce, which emptied the bottle, and folded it over. "Well, that settles it. The museum it is. Tomorrow, I will get my boss to hire you as a porter. Roll your eyes any more and they will be stuck at the back of your skull like a Midwich Cuckoo."

Reggie leaned back in her chair, stretched and put her hands behind her head. "You know, Loveday, I actually enjoyed my time working at the museum. It opened up all sorts of new avenues for me."

Loveday avoided Reggie's eyes as she retorted. "What, like working in the sticks, doing the books for a hideous upper-class family at the smallest aerodrome in the world, living in a council flat in Hertford, joining the women's institute of all things and being with a man who seems to have the personality of a marrowfat pea?"

Reggie stared witheringly at Loveday before stuffing the remains of a Yorkshire pudding in her mouth. "I will have you know it is a maisonette, not a flat."

Alfie, relieved Loveday's confrontation with Delice was dying down, changed the subject. "Thanks, girls, for the breakfast. It was utterly fabulous. Is there anything left?"

Loveday surveyed the carnage. "Four Yorkshire puddings, three sausages and tons of baked beans."

"Pile it all in the fridge, Loveday. You know your

mother is going to be away all week, don't you, so we'll be fending for ourselves?"

Reggie chimed in, "Dad, let us know which film you want to watch this afternoon and we will organise the roast beef timing to fit."

Alfie relaxed and let out a contented snort. "*Dynamite McQueen and the Buckingham Palace Brouhaha* starts at three o'clock and finishes at five so roast beef and more Yorkshire puddings any time after that would be great."

GloGlo and Reggie cleaned up the breakfast things and sorted out the kitchen chaos, while Loveday flitted about with a tea towel. Alfie, unable to move from the kitchen table, intermittently groaned as he delved further into the *Sunday Express* World Cup coverage. After ten minutes, he rustled up the courage to move to the living room sofa and lie down, clutching the newspaper to his chest, for a morning nap.

Once she could see the kitchen was being put back to rights, Delice headed off to pack her bags for the week. The sisters could hear her humming the Dynamite McQueen theme song to herself as she went up the stairs – a good sign.

Loveday feigned that her feelings were more hurt than they actually were. "I think you two could have been more supportive just now. In this family, I always feel like I am on the outside looking in as if you all know something I don't."

Reggie crinkled her all-seeing x-ray eyes and a smile broke through. "You know, Loveday, we think you are still Mum and Dad's favourite daughter which is why they ride you more than us. They admire your pluck, whereas I am so predictable and GloGlo is somewhere in between. Also, you are the spitting image of Mum as a young woman, so I think Dad always will have the softest spot for you. So don't kill them yet is what I am saying."

GloGlo chimed in, "Actually, Loveday, we were only letting you dig your own grave because Reggie and I have cooked up a plan, and for old times' sake, we were enjoying your amateur dramatics. Don't worry, your sisters will *save, save, save the day* as per usual. You are so much more than you let on. We know a lot of your behaviour is only an act. All you need is the right inspiration, and no matter what you might think of us or our opinions, we are here to help. Now, I can tell Dad is listening in from the next room, so let's talk later once the wrinklies have gone to bed. We should get the beef and veg prepped."

***

Looking back on the day, sitting at the kitchen table and watching his daughters peel vegetables was Alfie's favourite memory. GloGlo filled them in on how well the first two weeks were going of living with Ashwariya and the fun they were having turning the aerodrome's disused war-time control tower into a habitable love nest. She also told them excitedly about her plans to improve the summer fête's flying display, increasing the number of private planes renting hanger space, training more pilots, skydivers, and parachutists, and taking paying customers up for sightseeing flights.

Reggie nodded approvingly, knowing GloGlo was a central element of the aerodrome's recent financial success. She explained her new ideas for Cuffley Manor to start generating more income, including leasing more land out to farmers, renting out the manor for weddings and conferences and offering accommodation. "So many ideas and not much time to implement them, as the financial picture overall remains pretty dire, and the manor requires a major investment to stop it from becoming unsafe. But the aerodrome is going great, thanks to GloGlo, and the potential financial injection afforded by a film company renting out the manor this month will go a long way to fixing the roof. Dad, you are not going to believe it, but it is the latest Dynamite McQueen film which is coming to Cuffley Manor to film in August." Alfie looked excited and horrified at the same time, as he and Delice exchanged glances.

As cooking anything in the belling took ages, the roast was in the oven before the film began. The family squished together on the sofa while the BBC continuity announcer pompously droned on. Loveday leaned on her father and nudged him affectionately. "Tell us again why you like these films so much, Dad."

Alfie leaned back. "Well, my little Jaffa Cake, I remember them being a rare, bright spark during my growing-up years. I read all the books and saw all the films several times. They are one of the few things I feel nostalgic about, and I love the fact they are still making them. The action sequence before the credits always makes me smile. And I love it when they break into song and start dancing. Hush everyone, it is starting." The sisters had learned the theme song's lyrics by heart from their dad's incessant playing of his Dynamite McQueen soundtrack albums throughout their childhood. It had also gone down in MacGuffin family lore that when Alfie and Delice had first met, he had been startled by how much Delice had reminded him of the first actress to play Dynamite McQueen.

The Eighth Wonder Film Company presents Dynamite McQueen and the Buckingham Palace Brouhaha appeared on the screen before fading into the pre-credit sequence featuring Dynamite McQueen's alter ego, unassuming antique store worker, Penelope Knickerbocker, taking afternoon tea at The Trafalgar Square Hotel with Aunt Aspidistra who has announced that she has recently updated her will, leaving the antique shop to her niece. Aunt Aspidistra's handbag starts vibrating and she removes her compact. "I think this must be for you my dear," said Aunt Aspidistra, as she hands the compact to Penelope and takes a dainty bite of miniature pork pie. The message is from Mrs Dogsbody, Aspidistra Antiques' cleaner, alerting them that Buckingham Palace is under threat from several London buses with blacked-out windows, speeding down The Mall and to not to eat anything at the hotel as the pork pies have been poisoned. To Penelope's horror, Aunt Aspidistra slumps forward into the cake stand. Penelope calls 999, and once she hears the ambulance approaching, rushes outside to where the Aspidistra Antiques lorry is parked.

The back of the lorry drops down, revealing Dynamite McQueen's Thunderbolt speedster car. Penelope, now changed into her instantly recognisable Dynamite McQueen, Jewel Britannia, Union Jack dress, drives at high speed through Admiralty Arch and along The Mall to the Palace. Ahead of her, half a dozen double-decker buses are driving fast, aiming at the crowds gathered for the changing of the guard. Just when Dynamite has the buses in her sights, the Thunderbolt is attacked by a fleet of grocery vans, lobbing milk bottle grenades. Dynamite swerves skilfully through the explosions. Her eyes narrow, and she presses a big pink button on her dashboard. A large crossbow emerges from the roof of the Thunderbolt, firing lit sticks of dynamite into the lead grocery van and one of the buses, exploding them to smithereens and sending the remaining enemy vehicles careening into St James's Park pond. With the royal family looking on from the balcony, the Thunderbolt stops in front of the palace gates and Dynamite ejects into the air, opening her Union Jack parachute to land in the massed arms of the Palace guards who break into song as the opening credits roll.

***

Reviewing the film over roast beef, Reggie appreciated that the director of a big action film was a woman. GloGlo thought Dynamite's Art Deco wonder of a car (if only it were real!) was stunning. Delice had a soft spot for Fontaine de Havilland, the actor playing Dynamite's moustache-twirling nemesis. "I always enjoy a bad boy," she said as she squeezed Alfie's thigh. Alfie beamed as he could still see a Dynamite McQueen twinkle in Delice's eyes. Loveday applauded that each actress who had played Dynamite was a complete unknown, adopted the stage name 'Dynamite McQueen' while playing the role and then disappeared, never to be heard from again. Reggie and GloGlo thought this a silly conceit, *as if we couldn't work it out for ourselves.* Alfie and Delice just laughed.

Alfie requested a game of Monopoly. By not trading cards except with Alfie when it was to his advantage, the rest of the family conspired for him to win. After the game, the sisters looked at each other conspiratorially. "So, Dad, are you going to put it on? You know you want to."

In the living room, Alfie slid open the top of the Magnavox, carefully placed one of his Dynamite McQueen soundtrack albums on the turntable, and led Delice to the middle of the room, pushing back chairs as they went and before starting to swing dance.

"Alfie, I have no idea what you are doing. Your lead has gone to pot," giggled Delice as she tried to keep up.

"Pretzel," yelled Alfie as he raised his left arm and put his right hand behind his back. Alfie and Delice carried on dancing for several songs, mixing fast and slow, while their daughters chortled from the sofa, eventually getting up to dance themselves, sometimes together, sometimes apart when a song took their fancy. Alfie danced with each daughter in turn. He was so gratified to know his whole family could dance.

Knocked out by the excitement of roast beef, playing Monopoly, dancing up a storm, and expecting a busy week at work, Alfie and Delice drifted off to bed earlier than usual, leaving Loveday, GloGlo and Reggie to clean up before they too turned in. Squeezed back into their childhood bedroom, Reggie was in her Miss Marple pyjamas, Loveday in her Danger Mans and GloGlo in her Royal Air Force jimjams.

"How about we snuggle on the top bunk together like we used to?" asked Reggie. Once they were all pressed against each other's warm bodies on the top bunk, feet dangling over the side and pillows arranged so nobody's back was resting against the rails, Reggie threw the candlewick bedspread over all three.

Loveday rubbed her hands. "Okay, tell me your plan. Spit it out!"

Reggie nudged her sister. "Actually, it is GloGlo's plan. She came up with the idea and it is such a good one. I don't know why I hadn't thought of it."

"Well, Loveday, in a nutshell, we want to spirit you off to Cuffley Manor as Reggie needs someone to organise all the baking required for next weekend's fête," said GloGlo matter of factly.

Reggie explained, "Ancient Mrs Gascoyne, the manor's cook and housekeeper has prepared all the food for every fête since the end of the war. We thought she would be back by now but she is still in hospital getting her dicky heart sorted. Although I have the Maiden Combust Women's Institute ladies helping out, I would feel so much better if a professional could take charge. I know it in my bones; you could do it. So why not travel up to Hertfordshire with us tomorrow morning and spend the week out of Mum and Dad's hair?"

GloGlo chimed back in, "So, is it museum with Dad or Cuffley Manor with us? I should come clean and admit that my and Ash's place is more of a building site than a guest-worthy abode at the moment, so you would have to be happy bedding down in Reg's spare room. We would also make sure the Cuffley boys provide you with a solid reference which might help with your next job. Well, Loveday, what do you think?"

Reggie handed Loveday her notebook. "Actually, before you answer, have a read through of my thoughts on what needs to be done. If the scale of it makes you blanch, we can adjust the details." Loveday began reading.

1966 Cuffley Manor Fête.
Start Time: 2 p.m. Saturday, July 23, 1966
Two hundred and fifty afternoon teas (five shillings per head) comprising:
Scones with strawberry jam and cream,
Victoria sponge,
Fresh strawberries,
Mini pork pies,
Cucumber sandwiches,
Egg and cress sandwiches,
Rabbit paste sandwiches (Mrs Gascoyne has already made the rabbit paste).

The following supplies have been ordered:
Twenty-five loaves of bread,
Twenty-five pounds of minced pork,

Forty pots of clotted cream,
Twenty pots of strawberry jam,
Eighty punnets of strawberries,
Sixteen pounds of butter,
Eight pounds of lard,
Fifty cucumbers,
Eight bottles of salad cream,
Fifty dozen eggs,
Twenty punnets of cress,
Ten pounds of sugar,
Twenty pounds of flour
and two hundred and fifty napkins and paper plates.

Loveday grinned and her eyes sparkled. "And a partridge in a pear tree? Can I add a few personal touches as long as I stay within budget? I have always loved cooking in other people's kitchens, so it's a yes. Cuffley Manor – 1, V&A Museum – 0."

Reggie gave her sister a tight squish. "Oh thanks so much, Loveday, I promise you will have a great time, and yes, you can add your personal touches. Apparently, the afternoon tea is what everyone looks forward to. And the WI ladies will come over Friday and Saturday to help out and do all the serving on the day. Beaver will be on hand if anything goes wrong with the ovens. I know you are not a fan of the country, but I can make my box room comfy for you, and we can go to work together every morning. I thank our lucky stars that the fête is on the weekend before the World Cup Final otherwise no one would come. And if all goes well, I have another idea percolating which will keep you out of Mum and Dad's clutches over the long term."

GloGlo leaned over. "And this is from Ash and me." GloGlo handed Loveday a *Planning Your Visit to 18th Century Cuffley Manor* leaflet. On the front was a load of house history, which Loveday skipped over, and on the back was an annotated map of the area with the house, grounds, aerodrome, Maiden Combust village and surrounding villages, bus stops, train stations and a large *X* ringed by a heart, marking the location of GloGlo and Ashwariya's home in the aerodrome's disused control tower. There was also a large 'R' ringed by a star marking the hangar where Reggie's office could be found and an arrow indicating the footpath through the woods to the Ridgeway Council Estate and Reggie's maisonette.

"Thanks so much," said Loveday, as the stress of the day dissipated. Reggie's bladder was sending alarming signals from all the tea and gravy she had consumed, so she hauled herself off the bunk to the toilet. When she returned, GloGlo had also moved and was already snoring in the zed bed while Loveday lay in the bottom bunk, going over the leaflet and chewing on a pencil, thinking of more questions to ask and how she could make a big splash at Cuffley Manor. She listened to Reggie come back into the room, clamber up on the top bunk, unfurl herself on the mattress to lie flat on her back stretching her limbs, toss onto her left side and then onto her right, like she was grilling a sausage, before hearing her breathing start to deepen. Loveday was up to seventeen questions before her breath also deepened and slowed, and the pencil rolled out of her fingers and on to the floor.

Strangers on a Train

Loveday woke early. She was very happy to be delaying her museum fate by spending a week in the country, in the grandest house she had ever cooked in, even if she was only, in effect, making sandwiches, cakes and scones. Alfie and Delice came downstairs already dressed for work and exchanged glances, shocked that their youngest daughter was up before them two days running. Over tea, Loveday explained the plan the sisters had cooked up. Giving each other an infinitesimal nod, Delice said, "You know, Loveday, we think it would be lovely if you help out your sisters this week, and next week you can help your dad at the museum. Alfie will arrange things today. Are we making ourselves clear?"

Loveday held out her left and right hands to each of her parents. "Absolutely, crystal clear."

Seeing GloGlo and Reggie arrive downstairs carrying their bags, Loveday returned to the bedroom to finish packing, while Alfie whipped up five packages of cheese and pickle sandwiches which were sitting on the kitchen counter when Loveday came down.

"Thanks for the sandwiches, Dad, and good luck on your own this week. See you both on Sunday. Don't look at me like that Mum, how much trouble can I get into in the country with Reggie and GloGlo overseeing my every move? Where are you going again Mum? Anywhere near Cuffley Manor or Hertford?"

Delice looked rueful. "Oh, you know, checking up on British Legions all over the place as per usual. I won't be back until Friday night, so please phone your dad during the week. He should be fine though, given all the football on the telly and all the food in the fridge."

Reggie and GloGlo put on their raincoats as it was looking threatening outside. Loveday reached for her coat and started to head out. Delice called her back. "Actually, Loveday, take my pink raincoat and raspberry beret, as they are both waterproof. You might as well arrive looking gorgeous before you have to skivvy like Cinderella below stairs."

"Won't you need them this week, Mum?"

"No, you take them. I'll take my second-best, as it folds up smaller."

Loveday looked surprised. "Well, if you are sure, Mum. And don't worry, we will check in with Dad to make sure he will still be alive for your return."

"Loveday, you look the spitting image of Mum in that outfit." Reggie meant it as a compliment, but Loveday made a face.

The three sisters walked quickly down the road in the drizzle to Woodford tube station. On the tube, only Reggie noticed the man and woman surreptitiously watching them from the front of the carriage. At King's Cross mainline station, with ten minutes to spare before their train to Hertford North was due to depart, Reggie put on her serious face. "I have a favour to ask you both. Let's meet in the last carriage of the Hertford train on platform twelve in eight minutes. Before we do, whether you need to spend a penny or not, let us go together to the toilet. Loveday, before coming out, reverse the coat so the rainbow lining is visible and give Mum's beret to GloGlo. GloGlo, reverse the beret before you put it on so its green satin side can be seen and put on your reading glasses. And when we leave the toilets, let's go through turnstiles separately. GloGlo first, then Loveday, then me. Don't ask any questions, just do it, please?"

GloGlo agreed immediately, and Loveday's brow furrowed, as she tentatively nodded in agreement. With two minutes to spare, the sisters MacGuffin met up in the last carriage, and Reggie was happy to note they were no longer being followed. They grabbed an empty compartment and sat down. GloGlo made herself comfortable in the corner seat. "Here's your hat back, Loveday."

Loveday grinned, "Thanks, GloGlo. Such cloak and dagger! I hope Reg will fill us in at some point."

Reggie kept her counsel. As the train whistle blew, the sisters opened up Alfie's sandwiches and ate silently, lost in their own thoughts. With the cooking for the fête taken care of and the syndicate inactive since the explosion at Ravenwood Studios, Joan had encouraged Reggie to focus on the remaining fête preparations. Then she could turn her attention to the film company's arrival in early August. GloGlo thought more about the flying display, as she had some new ideas to share with the Cuffley brothers, Charlie and Cliff. Loveday was happy to be leaving the city's grime behind which surprised her. Could she be done with London after all?

The filthy culverts around King's Cross soon morphed into soot-coated Victorian buildings which loomed over every railway line out of the city. The relentless, sooty brick of the London suburbs, pockmarked by gasometers, thankfully became punctuated by more green space and trees. They were soon rattling through Cuffley and Bayford, slowing down for arrival at Hertford North. GloGlo exited first and led the way via the underpass to the Maiden villages' branch line platform, where a single carriage train was waiting. Two older women were sitting on the platform having a natter next to a carpet bag, two handbags and a hatbox that looked like it came from the ark.

As Loveday looked at the timetable, one of the women leaned in. "It should be leaving in about four minutes, dear. Oh, Reggie, I didn't see you there, are these your famous sisters? You must be the flying lesbian, and you must be the flibbertigibbet who can cook but can't make up her mind. I hope we will be seeing you both at the WI. We could do with some new blood."

GloGlo, suppressing a smirk, replied, "Actually, I am the flying lesbian. Lovely to meet you."

And Loveday got her shilling in. "And I am the flibbertigibbet who can cook but can't make up her mind. Call me Loveday. Charmed, I'm sure."

Reggie, looking horrified, managed a brusque but polite, "Good morning, Joan. Nice to see you again, Blessing. We should all get on board. It must be about to leave."

The sisters boarded the train as the whistle blew. Blessing and Joan followed, still in character, plopping themselves down on either side of Loveday.

"I didn't realise the service was so efficient," said Loveday breezily.

Reggie was about to steer the conversation when Joan launched in, "Now, you, young lady, have quite the job on your hands following in Elsie Gascoyne's footsteps. That kitchen is not the easiest, let me tell you, but at least there is food in the larder. You know, during the war, Elsie would have to go out and shoot rabbits and game to make their rations go farther. She even stoned robins and would roast them on a stick. What a terrific shot she was! The current Lord Cuffley and his brother do what they can of course, but it is not the same. They are hard workers though, doing their best to stop the place from going to rack and ruin, I will give them that. At least the aerodrome seems busy. You can't hear yourself think before another plane takes off, drowning out Woman's Hour, The Archers or Gardener's Question Time."

Loveday exclaimed, "Oh good heavens, look!"

They all looked out of the window to see a magenta, vintage biplane chasing towards the train across the fields.

"It's just Beaver taking the Tiger Moth out for a spin," said GloGlo. "I told him he could this weekend, as flying is the best remedy for keeping an old engine maintained. Hold on girls, Beaver's going to buzz the train."

"Beaver can fly!" exclaimed Loveday. "He has gone up in my estimation one thousand per cent."

"What's he playing at? He's coming straight for us. He's meant to be putting up marquees, not tossing about in the sky," blurted Reggie.

As the magenta Tiger Moth flew low enough for its undercarriage to almost touch the train, Beaver pulled up at the final moment, but not before everyone, apart from GloGlo and Joan, had ducked down in their seats. GloGlo was impressed. "Look at Showgirl One go, she's so much more responsive since we tinkered with her ailerons. Well done, Beaver. After you, Reggie, he is my star pupil." Loveday looked confused.

"Showgirl One is the biplane, Loveday," said Reggie with chagrin and an eye roll. "GloGlo is training both me and Beaver to skydive. It is Beaver's dream that we jump out of a plane together, one day."

Joan turned to Loveday. "He's that delightfully strapping young Canadian, if I do say so myself. I've seen him with his shirt off, digging in the gardens. He can tinker with my ailerons any time. By the way, pet, Blessing and I are going to be on Friday sandwich duty. It always gets a bit hairy before the fête but we get the job done. Are you thinking of moving here permanently? We could use the new blood."

"Let me get through this Saturday, and then we'll see," said Loveday, thinking an inquisition from two old biddies before she had even arrived was not what she had been expecting.

"Well, I for one do hope you will stay," leaned in Blessing. "You see, so much goes on here that would be of interest to a vibrant young woman like yourself. Have you read *Scandal in the Shires*? I have, seventeen times! It claims that Cuffley Manor was England's major fascist enclave in the 1930s where meetings, masked balls and what's-seen-at-the-party-stays-at-the-party weekends were held, regularly involving the glitterati from politics, entertainment, aviation, royalty and aristocracy, which is utterly Babylonian if you think about it."

Reggie looked alarmed, as it was possibly a little too much gossip and scandal for Loveday to process before she met everyone.

"The more scandal the better in my opinion," said Loveday. "I was thinking that living in the country was going to be quite dull, but I do like a nice skeleton in the closet, a black sheep in the family, a treasure trove buried in the garden, secret passages in the house, debauchery in the shrubbery and of course, a mad woman in the attic."

Encouraged, Blessing carried on, "Let me tell you that the current Lord Cuffley's father, may he rest in peace, the poor man, had grown up here surrounded by all this debauchery but he managed to escape when the war started. Apparently, he came back a changed man. He lived in the lodge, got married, had twin boys and moved into the manor with his young family in the late 1940s once the army vacated. No abusive boarding schools nor forbidding governesses for Cliff and Charlie, they went to the local primary school. His wife died when the boys were small, and he recently passed away himself late last year. That is when young Master Clifford became Lord Cuffley, the poor boy, only because he was born a few minutes earlier than his brother. Thank goodness for the support of his brother, Charlie, otherwise poor Clifford would have been completely overwhelmed. Oh, here's your stop. We are not getting off until Maiden St Genevieve."

The MacGuffin sisters waved at Joan and Blessing as they piled off at Maiden Combust station, and without Loveday noticing, both Joan and Blessing winked at Reggie and GloGlo, and Joan handed GloGlo an envelope which GloGlo stuffed into her pocket. "Welcome to Maiden Combust, Loveday, and your first piece of local colour," grinned Reggie.

"They were a scream," said Loveday. "I cannot wait to gossip more with them about their plans to seduce Beaver and bringing back debauched parties. Does Beaver know what a commotion he has caused?"

"He is, as usual, completely unaware, much to my relief," sighed Reggie. "Let's drop in at the aerodrome first and afterwards I can take you up to the manor. What have you got going on today, Glo?"

GloGlo looked excited. "More rehearsals for the display plus I am hoping some parts I ordered have come in. Ash has been working all weekend, splashing paint around the control tower. I can't wait to see what progress she has made."

Emerging from the woodland, Loveday could see three hangars clustered at one end of a grassy landing strip. The smaller hangars were on either side of a larger one which had *CUFFLEY* painted above the huge doors. As they started walking on the side of the landing strip, the magenta Tiger Moth flew over the trees towards them and turned upside down.

"Down!" Loveday felt Reggie's hand pull hard on her shoulders until they were all face down in the wet grass. The noise of the plane's engine grew louder and louder and it seemed to skim their heads, pierced by faint screams and whoops from the cockpit.

"That was amazing," said GloGlo, removing grass from her mouth and picking up her bag. "Beaver wants me to know he has mastered the art of flying upside down before he lands."

They all stood up. Loveday cast a hand over her beret and checked the buttons on Delice's coat. "Who knew the country could be so exciting, and I have only this moment arrived."

"Beaver is just showing off," muttered Reggie smoothing down her coat and retrieving her handbag from a knot of cowslips.

"I should go and find Ash to let her know I am back safely. She is probably under Bluebell," said GloGlo, rushing off, holding Joan's envelope in her hand.

Reggie was slightly disappointed when she and Loveday found the main hangar empty of people. "Before we go over to the house, why don't we drop our bags here?"

Beaver arrived flushed in his flying suit, looking exhilarated. "Hello, Loveday, sorry for flattening you earlier. Oh man, you should have seen your faces! Hey, Babycakes."

Reggie put on her stern face. "Beaver, don't call me Babycakes in public. What on earth were you doing playing about in Showgirl One when there are tents needing to be erected?"

"Oh, Reg, the tents and marquees are all up as we had a lot of help from the volunteers. Don't worry, we followed your instructions to a tee." He gave her a rakish salute. "And Loveday's not public, she's your sister!"

Suddenly GloGlo came in running. "You will all never guess what has happened! I opened the note from Joan. She was such an amazing pilot in her youth, as you know. All sorts of daredevil exploits. She has owned Tiger Moths for nearly thirty years, and wants to give me guardianship of Showgirl One to formally relaunch the Showgirl Squadron Flying Circus!"

Loveday looked puzzled. "Joan, one of the mad old biddies from the train? She has a biplane!"

GloGlo nodded emphatically. "It started with an idea by our dear sister to generate more income for the aerodrome. When I began planning the flying display, Reggie put two and two together and wondered if there was demand for organising flying displays for others and whether I could give skydiving lessons. Then I suggested wing-walking and barnstorming, and I got all excited. All we needed was a plane and *blah blah cockles and mussels alive, alive oh*, the Showgirl Squadron Flying Circus has been reborn. And not only has Joan provided the plane, she also has provided the first booking. You will never guess what it is. The Football Association wants to have a whole squadron of vintage planes to be part of the historic fly past prior to the World Cup Final at Wembley on the Saturday after next. They are going to pay everyone who participates and not only fuel expenses. Rehearsals take place at Duxford airfield on Friday week, the day before the match."

Loveday was gobsmacked. "You old scruntbag. You know, England has an excellent chance of reaching the final. Imagine what Dad will say when we tell him. You might even get to see the Beatles. They are rumoured to be part of the pre-match entertainment."

Reggie was thinking that even though the syndicate had remained inactive since the explosion at Ravenwood Studios, how canny it was of Joan to insert the Showgirl Squadron into the World Cup opening ceremonies in a way that provided a bird's eye view of the whole of Wembley Stadium. Maybe Joan was still worried. Reggie would have a private chat with her later.

***

As they walked through the woods to the house, Reggie prepared Loveday to meet the Cuffley brothers. "There is no need to stand on ceremony with them. They're about our age and both a bit shell-shocked from the death of their father last year, especially as they have finally come to realise the perilous financial state the estate is in. You will think Charlie is the elder brother as he will do all the talking, but it is Cliff who, surprisingly, is older. The Lord Cuffley title weighs heavily on him. It's quite endearing, but you will see Charlie doing what he can to protect Cliff from getting overwhelmed, as Cliff is quite shy but perfectly nice once he warms up to you and gains confidence. They both spend most of their time at the aerodrome. Charlie took over the actual running of the place while Cliff helps GloGlo with aircraft maintenance. Once I have introduced you to the brothers, I will need to get back to the aerodrome. Meet me back there a bit before five."

Loveday became increasingly awed as parts of Cuffley Manor came into view through the trees before the whole was revealed.

"Oh my goodness," exclaimed Loveday, "I didn't think it was so huge or so round. What an enormous, wedding cake of a house!"

Reggie looked perturbed. "The rotunda is huge, isn't it? It is going to cost an enormous amount of money to fix the roof too. A few thousand afternoon teas might just do it. Let's go round the back of the rotunda and down the stairs to the kitchen via the servants' entrance. The grand entrance out front is a bit too grand if you ask me. Even Charlie and Cliff don't like to use it. Oh good, look at all the tents and marquees on the lawn, ready for the fête, and it looks like the grocer's van is already here. Hello, Charlie, did they bring everything? This is my sister, Loveday, who I told you is going to help cook for the fête."

Charlie turned around from the back of the grocer's van and grinned at them both. "Loveday, lovely to meet you. Did your father's birthday go well?" He extended a hand and smiled at Loveday in an easy way. "Yes, Reggie, everything is ticked off the list. I am waiting for Cliff to arrive with the trolley and when he gets here, we can bring it all in. We are a bit behind as the kitchen needed a good scrubbing before being used by a professional. Don't tell

Aunt Elsie, I mean Mrs Gascoyne, but I don't think anyone has given it a good scrub since the WI did it before last year's fête."

Reggie smiled and her shoulders visibly relaxed. "I'll be heading off. Loveday, I cannot tell you how much easier this is all going to be with you here. See you at five. Charlie, I'll see you later back at the aerodrome."

Loveday nodded and turned her attention back to Charlie who was also looking relieved. "Loveday, once we get the food stored, we can gather our thoughts. Fête week is always like this. We have the best intentions in the world, but then everything starts to run away from us. Oh good, there's my brother. Cliff, this is Reggie's sister, Loveday."

"Hello, Loveday," he said, barely daring to look her in the eyes. And then he seemed to gather his courage. "That is an easy name to remember."

The kitchen was as big as the MacGuffins' whole house. The outside wall was built in the curve of the rotunda and met the inner wall at an odd angle, hidden by the enormous fireplace, situated next to a wood-burning stove, two modern ovens, hobs and three big sinks. The ceilings were twenty feet high, with windows high up on the curved wall, letting in long shafts of light. A formidable iron frame holding saucepans and pots was suspended over a big oak table which looked centuries old. On the table were gathered buckets, mops, dirty cloths, bottles of bleach, vinegar and Liquid Gumption.

Charlie summed up the state of play. "The clean-up is pretty well done. Cliff and I attacked the floors, the windows, the insides of the ovens, fridge and cupboards. We also washed up the utensils, cutting boards, knives and baking pans and made sure the ovens and hobs were working. And don't worry, we don't use this kitchen ourselves as we have a much more practical, smaller, modern one upstairs."

"You have done me out of a job," smiled Loveday, "I was planning to spend the rest of today and tomorrow putting the place to rights."

Charlie helped Cliff bring down the non-perishable items from the grocer's van, while Loveday corralled a pot of tea. Blowing over his mug to cool it down, Charlie explained about the fête, "It is always on a Saturday in July, from two until five in the afternoon. There is a bring-and-buy stall, a cake, pie and baked goods stall, a tombola, a raffle, games for the children and chicken bingo. We also go all out and serve afternoon tea."

"Chicken Bingo? What's that?" asked Loveday, as she wrapped her cold hands around her cup.

"It is much like ordinary bingo except you mark out all the numbers in a grid, on the ground, surrounded by a pen of chicken wire. Then you place a chicken in the pen and mark off on your bingo card whichever number it, you know, does its business on, until someone wins," said Charlie smirking.

Cliff chortled to himself. "If you pick the wrong chicken, it can take hours."

Charlie nodded and laughed. "Everything has to be ready for two o'clock when the Tiger Moth flies over to declare the fête open. At five o'clock, two biplanes put on another display to close the event. I hear you already were buzzed earlier today. Sorry about that. Par for the course here I am afraid, isn't that right, Cliff? On Saturday morning, we will fine tune the organisation of the tables, signage and balloons, and set up the loudspeaker system. The WI members organise the tea tent themselves. Do you have any questions?"

Loveday consulted her notes. "Because I don't have to clean up the kitchen, tomorrow could be a day for test baking for which I will need some guinea pigs. What do you think? Are you both up for sampling my delights?"

"Sounds great, Loveday, doesn't it, Cliff?" Cliff blushed.

Charlie offered to give Loveday a tour of the manor which she gratefully accepted, but Cliff made a request. He wanted to show Loveday his favourite room in the manor, himself.

"Because the manor and aerodrome were so far apart during the war, the army installed a pneumatic tube postal system, and it still works like a dream. And it goes with a tremendous *whoosh*," said Cliff with a trace of wonder as he took Loveday past the walk-in larder to the corridor on the other side of the kitchen walls and servants' entrance. They passed closed doors marked 'Housekeeper's Room', 'Butler's Room', 'Laundry Room', 'Ironing Room', 'Linen Closet', 'WC' and 'Cellar', to the one marked 'Post Room'. Inside was a large room with a big table in the middle. One complete wall was covered in over two dozen, six-inch-wide brass tubes, all disappearing into the wall. Underneath the table was a big box full of steel canisters, each the size of a banana. "You write your note on a piece of paper from the pad here, unscrew the top off the canister, put the note inside, twist the top back on and put it in whichever tube you want and it flies off to wherever you want it to go like a missile," said Cliff with unabashed enthusiasm.

Cliff took Loveday over to the wall of tubes, each of which was marked with a building name. "Write a note to Reggie and then we can send it." Loveday did as she was told, wrote a quick note, put it in a cylindrical canister and screwed it up tight. Cliff showed her how to lift the hinged cover at the top of the pneumatic tube marked 'Aerodrome Hangar 1'. "Each tube has a door to send the mail," said Cliff proudly. "You open the door, place the canister inside, close it and press this big red button. A fan at the other end of the pipe comes on, the air pressure changes, and *whoosh!* It's gone. Reggie should get it in a minute or two. Once she is back in her office, she will hear a buzzer, letting her know mail has arrived. When I get to the aerodrome, I will send a note to the kitchen. You probably won't hear the buzzer from the kitchen but there is also a red light in the corridor which alerts you when new post has arrived."

"My goodness, how nifty. This house is a marvel," said Loveday, pleased to see Cliff relaxed and animated.

Charlie poked his head around the door to chivvy Cliff to return to the aerodrome while Charlie carried on with the tour. "As you can see, the manor is a huge, ridiculous, eighteenth century rotunda which no one in their right mind would build if it was not already here. A lot of the best furniture, art and silver has been sold over the years when family members found themselves in financial difficulty. Some of the land was sold off as well. You know the Ridgeway Council Estate where Reggie lives? It used to be part of the grounds. Cliff and I live upstairs. Let's start with the servants' staircase which enabled the staff to move about sight unseen in the 1920s and 1930s when the family could afford staff."

Emerging up the hidden servants' stairs and out of a door hidden in the wooden panelling and into the rotunda's grand hall, Loveday looked up at the beautiful ceiling, and her mouth dropped in awe, which delighted Charlie.

"The servants' stairs take you right up to the roof, where you can exit and walk around, but be careful exploring up there as often a Tiger Moth will swoop down low and you end up thanking the heavens for whoever invented parapets. On this floor, there is also the ballroom flanked by the drawing and dining rooms. We hardly use the main floor at all. There is quite a lovely garden terrace off the ballroom with steps down to the formal gardens which are designed around a huge fountain, Long Lake and Cuffley Hoo, which is our grandfather's lunatic Hanging Gardens of Babylon pastiche. This is our grand stairway. On the next floor we have the library, study, billiard room and morning room. Further up are all the grand bedrooms and bathrooms but we don't use them. Cliff and I sleep in a couple of the smaller rooms near where our old nursery was. On the top floor, which is really a glorified attic, are the old servant bedrooms, access to the roof and several storage rooms."

On the third floor, Charlie opened a door painted in gold, lilac and white. "This is my favourite of the grand bedrooms. They all have themes, and this is *The Romanovs go to the Baltic* bedroom." He went over to the windows to open white and gold painted shutters. Light flooded in, illuminating walls painted in mauve and white stripes with gold filigree detailing, Scandinavian decorative accents and a huge brass bed covered in white linen. There were shelves and shelves of blue and white porcelain edged in gold, a collection of Russian lacquer boxes in an elaborate gilded vitrine and a decorative purple, mauve and white tiled stove in one of the room's corners.

"When I describe it to people, they think it sounds hideous, but as you can see it is quite lovely, and I feel as though we might see the Baltic Sea out the window instead of the church spires of Maiden St Genevieve, Maiden St Irene, and Maiden All Saints. We rarely come in here now, as this was the room where my dad died of a heart attack last year. Cliff found him. We don't know why he was even in here as it wasn't his bedroom." Charlie sounded wistful.

"I am so sorry Loveday, I thought I could show you this room without all the emotions about my dad's death springing up. I obviously need more time to grieve." His eyes welled up before he shook himself back to the present.

"Over there, you can just see the stables which used to house horses and carriages. We keep all the gardening and maintenance equipment there now. There are lots of follies throughout the gardens in varying states of disrepair. Some are quite beautiful and some are just barmy. The best of them are the ones which decorate Cuffley Hoo – the big hillock that dominates the garden to the rear. The original hillock was designed to allow the first Lord Cuffley to see all his land when the manor was built. About sixty years ago, it was made higher by my great-grandfather when they were digging out the chalk pits. He thought it was a cheap way to repurpose all the soil, gravel and stone they unearthed when he redid the gardens."

Charlie looked at his watch, grimaced and also sounded relieved. "Cripes, Loveday, I should get back to the aerodrome too. Reggie needs to have a discussion about the film company's plans while they are on location here. We can pick up the tour another time. Please feel free to wander about as you wish."

Checking her watch, Loveday saw it was already close to four o'clock, so she headed back down to the kitchen to get organised for the next day's baking. At a quarter to five, she picked up her coat and sauntered back to the aerodrome, finding Reggie at her desk looking harassed behind a tottering pile of files. "Oh, Loveday, is it already five o'clock? Gosh, this afternoon sped by. You will never believe what has happened. Because their soundstage at Ravenwood Studios burnt down, you must have read about it, the film company wants to arrive this week! And they want us to provide accommodation and food, if at all possible, for their key people! They are going to pay extra for the change of plans of course, so Charlie and Cliff are all for it and will organise the accommodation with Joan and Blessing's help. But we need someone to take care of the film crew's culinary needs. So, how do you fancy staying a bit longer and feeding some film stars?"

Loveday threw her arms in the air and hugged Reggie. "Of course I am going to stay!"

"Wonderful," said Reggie, "I have been on the phone all afternoon with Nobby, the film company's production manager. The film company will arrive later this week, on Friday afternoon, the day before the fête, to do something called a *press call* where the stars meet the press and the press take photographs. However, they will not begin any filming until next week, after the fête thank goodness, and won't be requiring any accommodation until then. Most of the crew are going to stay at various hotels, bed and breakfasts and pubs in Hertford and the local villages. They will need Ash to ferry the film crew between here and Hertford in Bluebell. Nobby has requested the director, her assistant and the leading cast members to stay at Cuffley Manor for a minimum of two weeks. Only four of the grand bedrooms will be needed. Although the film company is bringing its own on-set caterers, they have asked if breakfast and dinner could be provided for those staying at the house, with breakfast served in the large dining room at half-past six in the morning and dinner served late, around nine o'clock."

Loveday nodded. Her adrenaline was flowing at the prospect of mixing with the cast and crew.

Reggie added, "We will need to get two floors of the rotunda fit for human habitation. Do not worry, we will rope in the WI. However, can you start thinking about menus and making a list of all the food that needs to be ordered?" Loveday nodded. "And now, let us go home."

***

Reggie had banished Beaver for the evening so she and Loveday could be alone. Over a reviving plate of cheese on toast, Reggie turned towards her sister with her steely let-us-get-down-to-business look. "Have you ever thought why a former head girl of the Kitty Cadbury School for Girls of Distinction with ten A grade O-levels, four A grade A-levels, and a degree in criminology and politics, Air Cadet badges in parachuting, skydiving, explosives, incendiary devices, unarmed combat, map reading, codes and signals, not to mention all those Brownie's badges in survival skills, would end up working as a bookkeeper for a tiny aerodrome in the home counties?"

"I thought it was because you peaked when you were eighteen and had given up anything fun for Lent, which thus far has lasted almost four years. I thought you were just being pragmatic." Loveday frowned and slumped back with her arms folded. "Whatever happened to our girlhood daredevilry? GloGlo has found her niche I suppose, but what about you and me? You used to be the most fearless of all of us in air cadets. Remember learning to parachute, throwing ourselves out of planes, flying gliders? That was so thrilling! Now look at you, bookkeeping in the home counties."

Reggie changed tack. "Loveday, do you remember the day Mum was injured in the train crash?"

"Of course, I do."

"What exactly do you remember about that day?"

"Mum was away for the weekend, something to do with the British Legion. You were out at air cadets, Dad was outside washing the car and GloGlo was on a school trip to the Brabazon Aircraft Corporation. I remember playing in our room and no one answered the phone which kept ringing and ringing, so I harrumphed downstairs. It was the voice of a woman I didn't recognise, asking whether Mr MacGuffin was there. I left the phone hanging and went to get Dad, still holding my felt pens. After the phone call, he went all quiet and pale and took me into the living room and told me that the call was from the hospital and that there had been an accident with Mum's train and it was very serious. Mum was alive but injured and might not make it. He asked me if I understood what it all meant. I think I just nodded and thought about when Desdemona, the psycho hamster, died, and we buried her in the back garden and it had been all right to feel sad and eat fish and chips. Dad and I drove to air cadets to pick you up, and we all went to the hospital but were not allowed to see Mum until the next day. When we did see her, she just lay there. I was only young and did not understand what was going on. It was the one time Dad took us to the Wimpy, and we had egg burgers and Dad had the Wimpy grill. Why are we talking about this?"

"After the train crash, I figured out that the WI was not just the WI. When Dad sent me to pack some clothes for Mum to take to the hospital, I found a copy of this in her wardrobe." Reggie handed Loveday an envelope, stamped on the front with *On Her Majesty's Women's Intelligence,* containing several pages of foolscap stapled together. Each page was covered in tiny grey text, on paper embossed with the crest of the Government of Great Britain and Northern Ireland.

Official Secrets Act, 1911 as amended by the Act of 1920.

With a furrowed brow Loveday looked across at her sister. "Reg, you play your cards really close to your chest, don't you?"

"It is because I am really good at buttoning my lip, unlike you, and it is my job. To be honest, I am unsure this is what you or I should be doing right now but circumstances are such that I need the kind of help only you can give me, and I want you to be fully aware of the context and circumstances. There have been enough secrets in our family for far too long. If you are going to work at Cuffley Manor, you have to read this carefully, reflect on what it means and sign it. There will be no going back."

Loveday threw her sister a quizzical look. "Why am I the only one who can help you? Surely there are other cooks about."

"Loveday, this is only partially about cooking. You are the only person who can help me, because you are family, I can trust you, and you cook like blazes when you put your mind to it. I will answer your questions as best I can within the limitations placed on me."

"Limitations placed by whom, Reg?"

"Come on, Loveday. Look at the government crest on the headed notepaper and the envelope?"

Loveday snuggled down into the sofa's cushions. "I thought there might be something nefarious going on. That business at King's Cross station this morning, for instance."

She spent the next hour and four mugs of tea reading the documents. "When did you sign?"

"Two years ago."

"And you didn't tell me!"

"I did not, and now you know why. You cannot tell anyone, Loveday, ever."

"Ever?"

"Ever."

"Will you look after me if I sign?"

"Yes, I will."

"Okay, I am signing." Loveday put her signature on the final page, with Reggie signing as witness.

"Oh, Loveday, I am so excited you took the plunge. Thank you."

"So, your job is not about bookkeeping at an aerodrome and organising jumble sales for the women's institute?"

"It involves that but not only that. My job here is something bigger."

"So, spill the beans."

Reggie fixed her cushions so she could sit more upright. "After the Second World War, there were several years when the British government stared at the tealeaves, analysing the intelligence successes and the failures of the war and its aftermath, including when the Soviet Union recruited the Cambridge spies in the early 1950s and the country suffered a whole spate of terrible plane, train and bus crashes, shipping accidents, arson, flooding and other industrial and environmental disasters for which MI-5 had no advance warning. Are you with me so far?"

Loveday nodded. Reggie carried on, "The women who worked in intelligence during the war were unceremoniously let go in the latter half of the 1940s. However, thank goodness, one person in power was on our side. In 1955, due to the government's embarrassment over the Cambridge spies' security breaches, the prime minister was persuaded to relaunch the Women's Intelligence Service, now called WI-5, with a focus on surveillance, information gathering, analysis and communications. Across the country, you know, there are networks of women's institutes which do good works in every village, town and city. Not all women's institutes include WI-5 operatives, but many WIs are WI-5-equipped and supported with a subset of women focusing on the identification and gathering of information on activities which are potentially a threat to the security of the nation, sending the resulting information back to headquarters. Are you still with me? Is the penny dropping?"

"Oh my goodness, Reg, are you the Mata Hari of the home counties?"

Reggie laughed. "Yes, though there are many of us Mata Haris, mostly dressed in crimplene, polyester, wool and nylon rather than whatever seductive spy wear you are imagining. Maiden Combust Women's Institute is WI-5's Hertfordshire hub. We are in the midst of some major goings on which has everyone on high alert. Headquarters has been experiencing some communication leaks and certain things have not been going well, so I suspect not everyone can be trusted, but I know I can trust you."

"Oh my goodness, how exciting! Will I have to sleep with Russians after I cook for them?"

"Possibly."

"All the secrecy stuff on the train. What was going on?"

"It was a tactical response to some fairly ham-fisted evidence. We were being watched but I was not sure by whom."

"Oh gosh. Does GloGlo know about this? Wait a minute, has she signed too?"

"Yes, although only recently, in rather urgent circumstances with support from Ash, who has been working with me. You met another two of them on the platform today, Joan and Blessing. Good, aren't they?"

"Oh gosh, yes, I would never have guessed. Has Beaver signed?"

"No."

"Is Beaver really your boyfriend?"

"Yes."

"So, the security of our country is not in the hands of Beaver."

"No, it is not."

"So, what do you want me to do?"

"Actually, Loveday, as you have now signed on, I need you to come with GloGlo and me to WI-5's London headquarters tomorrow morning. I need to get both of you up to speed as soon as possible. Time is of the essence."

Bus Stop

All three MacGuffin sisters walked to Hertford North train station, under a welcome splash of morning sunshine. Reggie was feeling good that finally she could be completely open with both her siblings. Conducting surveillance on the film company's activities was going to be vital. Loveday was central to those plans and Reggie would need to keep her close. Loveday was happy she was going to spend an unexpected day in London. Feeling safe in the company of her two sisters, she became preoccupied with how she was going to squeeze four days of cooking into three. GloGlo was excited about preparing for the flying display, the film company's arrival at the aerodrome and the rehearsal for the World Cup flypast.

Reggie broke the spell first. "Loveday, how are you feeling about these revelations?"

"Pretty good, Reg. I am flattered you think I am up for this, and I am going to try my best not to disappoint," said Loveday, as she received a big hug from GloGlo, almost knocking her over as they walked.

"And me too," said GloGlo. "You know I suspected there was some deeper connection between Ash and Reggie, and now, I know. It is rather a relief."

"Oh my goodness, yes, Ash is the most experienced of all of us newish recruits. She has already been trained at HQ so she didn't need to come today," said Reggie matter of factly.

"Can you tell us exactly where we are going?" asked Loveday, as her mind whirled.

"Be patient," said Reggie enigmatically. "I want to see both your faces when all is revealed."

The train ride into London was uneventful, with each MacGuffin sister returning to her thoughts. At Kings Cross, Reggie led them outside to a bus stop which surprisingly, for the morning rush hour, did not have a queue. It was just a temporary white pole with the London transport sign on top and a notice stating the only bus stopping there was the 999. GloGlo registered the number and furrowed her brow. "The 999? I've never seen a 999."

"Don't worry. The 999 always goes where we want to go," said Reggie with a half smile and a glinty squint. "Welcome to my world."

They did not have to wait long before three buses went past and the 999 came along with a *Driver in Training* sign, and one woman got off. Although it was not full downstairs, Reggie headed straight upstairs to the front, knowing the unoccupied left front seat by the window was Loveday's favourite perch. She and GloGlo grabbed the seats in the row behind. *So far so good,* thought Reggie. *Loveday and GloGlo on time (not always a given), bus on time (almost always a given for the 999) and Loveday in her favourite seat.* Only Reggie was aware of the woman who leapt off the bus, grabbed the temporary bus stop pole and gotten back on board, heaving the pole into the alcove under the stairs.

To sit down, Loveday had had to push by a man thankfully sitting in the aisle seat, leaving her the window, and who she registered as quite acceptable looking. She caught a flash of brown-green eyes, a half smile and a decent pair of shoes. He fleetingly caught an eyeful of pink, gabardine coat, a flash of red lips and raspberry beret. *Quite arresting*, he thought. He shifted in his seat and pressed his toes into the soles of his shoes.

Loveday rested her bag on her knee and made a point of looking to her left out of the window as the engine strained to pull away from the kerb. She still had no idea where they were heading and was thankful Reggie was in charge of getting them there. Reggie had not revealed anything other than a few titbits and a sense of broader intrigue. Loveday squirmed in her seat to find the most comfortable place where the springs were not quite so prominent and the nubbly fabric not quite so worn down and inadvertently rubbed against the thigh of her seatmate who was reading *Strategy and Tactics of Monopoly*. *An interesting choice*, thought Loveday. Glancing over, she moved her bag off her lap, so it rested on her feet and pressed her knees and thighs together, unaware she was being demure. "Good book?" asked Loveday, as the bus moved surprisingly quickly along the High Road.

"I haven't got into it yet. Actually, let us not talk about books. I haven't seen you before. How come you are on the 999 this morning?"

"I am here with my sisters," replied Loveday, nodding to the seats behind them.

Tolly looked back over Loveday's shoulder. "Oh,

hello, Reggie, how's tricks?"

Reggie signalled for him to turn back around. "Never you mind, Tolly. Keep your eyes forward and mind your Ps and Qs. Loveday, GloGlo, this is Tolliver," said Reggie tersely before relaxing into a smile and returning the nod of one of the women opposite.

Loveday in a stage whisper said, "I am much nicer than my sister by the way."

Tolly leaned towards Loveday. "I don't doubt it. I like your hat; red is my favourite colour."

"Actually, it's raspberry. How do you feel about fruit?"

"I am fine with fruit, though I don't get the point of it. I am more of a meat and potatoes man," said Tolly with a grin.

Loveday returned the grin. "You don't get the point of fruit. *Mmm*, well your eyes are quite distinctive. Browny green, like a ripe pear; however, I cannot, for the life of me, figure out if they are Bosc or Bartlett."

"Is there a compliment in there somewhere?" asked Tolly, twinkling.

"I did say they were 'distinctive'."

"I am focusing on the Bosc – a particularly ugly fruit. You know, the asymmetry of your face from this angle is quite mesmerising," said Tolly.

"Is there a compliment in there somewhere?" replied Loveday, returning the twinkle.

"I did say you were mesmerising."

"My English teacher used to mesmerise our whole class with her knee-length red socks and clogs."

"She sounds not only mesmerising but bewitching."

Loveday twisted in her seat and held out her right hand. "Loveday Mundesley Penelope MacGuffin, pleased to meet you, Tolly."

Tolly shook her proffered hand. "Tolliver Culverhouse Pye but call me Tolly, please. Likewise, I am pleased to meet you Loveday Mundesley Penelope MacGuffin. Did you get lumbered with family names as well?"

"I was conceived in Mundesley, a seaside village on the Norfolk coast, on an extremely stormy, blustery day which is all you need to know about my parents and the drama of my life. Penelope is for my dad's heroine, you know Penelope Knickerbocker, the alias of Dynamite McQueen in the films, if you've ever seen one."

Rather than singing the Dynamite McQueen theme song which he could have done, Tolly surprisingly broke into *Gimingham, Trimingham, Knapton and Trunch, Northrepps, Southrepps, all in a bunch. Mundesley, Bacton, Walcott and Stow, Sidestrand, Overstrand, falling below.* He grinned at Loveday who was admiringly aghast.

"I thought it was only my parents who knew that ancient rhyme. They used to sing it to us as children. I am impressed."

"I had an aunt who lived in North Walsham, and she used to take me to the gas terminal at Bacton to watch the ships to keep me entertained. She was a retired civil engineer, and I found all the gasworks' piping quite bewitching, like your English teacher's socks. She also would bring me up to London to marvel at Beckton

Gasworks – the largest gasworks in the world."

As their bus reached the Cambridge Circus junction with Shaftesbury Avenue, Tolly's attention was suddenly taken by something outside. "Gordon Bennett, what is that?"

Another double-decker bus, with darkened windows, pulled alongside them. Suddenly the windows beside Loveday and Tolly emitted a loud crack. The glass shattered but held in place.

"Everybody down," yelled Reggie as she pushed GloGlo towards the floor and Tolly grabbed Loveday by the shoulders, folding her forward. Her head brushed past the metal sill of the window. Thank goodness Loveday's raspberry beret provided a semblance of padding.

Tolly reached across Loveday to wrestle under the seat to find and pull up the other end of a leather seat belt. "Take this and buckle it up tight!" Loveday glanced up at him with panic in her eyes. She could see the other passengers were bent over.

Reggie hissed from the seat behind, "Do what he says, belt up and bend forward." Loveday quickly secured the belt across her and Tolly's laps, pinning them to the seat and to each other. Tolly pushed Loveday further down so she was bent completely double, head pressed against her knees.

The bus accelerated and veered to the left. Loveday couldn't resist twisting her head to take a peek, eyes widening, as she realised they had hit the side of the chasing bus which was sent careening behind them into the awning of the Palace Theatre while their bus continued onto Shaftesbury Avenue.

"Keep your head down, we are not out of this yet. Thank goodness Fragrance is driving, and we are in Drusilla," muttered Reggie.

GloGlo looked at Reggie and mouthed, "Fragrance? Drusilla?"

Reggie returned her look, communicating excitement rather than panic as she whispered, "Fragrance is amazing, but it is Drusilla who puts the master in Routemaster."

Under Tolly's arm, Loveday was able to twist herself in a position to peek through the bottom of the front window. They were crossing Piccadilly Circus heading west, shooting past bus stops with long lines of people waiting with their mouths hanging open, pointing at the bus going faster than any other bus had gone before, overtaking cars, taxis and other buses with its horn blaring. Several grocery vans jumped across the central reservation, jackknifing in front of Drusilla, which Fragrance sent into a sharp turn, smacking into each van, scattering them across Piccadilly. Loveday's head slammed into the side of the bus as Fragrance took a sharp right turn into Hyde Park along Serpentine Road, mounting the kerb and causing pedestrians and a long line of orange traffic cones to scatter in all directions.

Loveday did not see the sign for 'roadworks' and the Serpentine Bridge fast approaching. Although Tolly was again using his hand to press her head down, she managed to twist to face him. He was grinning at her. "Having fun yet?"

On the road adjacent to the Serpentine, Fragrance

drove Drusilla towards the bridge, with her foot to the floor. Her voice yelled over the loudspeaker, "Everyone on the top deck descend to the bottom deck. NOW!" Within ten seconds, all the top deck passengers shunted downstairs. Reggie, GloGlo, Tolly and Loveday sat squished together in the aisle on the lower deck. Glimpsing out of the rear window as they rushed downstairs, they could see they were being followed by the same black-windowed bus which was getting closer as more shots were fired.

Drusilla lurched to overtake a line of cars backed up behind a road worker holding a stop sign. Practically standing on the pedals, Fragrance wrestled the steering wheel abruptly to the left, causing Drusilla to knock over another line of orange cones marking out a hole being dug in the road. Cars coming towards them along the single lane of road dove left and right, as Drusilla roared down on them. Immediately after the roadworks, half a dozen grocery vans in V-formation headed towards them across the grass from the right. Fragrance jumped the kerb and headed at full speed down to the wide pedestrian footpath next to the Serpentine. Loveday was peeking up through the front windscreen, blanched, and could only gasp, "Bridge!"

Over the loudspeaker, Fragrance announced, "Ready for top deck release." After several replies of 'Ready' from the lower deck, she commanded, "On three: one, two, three!"

Loveday could feel a series of deep, muffled, clunks and thumps vibrating through the bus as multiple heavy clips were released above her head, to the side, in front and behind her. Passengers who were in seats, folded themselves forward and placed their hands over their necks. Those in the aisles crouched down and folded themselves over. Loveday crouched under Tolly's bulk, and GloGlo clutched Reggie. Taking peeks through the back, they could see the armada of grocery vans catching up with them. Suddenly, a periwinkle blue coach loomed behind the grocery vans and pulled into a three-hundred-and-sixty-degree spin that hit the back of one, which careened into the others, sending them all scattering like skittles into the Serpentine. Hearing what sounded to be a familiar squeal of engine, GloGlo looked up and caught a glimpse of Ashwariya driving Bluebell.

Stonework filled Drusilla's windscreen. Loveday looked up horrified and Tolly pulled her back down just as there was an almighty crash. Drusilla's top deck hit the bridge. The noise was deafening, with an alarming metallic scraping screech down the entire length of the bus as the whole top floor slid clean away from the rest of the bus and landed in one piece on the tarmac behind them, completely blocking the road under the bridge. They were hit by a forceful, cold wind and Loveday screamed.

"Operation successful!" yelled Fragrance.

"Why aren't we stopping!" yelled Loveday.

"Stay down, don't move," ordered Reggie.

"Let go of me! Are we dead?" sobbed Loveday.

Reggie and Tolly released their grips on GloGlo and Loveday respectively.

"How come we are still moving?" yelled Loveday as

she looked up through the windows and a non-existent roof now open to the skies. A Hyde Park scene of parkgoers with mouths agape watched a London bus without its top floor drive up onto the road and across the bridge towards Kensington High Street.

"Hang on a sec, Loveday, we are nearly there," said Tolly. The bus raced down Exhibition Road and turned left into a side street and through the unmarked entrance to a double height garage, coming to a sudden halt by a loading dock.

Reggie leaned forward and clasped Loveday's shoulders. "Are you okay?"

"What happened, and where are we?"

Reggie looked at her and said, "Sorry to say this, my dear sister, but welcome to the Victoria and Albert Museum!" Loveday looked at her, shocked and uncomprehending.

In her underground V&A archives office, Morag looked at her watch, thinking the bus should have arrived by now. She called up Fragrance on her compact. "How did the test go? Did Drusilla break down?"

Fragrance was sounding out of breath. "Oh, Morag, there was another incident. Drusilla was fired at, and I had to take evasive action. Instead of doing the test on the roof, we were forced to try out the new manoeuvres in the field, in Hyde Park actually. Everything worked beautifully. We hit the Serpentine Bridge and the top floor came off."

"Oh my goodness, was anybody hurt? What happened? Was it the syndicate back in business, doing their usual target practice? How did they know?"

Fragrance's attention was taken by Drusilla's upper deck entering the garage towed by Bluebell, with the garage doors closing quickly behind them.

Still stunned, Loveday just about registered they were in a huge bus garage that did not look like part of a museum at all. She followed the others towards a door in the side wall between a brightly lit office and a loading bay. Tolly yelled up to the loading dock, "Parcel's arrived," and Alfie came out wincing and rushed to give GloGlo, Reggie and a still speechless and shaking Loveday, hugs.

Alfie tried to sound as if he was not shocked. "Well, wasn't that was one for the ages! Loveday and GloGlo, we wanted to give you a proper welcome, but having you attacked was not part of the plan. Are you all right? What am I going to tell your mother? I might have to rethink my support for this family escapade."

Loveday was starting to gather her senses. "Reg, what is going on? I thought you said we were going to a headquarters? Why is Dad here? Why are we at the museum?"

Reggie put a calming arm around both her sisters' shoulders. "Welcome to the V&A, which also doubles as the headquarters of WI-5. Dad works here too. Surprise!"

Behind the Scenes at the Museum

"Oh thank goodness," said Loveday, starting to calm down. "I thought everything might have been some hideous ruse to get me into a museum job. Well, Dad, we were shot at, hit a bridge, the bus came apart and my heart is still racing. I think we deserve a cuppa."

Alfie looked relieved. "Kettle's already on. And how is everyone else?" Reggie, GloGlo and Tolly nodded and gave the thumbs up.

Ashwariya came through the doors and hugged GloGlo. "Oh, Glo, thankfully I was there to defend you. Reggie reminded me it was your first trip to headquarters and I wanted to be part of it, but I had no idea I would be in on the action itself!"

Fragrance entered and handed a pile of paper forms to Alfie. "Hello, Ash, Reggie and Alfie. Everyone else, I'm Fragrance Yeoh, in charge of WI-5 ground transportation. Alfie, get each of your charges to fill out one of these incident reports this morning, and hand them back to me. We need to collect everyone's description of what happened while it is fresh in their memories. I will compile a report for Morag. I will also put the word out that we are suspending all bus operations for the rest of the day pending the investigation, and call all buses to come back in."

Alfie grabbed his three daughters. "I am so relieved you three are all right. Your mum is going to have my guts for garters if she ever finds out the danger you were in. Welcome to the V&A. Not quite what you expected, is it, Loveday?"

Tolly went to find a quiet spot to fill out his form. Fragrance spirited Ashwariya to Morag's office for a debriefing, while Alfie steered his daughters to his cubbyhole where they hutched up on stools while he made tea. After five minutes of sitting in silence, waiting for the tea to steep and staring at their much younger selves in the MacGuffin family photograph Alfie had stuck to the wall, they gratefully took their mugs of tea and looked expectantly over the rims at Alfie.

"I want to apologise to you all. If I had known that this morning's demonstration of Drusilla's new capabilities was going to be sabotaged, I wouldn't have allowed any of you into the line of fire. Are you all coming back to life? Rest assured, Loveday and GloGlo, you won't get shot at every day. I know this might come as a disappointment to you both."

"Thanks, Dad, good to know. I need some aspirin first, and then I have so many questions," said Loveday. "But are we going to get any answers?"

Alfie and Reggie looked at each other before collectively nodding at Loveday.

"Thanks." She tossed back a couple of proffered aspirin with a big swig of tea. "My first question is the same as yours, Dad. What exactly happened this morning?"

Fragrance, who had reappeared to check the sisters were being well looked after in Alfie's care, heard the question and began, "The V&A has been a key part of the intelligence services since the Second World War, when this location was used by the secret service to train operatives to be dropped behind enemy lines. Since 1955, WI-5 has overseen all secret service ground and air transportation in London, and acts as the hub for information collected from all the regional coach networks which includes the Hertfordshire network, now led by Ashwariya, based at Cuffley Manor. WI-5's job has been to move documents, files and people secretly around London, between London and the regions, not only getting the information to where it needs to go but also tracking it and maintaining a copy in our central files stored in acres of filing cabinets stacked in all the corridors here. Whenever you see a London bus or regional coach which is 'Not in Service', 'Driver Training' or 'Mystery Tour', it is usually one of ours – full of boxes and people. Although this started during the war, it continued and grew quickly once war ended, as the need for information to move speedily and stealthily became even more acute. We already have over fifty buses in service in London alone and two hundred coaches throughout the regions, all of them loaded and despatched from the bus garage behind the museum. We also do all the maintenance and the driver training. This morning was meant to be the first road test for WI-5's Routemaster warhorse bus, Drusilla, which has had some novel capabilities added. In the past six months, several buses and coaches have been intercepted, and so the ground transportation team has been working on expanding WI-5's defences. Drusilla was the first prototype bus to incorporate a weapon and the ability to release the top deck to block the road if being chased. There is a road-testing circuit on the bus garage roof next to the V&A, where any new vehicle is put through its paces, and that was the plan this morning. We always get lots of volunteers when we are testing buses. The original plan was to pick up passengers, drive Drusilla on to the roof here, test her machine gun on a pile of boxes and have her run into a mocked-up bridge to knock the top deck off cleanly to block any chasing vehicles. However, no one expected us to be intercepted by a hail of bullets out there in the street. Based on recent events I think the attack is clearly the work of the *Fleur de Lys Crime Syndicate* which we thought had been put out of action last month but apparently not so." Fragrance trailed off, lost in thought, and then her attention was caught by Ashwariya, who had appeared in the doorway. "Ash, do you want to summarise what happened from your perspective?"

Ash nodded. "As a surprise for GloGlo, I was following in Bluebell at a safe distance behind Drusilla. Fragrance had noticed Bluebell in her mirrors soon after we left the railway station. Once she noticed Drusilla being chased, Fragrance alerted me of her Hyde Park plan. I then alerted Joan and Blessing at the manor that something was up. As soon as I saw the convoy of grocery vans approaching Drusilla across Hyde Park, I prepared to deploy my lethal three-hundred-and-sixty-degree handbrake turn. When Drusilla had escaped their clutches,

I used Bluebell's tow rope and trailer to remove the upper deck from the scene. I agree with Fragrance. This morning's attack was the work of the syndicate, and someone among us must have shared information with them. The mole is active once again."

Everyone reflected on what they had just heard until Loveday spoke up. "Tea top-up please, Dad. Another question! How do you not get the attention of the press, blowing things up on the roof of the V&A and spraying gunfire in Hyde Park?"

"That is an easy one to answer. We just pretend a film crew has been working. We actually had a film crew shooting a chase sequence on the V&A roof once and this gave us the idea. We have a dedicated film liaison person who handles any actual filming requests and smoothing over any ruffled feathers with the authorities."

"Okay, good answer," said Loveday, looking serious. "Why specifically were we shot at this morning?"

Reggie put her mug down. "We do not yet know. We are going to go into a huddle with Morag as soon as she calls down to discuss that very thing, so hopefully we will have more answers later. The syndicate has been trying to disrupt the work of WI-5 for a long time so this is all part of a pattern. I think we were all wrong to think that the Ravenwood Studios explosion put them out of business."

There was a ring of the doorbell outside the cubbyhole. Alfie leaned forward, cradling his mug. "It will be the bakery with my grub order."

Loveday chimed in, "What is as interesting to me as being shot at and nearly dying is that all the mechanics I saw in the bus garage were women and, apart from Dad and Tolly, women seem to be playing all the major roles. I think that is great! Care to illuminate?"

"Well, Loveday," continued Reggie, "very rarely does a man come along with the skills WI-5 needs. Dad was involved near the beginning, and he's still here, like an old cushion or a piece of furniture. Sorry, Dad. Tolly came along and became Dad's unofficial protégé. Dad is surrounded by women at home and work, so I think a bit of male company is good for him."

The phone rang. It was Morag, announcing that Joan and Blessing had arrived from Hertfordshire and she was ready for her meeting with Reggie, Ashwariya and Fragrance to review the incident and plan next steps. GloGlo and Loveday would meet her afterwards so they were the only ones remaining in the cubbyhole when Alfie opened up a large cardboard box laden with iced buns, sausage rolls, spinach and potato knishes, falafel, lamb samosas and cheese and onion pasties, licking his lips. "Lunch," he announced.

***

Between mouthfuls, Loveday asked, "I know GloGlo and I are too new to this to be of much help at whatever meeting they are having, but what about you, Dad, why can't you be there?"

"Well, my little scrawnbag of a chook, they are quite the well-oiled team and need to put their heads together to figure out what to do, and I wasn't on the bus nor had any involvement in the adaptation and testing of Drusilla. Also, I like being a backroom boy, keeping my head down, so no near-death experiences for me I'm afraid. Don't worry, we will get the call later to go downstairs once they have worked through their agenda, probably in an hour or so. After all the excitement of the morning, seeing what goes on behind the public face at the V&A might be a tonic for you. Let me go and find Tolly. He does keep wandering off."

Alfie reappeared two minutes later with Tolly, sheepishly in tow, and poured him a tea. "Tolly is my current project, though it is taking a while for him to find his feet, isn't that right, Tolliver, my boy?"

Tolly replied with chagrin, looking at Loveday and GloGlo, "London's pollution is not good for my respiratory system. I have bad asthma, and sometimes I have to go home early or not come into work to rest my lungs. Luckily, WI-5 is giving me lots of time to complete my training, and the V&A lets me work part time with a lot of flexibility. Three days a week at the museum and two days studying for civil service exams. When Alfie retires, I hope to fill his shoes in administration, at both WI-5 and the V&A, but if I am not up to snuff with WI-5, I can still work full time at the museum. I have to work in every V&A department before I can earn my stripes. I am usually down here with Alfie doing a bit of loading-dock lifting and portering, but sometimes I get whisked off to another department with no notice. Isn't that right, Alfie?"

Alfie nodded with a half smile, half grimace, perfectly communicating his thoughts on the less-than-satisfactory situation of having Tolly sent to other departments and leaving him on his own.

"Don't worry, Tolly, we'll get you in the field soon. Some country air will do you good, and you might be a completely different man without London's pollution holding you back. Why don't you give Loveday and GloGlo your grand tour of the V&A labyrinth? To build our strength back up, how about we finish putting a great big dent in these delicious treats? We can take any leftovers down when they call us. Does anyone want a Tizer or a Vimto? I have a secret stash in my little fridge."

Loveday grinned at her father. "You know, Dad, I think I am ready for my museum tour."

Alfie took a samosa. "Tolly, do you want to give them the overview? You've heard it from me often enough."

Tolly winked at his audience. GloGlo inwardly rolled her eyes while Loveday's heart skipped a beat. "Well, from this office, Alfie oversees the delivery and receipt of all V&A parcels and WI-5 intelligence boxes and packages. Every WI-5 bus has a team of four women: a driver, a conductor who keeps track of packages, and two security officers who are also good for lugging boxes. Shall we get going? Don't worry, we won't get lost in the seven miles of V&A corridors, as doing this job you get to know the labyrinth like the back of your hand. Well you do if you are Alfie. I'm still learning, and count myself fortunate if I don't get lost more than twice a day."

Alfie handed Loveday and GloGlo brown porter coats and gave Tolly a trolley of packages to deliver. As they trundled along dark corridors, Tolly stopped to chat with the other porters. Loveday and GloGlo learned the V&A buildings covered a hundred acres and were built in 1852 as a permanent successor to Crystal Palace's Great Exhibition of 1851. With much to occupy their minds, an hour went by quickly, before they returned to the loading dock.

"Hello, Dad, how's tricks? That was so interesting, quite the maze. Have we been called downstairs yet?"

Alfie grabbed his clipboard and stood up. "Actually, Morag just called up, so follow me. Tolly is going to look after the loading dock. If you get into trouble, Tolly, call down to Morag."

Alfie took GloGlo, Loveday and the remaining bakery treats down in the freight lift to the lowest level of the museum's basement and along a dark corridor filled with filing cabinets along one wall, broken up by glass-paned doors which opened into rather gloomy rooms. They stopped at the only door through which light was shining and entered an anteroom filled with yet more filing cabinets. From behind her desk, a woman wearing large, thick, owly glasses and staring at a clipboard introduced herself with a pronounced Scottish accent. "Morag Fyfe, at your service. Hoping to sneak in, were we, Alfie, you rapscallion? What have you got there? Some shortbread for me perhaps? Are these your daredevil younger daughters I have heard so much about? Girls, he is so proud of you both."

Loveday and GloGlo blushed as they followed Morag into a much larger room where several women were standing over two enormous maps, one of London and one of Great Britain, covered in large red, yellow and green wooden blocks, each with a numbered flag on top. On the side of each map was a key identifying a list of women's institutes in alphabetical order and in flag number order. Reggie, Ashwariya, Fragrance, Blessing and Joan were clustered to one side poring over the London map, tracing the route of the bus chase.

Three young women of about Loveday's age, wearing headphones with microphones, surrounded the Great Britain map, each holding what looked like a snooker cue. They were all talking softly into their microphones, leaning over with magnifying glasses and moving the blocks with their cues.

"Welcome to the hub of WI-5 operations," said Morag. "This is the room where it all happens. Do you need to have a sit down because of the shock or can I march on and bring you up to speed? By the way, let me introduce April, May and June." Loveday and GloGlo both nodded at the three women who acknowledged them and returned to speaking with WI-5's field operatives. "Come in Mickle Trafford. Receiving you Sonning Common. Could you repeat that Leicester?"

"Ooh is that an iced bun?" Morag grabbed one and took a big bite. "Britain's intelligence model got its start during the First World War and evolved into multiple intelligence departments all mystifyingly numbered in a way not only guaranteed to confuse the enemy but also all of us. It was so confusing and nonsensical, only a man could have come up with it." She looked at Alfie pointedly and raised her eyebrows as if Alfie was responsible.

Alfie held her stare as Morag smiled and continued. "I was initially recruited into MI-4, because I was looking for the ladies' loo in the wrong stairwell at the Ministry of Defence, but they liked the cut of my jib and so that was that as they say. Girls, never underestimate the power of a random event. Originally, MI-1 and MI-17 were the secretariat for all MI departments. MI-2's focus was on the rest of the world outside Europe which was also MI-3's territory, except for Germany, which was MI-14's responsibility. MI-4 focused on cartography, geography and aerial photography which was also overseen by MI-15. MI-5 focused on Great Britain. See what I mean about the numbers? They make no sense other than indicating the, shall I put it kindly, organic way the departments were created. Bear with me, there is more. Legal, economics and finance were the bailiwick of MI-6. MI-7's role was propaganda. MI-8 led communications and signals interception. MI-9 and MI-19 focused on interrogation. Don't ask me why there are two of them. Alfie, any ideas? No! Thought not. MI-10 led weapons engineering. MI-11 was responsible for security of agents in the field. MI-12 oversaw censorship. Thirteen was never used, presumably for superstitious reasons. Imagine! Why eighteen was never used is beyond me. MI-16 focused on scientific research and technology development. Over time, this overly complex structure led to poor communication and competition for resources between departments which led to many intelligence failures. Studies of these failures after the end of the Second World War led to a plan to amalgamate everything into the three departments, MI-5,

MI-6 and WI-5, which was formally relaunched about ten years ago, though we had kept skeleton operations going here at the V&A and in the field, between 1945 and 1955. Maintaining already trained operatives was far cheaper then than recruiting and training a new batch; however, as you can see, we do need an injection of fresh blood, hence why you were all recruited. Blessing, can you explain about the creation of WI-5's ring of defence around London as it leads directly into this morning's attack and our agenda today?"

"Absolutely," said Blessing decisively. "Early in the Second World War, all MI departments and sections, except MI-1 were moved out of the city to secret locations in the countryside around London. It was too unsafe to have them in London with all the bombing. They were moved to stately homes which the army and air force had already commandeered and requisitioned, as the houses had a lot of land for training the troops, good connections to London and were often encircled by woods to keep activities out of sight. MI-1 stayed here at the V&A to be close to government.

"When plotted on a map, all the sites that had been commandeered form a ring of defence around London. Cuffley Manor is the keystone of the ring. Other important houses include Goldings, Balls Park, Audley End, Bletchley Park, Blenheim Palace, Highclere Castle, Polesden Lacey, Chartwell and Knole. Efficient communications between each of these sites and MI-1 was vital, and at first, this was an utter disaster. Joan, Morag and I were tasked with improving communications, so we developed a plan which grew into our approach today, to ensure the secure movement and tracking of sensitive documents, files, people and information, seamlessly and secretly between all sites, using buses and coaches driven by trained operatives who radio in their locations to this room. Always humming, always buzzing, this room runs twenty-four hours per day, seven days a week. Over the years, many famous faces have been involved, including Princess Elizabeth. Recruited in 1943, we taught her to drive a bus and coach, trained her in map reading, surveillance and the basics of engine maintenance and repair. "Once she was crowned, the queen was instrumental in expanding WI-5's role and budget. Shall I stop there, Morag?"

"Yes, pet. Thank you and here endeth the history lesson, for now," said Morag with a glint. "Now, let's focus on today. On the maps in front of us, we are tracking the surveillance activities of all women's institutes across the country. Green means normal activity, nothing suspicious, yellow identifies something is possibly awry, and red indicates evidence of enemy activity. For yellow and red blocks, I am in daily communication with the relevant WI Cloak and Dagger Committees regarding status and planning."

GloGlo looked at the maps in amazement. "Gosh, you are not only tracking buses, coaches, lorries and bread vans but also WI surveillance activities. Look at all the yellow and green blocks all over the country. Only a few red ones though, thank goodness."

Morag nodded, pointed at the map with a stick and

continued, "Absolutely spot on. If you look here, you can see Maiden Combust Women's Institute has a red block. As you know, Joan runs the show there. Most of the other red blocks relate to women's institutes near Wembley Stadium. We have Hanger Lane, Preston Road and Neasden WIs surveilling the stadium, inside and out, and the surrounding areas. Spare a thought for Cricklewood WI as they have their waders on in the sewers. Feltham, Worth, Bishops Stortford and Markyate WIs are keeping an eye on London, Gatwick, Stansted and Luton airports. Nothing will get through. Joan's team, of which you all are now part, has been monitoring goings on at Cuffley Manor and aerodrome, but things have been pretty quiet until the Eighth Wonder Film Company came a-calling. In the recent fire at the film studios, all syndicate inner circle members but one were killed. Two people were seen leaving the scene just before the explosion. We believe one was the last surviving inner circle member who ran out of the soundstage and jumped into the back seat of a silver Rolls-Royce which headed into Black Park and disappeared. The other was Babette Kohlrabi, the head of the Eighth Wonder Film Company, but alas, she has also disappeared. We need to find them both. Our best lead is the silver Rolls-Royce which will be conspicuous wherever it is hidden. The rather ham-fisted bus attack this morning leads me to think we might be closing in on information the syndicate would rather us not know. Because the film company has moved its filming schedule to start before the World Cup Final, the key to all this must lie at Cuffley Manor."

Reggie picked up the cudgel. "Cuffley Manor having an aerodrome, distinguishes it from all the other stately homes which ring London. Although the current Lord Cuffley and his brother seem to be straight arrows, their predecessors were a suspect lot, especially their grandfather, who was known for harbouring extreme political sentiments and being involved in criminal activities. There are also military records suggesting planning for some major construction projects on the grounds before, during and after both wars, but nothing came to fruition. Finally, there is also a historical connection between Cuffley Manor and the V&A. Dad, over to you for a bit more history."

Alfie rubbed his hands. "Once London started to be bombed, the powers that be decided it was too risky to keep the whole V&A collection of art and artefacts at the museum. The grand plan that they cooked up was to move the collection to Cuffley Manor, and use the rotunda and the chalk pits on the grounds as storage. Some items were so big, they either couldn't be moved or ended up in the underground tunnels near Aldwych tube station. I began working at the V&A then. We sandbagged and bricked up the artefacts which couldn't be moved. As a junior porter at the time, I spent six weeks filling sandbags and mixing mortar. For all the artefacts going to Cuffley Manor, we must have had a dozen lorries. I was one of the irks who loaded and travelled with them to Hertfordshire. In '42 it was. I think Cuffley Manor was chosen because it had the closest, large amount of storage space found in a pinch. Colossal great place. I didn't like it much though. There was a terrible gloomy atmosphere, like bad things had happened there. There were several nissen huts scattered over the grounds behind the manor. I saw a lot of young women in uniform running between them. Apparently, most of the V&A's collection of smaller furniture, textiles, books and metalwork was moved into the house. Anything which was too big to fit inside, went to some huge caves in the chalk pits at the edge of the grounds beyond the aerodrome. Later on, the house had an attack of moths so we subsequently moved the textiles and books down into the chalk pits too."

Alfie paused for breath. "Once everything had been moved out, the V&A was completely taken over for war work. A lot of government departments had been kicked out of Whitehall by the Admiralty, so they came here. I was kept on as one of the caretakers. The ministry did make a mess of the place though. You can still see remains of the camouflage paint they used on the outside walls, especially when it rains. The South Court became a canteen for the Royal Air Force, the bomb squad and the bomb damage repair squad. Some of the galleries were also used as temporary housing and schooling for children evacuated from Gibraltar of all places. The sheds out back were used by the army for storage. It was quite exciting wasn't it, Morag? You were in the central office, keeping track of it all. Nothing much changes with you, does it? The old Royal College of Art building was where our men and women who parachuted into France were trained and kitted out." He mouthed the word 'spies', and tapped his nose. "Careless talk costs lives. I hope I don't need to tell you to not breathe a word of all this, otherwise Morag might have to kill you." Morag rolled her eyes and threatened to poke Alfie in the ribs with her iced bun.

GloGlo leaned in. "Carry on, Dad. This is fascinating stuff. What was that about Aldwych tube station? Tell us about what went on in the tunnels."

"Aldwych Station was closed to trains. It was only a branch line, so I don't think it caused any major disruptions. One platform became an air-raid shelter, but it was the tunnels that they used for storage. It was the British Museum's idea to use the tunnels for storing their big pieces, like the Parthenon Marbles."

Loveday's jaw went slack, as she often travelled on the tube through Aldwych station and never had any idea of its secret wartime role. GloGlo grabbed a lingering knish. "How did they transport everything down there, Dad? The marbles are huge. They must weigh hundreds of tons."

Alfie continued, "I was seconded for a couple of days to the British Museum to help them out with moving their stuff. The marbles were loaded onto a huge, wide-load lorry and taken to London Transport's rail depot at Lillie Bridge, right by West Brompton tube station. They were then lifted onto railway wagons and moved along the rail line to Aldwych. They did the same thing with the Boy David statue."

Loveday and GloGlo exchanged raised eyebrows and smirks. "That must have been a sight," they whispered.

"Alfie, I remember dealing with the British Museum. They looked down on us, the supercilious bunch of

Tunnock's Teacakes," said Morag scornfully.

"Some of them were all right. The toffs were hard to deal with, but the workers were great. Anyhow, after the war ended, the V&A wanted to repatriate all its artefacts. After the museum reopened in 1946, we retrieved most of them from Aldwych and Hertfordshire. It took a couple of years; we weren't done until 1948. We thought we had collected it all back, but it was common gossip about items being mislaid or completely missing. Nobody knew exactly what, and after a while, we had other fish to fry."

"We think there might be some unaccounted-for V&A artefacts still in Cuffley Manor or in the chalk pits," said Morag. "While Eighth Wonder is shooting its film there, we will be able to use this as an excuse to look for any lost items and have a surreptitious poke around. This week, Alfie and I are going to double check the old records with the current inventory. Reggie, how are your plans to conduct surveillance on the film company coming along?"

Reggie swallowed the rest of her sausage roll and took a final swig of her now-cold tea. "Now that the Eighth Wonder Film Company will be arriving at Cuffley Manor before the World Cup Final, we think the syndicate's plans have changed and Cuffley aerodrome could be used to launch an attack. The company plans to arrive at Cuffley aerodrome on Friday for their press conference and then they leave the same afternoon. We will not see them again until the next Tuesday, which means, fellow WI members, we should have a clear run at getting this weekend's fête out of the way without a hitch. Next week, most of the film crew will be staying in the surrounding villages or in

Hertford but a core group will be staying in the manor. Nobby, the production manager, tells me they will be having dinner in Hertford at the Salisbury Arms on their first evening, so Loveday, from next Wednesday onwards, you will be providing breakfast and dinner every day for the cast and crew members staying in the manor. Do not worry about serving meals in the manor by yourself. Joan and Blessing will be helping you out. Nobby did say there may be some cast members with special dietary needs. I will find out and let you know. Nothing you can't handle! For the rest of us, the key issue will be surveillance while the film crew are in the manor, on the grounds and at the aerodrome. I suggest Joan and Blessing take the lead on keeping an eye on activities in the manor and grounds when filming is not taking place. Loveday can take the lead when they are filming indoors and outdoors, as she can use food deliveries to gain access to the set. GloGlo and I will keep an eye on their activities at the aerodrome. Ash will be ferrying the cast and crew back and forth between Cuffley Manor and Hertford so she can keep an ear out when they are in transit. The current plan is to place listening devices in their rooms and have Blessing monitor their conversations from an attic room. Morag is providing the bugging devices which Blessing and Joan will install. Morag is also creating biographical files for each of the principal cast and crew members, including photographs, so you can identify everyone. We will have our own professional photographers at the aerodrome for this Friday's press call, so hopefully they can get some good shots of everyone. Every night, write down whatever conversations you managed to overhear between crew and/or cast members. Give your notes to Blessing to document, categorise and analyse. If Blessing is otherwise engaged, give them to me, and I will make sure they get where they need to go. How does that sound?" They all nodded.

"But first, we need to give the manor a good clean. Let us try to do this before Friday afternoon's press call. Even though only four of the grand bedrooms will be needed, let's take the opportunity to clean them all. The rooms on the main floor and second storey haven't been used for years, so they all need a good scrubbing and dusting, as well as planting the listening devices. All the bathrooms will also require some elbow grease. Ash and Glo, I know you have the airshow and a tour group to organise, so no cleaning duties for you. We can rope in Charlie and Cliff to move furniture and throw around the hoover. The WI volunteers can do the lighter cleaning, dusting and making the beds. I will tackle the toilets and bathrooms. Beaver will check to see if the plumbing and heating are working and fix them if not. What I am thinking is to get the cleaning crew to meet in the manor kitchen tomorrow where all the cleaning supplies are. Loveday, can you be in charge of keeping the food areas clean? Beaver will also help us clean if he has any time left over. Maybe you could do that too, Loveday? And by the way, I have at least five WI ladies to help you out on Friday and Saturday with the fête food. Charlie phoned the hospital this morning and it looks like Mrs Gascoyne will be coming home today, but I think she will need to rest. I suggest that those of us who can, meet tomorrow morning at eleven in the kitchen and get scrubbing." Reggie sounded satisfied at the plan of action.

Morag leaned back in her chair. "Well, everyone, I think we have a plan. Shall we finish up here? You girls still have to get back to Hertfordshire after what must have been an exhausting day, and Alfie and I have some filing cabinets to delve into."

As they were putting their coats on, Loveday called to Alfie, "Dad, by the way, what does Mum know?"

"Mum, as per usual, gets told nothing and knows everything. And we need to keep it that way."

Cooking up a Storm

Loveday woke early, her mind buzzing and muscles stiffened from having been thrown around the bus, the day before. She treated herself to a restorative bath while Reggie and Beaver slept. She could hear Beaver's heavy breathing and Reggie's lighter rhythmic exhaling through the walls, as she rinsed out some knickers in the bath water (she must find out how to work Reggie's washing machine), pulled a comb through her unruly hair, looked askance at herself in the mirror, shrugged and headed down to the kitchen to put the kettle on.

On hearing Loveday emerge from the bathroom, Reggie roused herself. Loveday had made tea and was turning on the coffee pot for Beaver when Reggie appeared and sank into a kitchen chair. "I am horrified you had to experience the attack yesterday, Loveday. I expressed my fears for your safety to Morag. She allayed them by highlighting that the syndicate has only attacked WI-5 assets in London. As long as we keep you in Hertfordshire, you will be safe. How is that for irony? Also, I am so happy you finally know Dad, Joan and Blessing are not just the fluffy old people they appear to be, though Dad still has his fluffy moments. Hence why he is happy just being on the loading dock. Joan has been around since the year dot, has an incisive mind like a bread knife, is quick on her feet and in the air, drives and flies like a demon and, because of her long history, is supremely well-connected with politicians, the gentry, the police and military intelligence. Keep on her good side, as she can knock you out with a well-timed high kick before you know it. Blessing is our queen of all things information-related. She has a photographic memory and knows every shelf of Hertford Library. She is also a whiz with codes, patterns and seeing the connections where the rest of us see none. And you know, by looking after our stomachs you are contributing to the security of the nation."

Over tea, Reggie looked at Loveday's first draft of her food order, asked a few questions, made some suggestions and handed it back to her. She took Beaver's coffee up to him. *He must be so tired for the smell of coffee percolating to not rouse him,* she thought. After having dressed, the sisters' energy was still somewhat low, so Reggie decided everyone needed a shot of sugar and whipped up some thick Canadian pancakes, proper French toast and bacon. She found golden syrup and added some almond flavouring, hoping it would pass for maple syrup.

Beaver appeared and, contentedly sitting in his pyjamas at the table, worked his way through a huge pile of food, soggy with fake-maple syrup. "Oh man, this is great!" Once he was on his third plateful, Loveday and Reggie walked to the aerodrome along the newly familiar route, past the dump, through the rabbit warren, across the fields and through the woods. Reggie took Loveday's arm.

"Loveday, I know everyone will enjoy having you around. Your presence, energy, spirit and your personality will help us all. You have had virtually no time to process everything, including the attack yesterday, and yet you are ready to plough ahead like a real trouper, taking it all in stride. I think you may have found your calling! I am so happy we get to keep you for at least another couple of weeks. If we can get through the clean-up of the manor and survive the fête, then we can concentrate on the arrival of the film crew. However, there is one fly in the ointment I should warn you about. Tansy Brockett-Storrs is turning up on Friday morning to help out with preparing the food for the fête and will probably stay for the photo call. How she heard about it, goodness only knows, but she will be there along with the WI ladies, and she is a bit of an acquired taste. Tansy is related to one of the former Mayors of Hertford, is the new leading lady of the Old Hertfordian Amateur Dramatic Society and has recently returned empty-handed from chasing moneyed marriage prospects on the continent. She is quite frankly a piece of work, if you catch my drift, and to the horror of all concerned, she has her sights set on becoming the next Lady Cuffley, so be warned."

"Crikey! Shouldn't you be warning Cliff instead?"

***

As they walked along the perimeter of the landing strip, they could tell the aerodrome was abuzz. "I think there are more fliers here today because of upcoming fête," said Reggie. "Weekends are usually the busiest time but fête weekend cranks it up an extra notch. The weekenders are a real community, and some of them are quite likable. Mostly men, but still. Escaping from work and family, they love to come to fix up or fly their charges and chat with each other. On fête weekend, they know they're likely to get roped in to volunteer, so they make a long weekend of it. They adore GloGlo, as she has usually tinkered with and spruced up their treasures during the week. They don't adore me, as I send them invoices and harangue them for payment. I am glad GloGlo gets some appreciation though. She deserves it."

Although many small planes were parked outside the hangars and their owners were milling around in overalls carrying cups of tea and toolboxes, the landing strip was quiet. As Loveday and Reggie were cutting across the corner of the airfield, they heard a great yell and whoosh of air. Looking up they could see a bright pink parachutist with an equally brightly coloured parachute bearing down on them. "Down!" yelled Reggie who pushed Loveday and herself to the ground, this time quite a bit more comfortably than when they were on the bus, as they landed on some nubbly, springy clover. They looked up to see a magenta flying suit land gracefully, and with great control, thirty feet in front of them. GloGlo released her parachute and ran up to them. "Oh my gosh, did I give you a scare? Loveday, I could see Mum's raspberry beret from way up there."

"Crikey, GloGlo, we've our work clothes on. If there's a grass stain, you are getting out the Daz tonight for some emergency spot cleaning," said Reggie, grinning, as she rubbed down her coat.

GloGlo removed her goggles and helmet. "Sorry, girls."

Loveday wiped down her skirt. "Wow, what an entrance, sister dear. That is quite an outfit. You match your plane!"

GloGlo was expertly gathering up her parachute, starting with the riser, the lines and finally the canopy. Tucking it under her arm, she held out her hands showing off her painted nails. "It is for the flying display. I am the Magenta Baron! Handbag, shoes, plane, parachute and even nails to match – not bad for the slovenliest of the MacGuffins, including Alfie. Charlie let me really ratchet up the stunts this year, as the weather is so good. Sunny skies, not too much wind or cloud – perfect for flying. Loveday, did Reggie tell you about what is new for this year? We have a never-before-seen stunt planned, designed to set the locals chattering for days."

Reggie grinned at GloGlo. They entered the largest hangar via a back door. Showgirl One, GloGlo's magenta Tiger Moth, was sitting, gleaming in the centre. "Beyond Ash, Showgirl One is my favourite thing in the whole world. Actually, she is running Ash quite closely for first place, but don't tell her that. The centrepiece of the display will be a hopefully dramatic dogfight between Charlie in Air Force blue in his Tiger Moth, named Virgil, and me as the Magenta Baron in Showgirl One. We will perform a series of choreographed manoeuvres away from the sun so the crowds can see the action. Reggie and Cliff are going to be gunners operating wooden machine guns mounted on their respective fuselages."

Loveday exclaimed, "Reggie, you are going up in that fantastic magenta biplane! I wish I were you."

GloGlo continued, "Beaver is in charge of the public address system playing the sound of machine guns firing at opportune moments. We have also added a much more dangerous stunt, whereby both planes fly horizontally towards each other from opposite sides of the aerodrome, which to the crowd will look like a certain head-on crash, but in reality, we will be safely quite far apart and then finishing with a synchronised loop-the-loop. We have already done a practice flight to make sure Cliff and Reggie can hold the wooden guns and test if our seat belt modifications enable them to turn safely and smoothly. Hopefully, the crowd will get excited. I always get a buzz hearing the crowd cheering. Oh listen! That's Charlie coming in. Shall we go and watch him land?"

Reggie looked at her watch. "Okay, but soon Loveday needs to get going in the kitchen. Okay with you, Loveday?"

Loveday nodded, and as they followed GloGlo over to the landing strip she asked, "So how long have the flying displays been going?"

"I think Charlie's grandfather started it in the 1920s. He's the one who put in the aerodrome in the first place. But Charlie's father took them to the next level after the war. In 1948, the first post-war fête was held, and Lord Cuffley sprung a surprise flyover, flying low enough to rattle the teacups and saucers. This became the most talked about part of the event, and it is the most looked-forward-to element – other than the afternoon tea, of course! In the early years, I think Lord C would only do a fly-past trailing red, white and blue smoke. Since Charlie is now in charge, we want to close the fête with something more and more spectacular each year. We don't want the villagers getting bored, or there might be revolution! Oh, here comes Charlie."

As Charlie's blue Tiger Moth approached the landing strip, Loveday looked at Reggie with something akin to amazement. "You are a lucky dog, Reggie, getting to be a gunner."

Reggie chagrinned back. "I am trying to feel the same. I really haven't felt confident in the air since the accident in air cadets at school. Under GloGlo's guidance and support, however, I am overcoming my fears. She wants me to get back to my cadet-level parachuting and skydiving. So far, I have only acquiesced to a couple of jumps whilst attached to her, so grasping a wooden gun, grimacing madly while sitting in a plane, is not so bad."

Reggie shook off her discomfort via a sudden epiphany that she felt more fearful sharing how she felt than she feared flying. "Let's get on, Loveday. Once you are done with your kitchen duties on fête day, you can be a free agent for the rest of the afternoon to enjoy yourself. The whole event should be almost over by the time the aerial dogfight gets going at five o'clock. The crowds will then quickly pack up and drift home, either walking through the woods and across the fields or heading to their cars parked along the drive and in the lower field."

Charlie landed and taxied over to where the sisters were gathered and bounded out of the plane with a flourish followed by a theatrical bow. "How was that, GloGlo?" GloGlo gave him the thumbs up while Reggie smiled at him seeking GloGlo's approval.

"Hello, Reggie, Loveday," said Charlie as he took off his helmet. "Actually, Loveday, I was wondering if we could ask you a favour. Once your cooking is done on Saturday afternoon, it would be great to have an extra pair of hands to help with the pre-flight checks. If you come here at three o'clock, does it give you enough time to have finished all your food preparation duties and explored the fête?"

Loveday nodded. Reggie looked a bit askance at a new recruit, Loveday, being asked to be part of pre-flight checks which were designed solely to keep an ancient plane she was a passenger in up in the sky. "What time do I need to arrive here Saturday for my gunner duties?"

GloGlo looked at Charlie questioningly, as she figured out the timing. "I was thinking about four o'clock? The landing strip will be completely closed to the public between noon and six on Saturday. By four o'clock, we should be done with the pre-flight checks and we can also do a final display briefing. At the same time, we will also check on the wind speed at ground level and estimate it for all the heights at which we will be flying, so we can make allowances for drift during each manoeuvre. And of course, you need time to put on your flying suit."

Charlie nodded, happy at the timing and GloGlo's rationale. He continued. "I will prepare the two extra safety parachutes for Reggie and Cliff and also their secondary chutes. All we have to do today is use a bit more elbow grease to clean up Virgil and Showgirl One, replenish the fuel tanks, double check the engine oil, reaffix the fake wooden guns to the fuselage behind the rear seats, give the windscreen a final scrub and make sure all intakes and vents are clear of debris. Oh, and I almost forgot…" Charlie dug into his pocket and pulled out a plastic bag full of pound notes. "… Reggie, here is the money for twenty afternoon teas for the aerodrome volunteers on fête day. Do you think, Loveday, you could bring them over using the trolley when you come over here at three o'clock? It is not only the planes which need refuelling before the display."

***

For two days, Cuffley Manor exploded in a frenzy of the domestic arts. Loveday cooked up a storm, her mind still going a hundred miles an hour with everything she had learned. It was a relief to focus on something familiar like pastry and scones. She also had to think about the culinary demands of the film crew, so she started revising her menus and the list of ingredients required – a list which would need to be double and triple checked by Reggie before she placed the order. With Reggie's encouragement, Loveday had picked the dishes she liked to make which could be served hot or cold depending on the weather. Summery soups, cheese tarts, smoked haddock and spinach pies, fish cakes, her famous lamb scotch eggs could all be served hot or cold. Menus were also pencilled in, built around dishes which would keep hot without spoiling, such as kedgeree, celebration rice, chicken, ham and leek pie, lentil loaf, vegetable chilli con carne, and butter chicken, which everyone found to be quite exotic but was dead simple with the right spices. Side dishes and salads could be made fresh based on what was in season, so all she needed to do was figure out puddings. Baked apples would be good and forgiving, and could be reheated. She could also make meringue nests, chocolate sponge, a plum cake and a blackberry and apple crumble. Also useful would be a veritable lake of cream and custard and a whole load of biscuits to keep the cast and crew from starving between meals. If she could spend the first two days of next week preparing their needs for the rest of that week, she could focus on finishing all the food for the fête.

Each morning Loveday put the kettle on for the cleaning crew and dug out all the cleaning supplies from under the sink and the various cupboards and closets. There seemed to be enough buckets and rubber gloves for everyone. She also added vinegar, bicarbonate of soda, oven cleaner and some of the older, rattier tea towels to the pile of cleaning supplies.

Cliff and Charlie arrived early on Thursday morning with armfuls of clean bed linen, looking cheerful despite having stayed up late the night before, watching football.

"It is so nice seeing you here, Loveday. The kitchen smells marvellous with all the baking. It's a bit like when Mum was here, but you don't ask us about homework. Is the tea ready to pour?"

"Thanks, Cliff, I am extremely happy to be here. This film crew business is so exciting. We are going to need to keep our strength up. Not being part of the cleaning brigade makes me feel guilty, so I should make us all something yummy for lunchtime – fuel for the troops. What do you think would be good? Or shall I just make something up?"

After a few sips of the best drink of the day, Charlie sighed happily. "Anything you make would be delightful. Thanks to you and your wonderful sisters, I am feeling confident about surviving the fête weekend and the financial future of the aerodrome. With the film crew coming, I am also starting to feel seeds of optimism about the financial future of the manor. I feel like all the MacGuffin sisters are casting their magic over the whole place. Things are looking up, and I am actually looking forward to cleaning today. Cliff and I love feeling like we are part of a team. We have spent so much of our lives feeling like we are on the outside looking in, haven't we Cliff?"

Both Cliff and Loveday nodded, one in brotherly affection and the other in empathy. "That is a lovely thing to say. Thank you. I also feel like that, as my sisters are so accomplished and always seem to know what they want whereas I faff about in the background. I often feel like the odd one out who just wants to be on the team. I am also a bit nervous. My plan is to fill the manor with food, including extra items which can be easily defrosted and reheated, so nobody starves even if more people turn up or the caterers aren't able to manage. I might get discovered, and then you will have to sing for your suppers!"

Cliff, who was sitting next to Loveday, put his hand

on top of hers and said solemnly, "Please don't get discovered. You can always be on our team."

They all looked up on hearing the screech of tyres on gravel. The WI volunteer cleaning team had arrived. Cliff and Charlie continued to attack the ground floor of the rotunda, removing all the dustsheets, moving furniture, doing sterling work with the hoover and wet mop. The WI attacked the dusting and brought up all the clean linens to make the beds, before ensuring the library, billiard room, drawing room and the other main floor rooms were put to rights. By the late afternoon on Thursday, the entire manor was looking quite presentable and ready for guests. The same could not be said for the cleaning crew who went home wearily after their labours.

Loveday walked over to the aerodrome delivering test bake items. A flustered Reggie was hiding behind a slightly smaller mountain of paperwork on her desk than before. "Sorry, Loveday, I know you probably want to talk, but can it wait? I have a lot to catch up on to prepare for the arrival of the film company, review in detail their filming schedule and needs and type up all the invoices. Also, GloGlo and Charlie want to take Cliff and me up for another flying display rehearsal, so we understand our rear gunner visual references and cues. Is that all right? Do you mind? You must be exhausted. I know I am. Feel free to just go home and rest. You will have the maisonette to yourself all evening as Beaver is preoccupied with wrestling the manor's boiler into submission."

Loveday was indeed exhausted. She hugged her sister, wished her well and slowly walked back to the flat on her own, allowing her mind to meander surprisingly towards the subject of Tolly, who continued to intrigue her, though she wasn't sure why. Maybe it was because they could have died together shortly after flirting. She scolded herself, however, when she had to retrace her steps, having missed the turning to the council estate through the woods.

The empty maisonette meant she could telephone Alfie without interruption, timing her call for after the evening's World Cup match.

"Oh, Loveday, it's so good to hear your voice. I have been wondering how you have been faring since your trials in London. How are you feeling? I think you had better stay away from London from now on though I do worry about you in Hertfordshire. The film crew arriving when all my daughters are there really bothers me."

"Dad, although I cannot yet quite wrap my head around what happened, I know I am in good hands here and will be safe. Remember I used to say nothing exciting ever happens in Hertfordshire. Well, now I say thank goodness for that. I also want to apologise to you for my past behaviour. I had no idea you did anything interesting at your job. I take it all back. I am sorry I have been such a scourge to you and Mum."

After chatting with Alfie for fifteen minutes, they both yawned down the phone at each other and said their goodbyes. Loveday hit the hay and fell into an immediate, deep sleep, undisturbed by Reggie and Beaver tiptoeing in late.

There's No Business Like Show Business

When Loveday arrived in the kitchen on Friday morning, Joan, Blessing and a handful of WI ladies whom Loveday did not recognise were already there, with who she thought must be Tansy Brockett-Storrs cracking the whip, literally, as she was dressed for horse riding. More than her first impression of Tansy, what alarmed Loveday was that Joan and Blessing already looked quite frazzled. Could it be that the high-kicking, high-flying women who could see off attacks by a deadly crime syndicate without breaking sweat had met their match?

Tansy held out her hand, palm down. "I am the Honourable Tansy Brockett-Storrs and you must be yet another Miss MacGuffin. Cuffley Manor seems to be positively swarming with more and more robust, young women every time I visit. How many of you are there, and where do you all keep popping up from? Anyway, it is simply lovely of you to finally grace us with your presence this morning. It is half-past eight already, and I was beginning to wonder if our *professional* chef had changed her mind. This place was an appalling mess when I arrived an hour ago, absolutely ghastly (which came out of her mouth as *gharzeley*), a complete fright, worse than my stables, so I rolled up my sleeves. I imagine I am the first person to make a decent effort at cleaning up your place of work since Mrs Beeton scrubbed out her first oven, *har har har*!"

Loveday bit her tongue.

"Luckily the others were here on time, so I put them to work scrubbing the floors and cleaning out the insides of the fridges, ovens, cupboards and behind the freezer, which was positively shocking. Delegation is a forte of mine in case you are wondering. I couldn't have the poor state of the kitchen undermine the excellence of Cuffley Manor's afternoon tea. What would Lord Cuffley think if we served up something second rate? We need to wait for the ovens to reach three-hundred-and-fifty-degrees, and we will be ready for baking, baking, baking. I must insist that we make quick work of all this, as later I have my dressage lesson, a face peel and a heart-to-heart with darling Lord C about my opening speech for the fête, though not in that order, *har har har*."

What would Reggie do… what would Reggie do? thought Loveday, as she put on a mask of civility much as it shrivelled her soul to do so. "Thank you, Tansy, it all looks super smashing. I cannot tell you how much easier today is going to go with you all here."

Tansy turned to the women and introduced them, not caring whether Loveday had met them before. "This is Mrs Spatchfork, Mrs Kill-something, Mrs Thing and the cream of the WI. If you deign to join us, you will see them all tomorrow in the tea-tent where I will once again be in charge, thank goodness, so something will go right and be perfectly executed in, what I expect to be, a completely gharzeley amateurish event. The tea's the thing!" announced Tansy, as if she was orating Hamlet on opening night.

Loveday decided to meet fire with a little fire. "The kitchen looks so sparkling clean, thank you all so much. The pork pies were cooked yesterday and are in the larder. Let's concentrate today on making sandwich fillings, baking the cakes and getting all the serving dishes and so on ready. Here are the sandwich filling recipes. Tansy, you can be in charge of those. I will oversee cake preparation. Let me get you a pinny, Tansy. It would be a shame to mess up your equestrian couture."

For the rest of the morning, Loveday and Blessing focused on the cakes, while Tansy, Joan and the others attacked the rest. Loveday kept everyone on task while flattering Tansy as being vital to operations and making sure there were always lashings of tea on hand. Loveday also ensured the ingredients were all available as needed, and no one could complain about not finding a suitable bread knife or stirring spoon. Everything was washed up as they went, and Loveday kept an eye on timing. Mercifully for them all, during elevenses Tansy discarded her pinny on the floor and disappeared upstairs to find Cliff to see if *dear Lord Cuffley would appreciate going over the fête details, as I have one or two tweaks to suggest*, and was not seen again for the rest of the day.

Just before lunchtime, there was a great sudden roar from the ladies, as the door opened and in walked a very unsteady Elsie Gascoyne supported by two walking sticks.

She declared that her heart was one hundred per cent healthy and nothing was going to keep her in hospital another day. Her heavy breathing belied her heartiness claims, and she settled into a proffered chair heavily and unsteadily. "Admittedly, I do get a little tired out, but I am absolutely able to look after myself and my duties here."

Elsie had slept in her own bed in the manor's lodge last night, and was clearly determined not to miss out on the fête preparations or greeting the arrival of the film company later in the day (*that news travelled around quickly*, Loveday thought). When Elsie paused rather breathlessly, Joan introduced Loveday as the interim, temporary, volunteer, kitchen help. Loveday was not offended as she knew Joan was pouring oil on potentially troubled waters. Elsie stared at Loveday, looking completely shocked and discombobulated, as if Loveday was a ghost. Aware that she was encroaching on Mrs Gascoyne's turf, Loveday tried to paper over the cracks by pouring Elsie a large cup of tea and emphasising that Mrs Gascoyne was free to come and go as she pleased, of course, but must rest easy and not to do any strenuous work, except would she mind sharing her expertise to help her conquer the eccentricities of the ovens and keep the teapot full.

One good thing about Tansy cleaning up the kitchen meant Loveday wouldn't get blamed for any changes Elsie spied on her turf. Whenever Elsie looked askance and *tut-tutted* about things having being moved, Loveday was happy to drop Tansy in the muck to keep Elsie onside. Once the cakes were cooling and everyone was lubricated by more tea, there was much discussion about the fête, the film crew and getting Loveday to join the WI (*a new face – exactly what we need*). As Elsie could see that her position, experience and expertise were being respected, she relaxed and admitted that Blessing's son, Dr Innocent Otukile, had ordered her to step back from her housekeeping and cooking duties over a year ago. When Blessing raised the idea of Loveday helping Mrs Gascoyne out in the kitchen over the longer term, Elsie was not overly enthusiastic but not adamantly against it, having seen the quality of her baking and lulled by a bit of flattery.

"I need to think about that. I have been slowing down, you know, and the boys haven't been doing too well without me. At least they have been able to rustle up canned pies in the oven fairly regularly, along with baked potatoes covered in butter and Bovril." Elsie shook her head as she informed Loveday. "The boys have been told time and time again of the need to ensure their dinner plates always contain something green, something orange, something white, something brown and something grey. So, a Fray Bentos pie covers all the bases."

Loveday did not know what to say, so she smiled and said, "Do you think we should expect rain by supper time?"

Elsie looked again at Loveday, as if seeing her for the first time, and peppered her with questions. She showed great interest in the young woman's history, her parents and where she learned to cook. Loveday thought Elsie's interrogation was a bit much, but she went along with it, as it would enable her to reciprocate. Elsie's estimation of

Loveday rose when the younger woman respectfully addressed her as *Mrs Gascoyne*. Joan's far-too-informal introduction had not been appreciated. Loveday's estimation of Elsie went sky high when Elsie asked if she had discovered her secret, emergency supply cupboard.

Knowing she might be out of action for a while, Elsie had thoughtfully stocked a heretofore undiscovered-by-Loveday storeroom on the other side of the tube post room with non-perishable food 'for the boys', including canned pies, puddings, meat, fish, vegetables and fruit, as well as dry goods, biscuits, preserves and copious bottles of brightly coloured fizzy drinks, all of which would be invaluable in the coming week. According to Elsie, the boys must be so sad having to forego for yet another week of her fortifying menu of cottage pie, devilled kidneys, creamed kippers, baby maud and spotted dick.

Throughout the early afternoon, there was much discussion of the minutes from the previous month's WI meeting held before Mrs Gascoyne had gone into hospital, the progress of the communal quilt which was collectively being made as a raffle prize for the Watton-at-Stone (she called it *Rotten-Old-Stone*) village autumn fair. There was also talk about the future of the Molewood railway museum, the need for the sewing group to meet more regularly and which Dorothy L. Sayers, John Dickson Carr, Agatha Christie and John Buchan book they were each reading. Elsie also became quite hot under the collar discussing the prospect of the film company's presence turfing out the WI from their every second Wednesday meeting slot in the rotunda as you never know 'what kinds of debauchery the acting profession, if you can call it a profession, will get up to.'

Once Elsie had disappeared to the lodge for her afternoon nap before the arrival of the film company, Loveday, Joan and Blessing cleaned up the kitchen and themselves with great gusto, in anticipation of witnessing the press call.

The buzzer in the tube post room alerted them to their previously arranged ten-minute warning from Reggie, indicating the film company's plane would soon be arriving. They removed their pinnies and scurried over to the aerodrome. The press had already gathered as had Reggie, GloGlo, Ashwariya, Charlie, Cliff, and Mrs Gascoyne resplendent in knee-length shrimp with matching hat.

The Eighth Wonder Film Company's Brabazon Speedbird twelve-passenger plane appeared over the trees and landed on the landing strip, taxiing towards the small crowd. A side door opened and a young man in jeans emerged, who Ash, Reggie, Joan and Blessing recognised as Nobby. Nobby stood by the passenger door to help Vesta Currie step out, followed by a man in a white suit and fur coat and a taller woman with platinum blonde hair and a fur coat to match. "Good lord! That is Dynamite McQueen and Fontaine de Havilland right in front of us!" exclaimed GloGlo. "I didn't expect film stars to look like film stars in real life."

While Loveday was imagining Alfie's screech of joy when he heard how all his daughters had seen Dynamite McQueen in person, Reggie was reflecting on how fortuitous it was having the press in attendance. Although Blessing was wielding her instamatic camera, Reggie whispered to Joan, "Let us hope we get a lot of good close-up shots so we can update all the suspects' photographs and send them to headquarters as soon as possible."

The press and Blessing leapt forward taking pictures as Dynamite and Fontaine posed in each other's arms, giving their best ten-thousand-watt smiles. Tansy Brockett Storrs, in full Ascot Ladies Day ensemble complete with wide-brimmed hat, had miraculously appeared and stood next to Cliff, Charlie and Mrs Gascoyne, *oohing*, *aahing* and gurning, showing her teeth, in case she was caught on camera. Cliff looked miserable in his suit. Charlie looked nervous, holding on to Mrs Gascoyne's arm. After ten minutes, Charlie stepped forward and said loudly, "If the members of the press from the Hertford Gazette, the Stevenage Optimist, the Cuffley Telegraph, and the Home Counties North Argus have taken their pictures, I will ask them to remove themselves quickly. Thank you very much."

Nobby then stepped forward and introduced Cliff to the company, clearly enunciating, *Lord Clifford Cuffley of Cuffley Manor*, with a small formal nod, which made Cliff blush even more. Charlie and Reggie were then individually introduced to Dynamite, who politely introduced herself, and Fontaine, who did not, while Vesta berated an elf of a woman with a huge clipboard and a beleaguered expression who had remained in the plane, seemingly forgotten. She was clearly Vesta's much put-upon assistant, Phoebe, and looked almost as uncomfortable as Cliff was feeling. The two of them shared a deer-in-the-headlights look of mutual misery. Vesta was interrupted by Fontaine taking her by the arm. "Three hours in hair and makeup and all we get is the Home Counties North Argus to greet us. Where was The Times? The Guardian? Variety? I will be calling my agent. What am I going to do for two weeks in this provincial backwater? You had better not be expecting me to stay in some hovel."

Having said his piece, Fontaine harrumphed and stomped sulkily, in his add-height shoes, back to the plane. Showing great control, Vesta shepherded everyone else back on to the Speedbird and as suddenly as they arrived, they were gone. Charlie looked at Reggie and whispered, "Good Lord, what have we let ourselves in for?"

"Indeed," said Reggie, who was thinking to herself that surely the horrifying parade of theatrical waxworks she had just witnessed could not be the work of the syndicate, or could it?

The Fêteful Weekend

On the morning of the fête, Loveday, Joan and Blessing gathered in the kitchen to attack the sandwiches in three separate stations: cucumber, egg and cress, and Elsie's rabbit paste – the recipe of which she would not share. Anyone needing a change of job was tasked with slicing fresh strawberries.

When the others broke for coffee, Loveday filled the Victoria sponges with the strawberries and cream, dusted them with icing sugar and whipped up the dough for the scones. The tea urns, cups, saucers, serving platters and all the other crockery and cutlery which needed to be set out for the WI ladies of the tent were organised. The kitchen team then put together the boxes for the aerodrome volunteers with paper plates, napkins and cutlery.

Elsie arrived for elevenses, mouth pursed and eyebrows disappearing into her hairline, as she shared the hot-off-the-press gossip regarding Tansy having been seen in Hertford that morning, having a scandalous manicure and hat-fitting so she could look her best for poor, lamb-to-the-slaughter Lord Cuffley. "I think she fancies herself already as Lady C," said Elsie, obviously thinking no one was good enough for the job.

By noon, all the food was organised, and Loveday had bagged up the bread crusts to freeze for future stuffing recipes. The team fortified itself throughout the morning by snacking on the misshapen or overbaked mini pork pies and scones deemed unfit for public consumption. Elsie had put a few select items on a plate for Loveday, who was pleased that everything, including the 'rejects', tasted good. As they were finishing up, Cliff came by to give Aunt Elsie a welcome-back hug. He promised he and Charlie would visit her in the lodge once the fête was over. Before scurrying back to the aerodrome, Cliff surreptitiously snatched a rejected pork pie from Loveday's plate with a shy smile.

At one o'clock, the trolley was loaded up and trundled to the tea-tent where Tansy was in full lady-of-the-manor regalia, including another inappropriately huge showstopper of a hat more suited to finals day at the Henley Regatta. As the last of the food was unloaded, they could hear the tannoy scratching into life, tested briefly by Beaver, and much more lengthily by Tansy as she rehearsed her braying opening remarks, referencing the crème-de-la-crème of Old Hertfordian society, the generosity of the valiant, recently orphaned Lord Cuffley and his poor brother and her desire to *Return Cuffley Manor to its Rightful Place as the Jewel of Home Counties North.*

Luckily Cliff and Charlie heard none of this as Cliff was watching GloGlo's Tiger Moth get ready to take off with Charlie strapped into the wing-walking frame, ready to grab the flag and open the fête. Reggie's plan was to be present at the tea-tent at the beginning to make sure everything was running smoothly, relinquish the clipboard to Tansy and enjoy the fête as a proper guest before heading over to the aerodrome with Loveday to deliver the food to the volunteers. Fêtegoers were already starting to line up at the tea-tent to ensure they secured a good table to view the opening flypast.

The queue was led by members of the Jane Austen Appreciation Society. Ashwariya had been driving them around Hertford in Bluebell all morning to the sites where Jane Austen had set *Pride and Prejudice,* including Hertford's Shire Hall and Bull Plain, Hertingfordbury, and Goldings, and they were all famished and parched. Ash could relax, as she was not due to pick up her charges until half past four, when she had arranged to drive them to a special cordoned-off VIP section of the grounds to watch the closing flying display before taking them home. She sat with them with the intention of making her way over to the aerodrome to see GloGlo once she had landed.

At the tea-tent, the WI team dealt with the great Hertfordshire public, with Reggie and Loveday in the background, loading plates until the initial rush was over. They could hear the deafening rumble of the magenta Tiger Moth and poked their heads out of the side of the tent to see Showgirl One fly low over the forest, and head straight up the great lawn, turn expertly upside down so Charlie could capture the flag from the roof of the manor, waving it over the crowds before hearing Tansy's voice, "I declare this year's glorious Cuffley Manor fête open!"

This was the cue for the Maiden All Villages Brass Band to begin the overture to 'The Women of the WI' as sung by the Hertfordshire Women's Institute choir.

We are the women of the WI,
No glass ceiling, just blue sky,
As we declare the fête is open,
A great afternoon tea, we are hoping,
Come along, join the fun, you will fly high.

The WI is more than jam and jumble,
Mystery tours, fêtes and mustn't grumble,
In the cut and thrust of country life,
Joy we spread with a great big butter knife,
Come along, we will pick you up, if you stumble

We are the women of the WI,
No glass ceiling, just blue sky,
We are on the lookout for new members,
To partake in all our splendours,
Grasp the nettle, we'll show you how,
Women together, is our vow
Don't dilly dally, come along and join us now.

Reggie and Loveday returned to the kitchen to load the trolley with the afternoon tea boxes for the aerodrome volunteers and wheel it along the footpath to the aerodrome for three o'clock. They could see that, although Showgirl One had already landed and was taxiing towards the hanger, everyone's attention was elsewhere – around someone lying on the ground.

They rushed over to find Cliff collapsed and moaning on the grass outside the hangar, being tended to by Beaver and a few aerodrome volunteers. Charlie and GloGlo alighted from the biplane and ran towards the commotion. Mercifully, Cliff seemed to come back to life just as they arrived and was sick on the grass. Charlie, shaken and worried, knelt by his brother and asked, "Please, can someone call Innocent over the tannoy? I mean Dr Otukile. I know he is somewhere on the grounds."

Ashwariya surreptitiously called Blessing on her compact and told her to bring her son to the aerodrome as Cliff needed medical attention. Joan drove both Blessing and Innocent over in her Hillman Minx. Innocent conferred with Charlie before checking Cliff over to see what the problem was. They were all relieved when Innocent shared his thinking that Cliff had suffered from a gastrointestinal issue that was not life threatening. Charlie, especially, was visibly relaxed.

"I don't think you should be flying this afternoon, Cliff. Any volunteers to be a replacement gunner in Virgil with me?" asked Charlie to the crowd.

"Yes, I'll do it," yelled Loveday over the hubbub. "I can grasp a wooden machine gun like nobody's business." A murmur went around the group, and Reggie went pale, but Charlie didn't notice. Innocent and Charlie managed to lift Cliff into the rear seat of the Minx and Joan drove them back to the house in record time.

GloGlo suggested to Reggie that she and Loveday swap planes which Reggie agreed wholeheartedly to. "I can look after Charlie who will be so worried about Cliff, and Loveday will look radiant in head-to-toe magenta with you – like two bottles of radioactive ketchup."

GloGlo spent the next half hour preparing Loveday for what to expect up in the sky. "Don't worry about playing the part, the crowd below won't know. Think of yourself as providing ballast for the plane. Prepare yourself for the stunt at the end, though. Showgirl One will fly at five thousand feet before diving to gain maximum speed of about one hundred and forty knots at a forty-five-degree angle downward before levelling off, aiming at Charlie and Reggie who will be coming from the opposite direction, before starting our loop-the-loops. At the top of the loop, you will need to prepare for the feeling of floating upside down. You will be wearing a parachute. I hope you can remember your air cadets training?" Loveday nodded and her eyes shone, as GloGlo showed her around the plane and gave her the pink flying suit to change into, going over the safety plans over and over again: what to do in case of fire, and using the parachute.

Charlie returned from the manor where Cliff was being looked after by Innocent. Once Cliff had come to, he remembered he had not eaten breakfast, not even had a cup of tea, but had scarfed a pork pie snuck from Loveday's plate in the kitchen. With Innocent's help, Cliff was feeling well enough to sit on a lawn chair on the roof of the manor with a hot cup of tea and wrapped in a light blanket, ready to watch the closing flying display. Charlie had tried to find Elsie to sit with Cliff, to give Innocent a break. He was sure she would be at the fête, no doubt well ensconced in the tea-tent, but Elsie could not be found. Charlie phoned the lodge, and when she eventually picked up, he explained that Cliff had been taken ill and they were wondering if he had had a bad reaction to a pork pie. As two hundred and fifty pork pies had been eaten that afternoon with no one else getting sick, Charlie wondered if there might be another reason. After a long pause, Elsie replied, sounding shocked, and asked Charlie to confirm whether it really was only Cliff who had been taken ill. She then promised to come up to the manor to look after Cliff, grabbed her shopping bag on wheels and a walking stick, and headed out her front door.

***

As he walked to the aerodrome, Charlie continued to feel guilty about the turn of events, worried he was asking too much of Cliff, encouraging him to go out of his comfort zone in a crowd of people and having to make conversation with Tansy, the person who alarmed Cliff the most. He was snapped out of these thoughts by discovering Beaver, GloGlo and Loveday had already completed the pre-flight checks for the closing flying display, with GloGlo and Loveday resplendent in head-to-toe magenta, complete with matching magenta lipstick. GloGlo was painting Loveday's nails the same shade to provide the finishing touch. Reggie was feeling relieved to be in a much more sober air-force-blue flying suit.

As Charlie put on his own blue flying suit over his clothes, he apprised everyone of Cliff's condition being careful not to include any rumours of food poisoning for Loveday's benefit. He smiled at the sisters while he inhaled the fumes of the nail polish which reminded him of his mother. "I see all the world's a stage, even in the sky. Thanks for filling in for Cliff, Loveday."

Loveday waved her hands to encourage the gloopy nail polish to dry. "I am glad Cliff is feeling better. I will do everything in my power to be a decent replacement gunner and do him proud."

"And do you know how the fête is going?" asked Charlie. "How is the tea-tent faring with the onslaught?"

Reggie stepped in. "The fête is going great guns. Beaver told me the lower field is so full of cars, they need to park on the overflow verge in the lane. All the afternoon teas are sold, all the tombola tickets are gone and the raffle tickets are nearly all sold, so I would say it's a roaring success. What do you think happened with Cliff? Loveday, did you poison him with a dodgy pork pie?" She giggled at Loveday's horrified reaction.

Charlie looked at his watch "Cripes, we had better get going, time is ticking." GloGlo grabbed a box of Loveday's food to take up into the skies for a snack. She stuffed the provisions into her metal lunchbox and headed out. Beaver and his team of volunteers followed him to where the blue and magenta biplanes were waiting at the side of the landing strip.

"Let us get this show on the runway!"

***

The two pilots and two gunners clambered into their seats. Beaver snatched a kiss from Reggie and told her to *Break a wing, Babycakes!* which made her blush. He and the others helped give both planes a push start so they could taxi to the edge of the landing strip. Charlie and Reggie in heroic blue Virgil, followed by GloGlo and Loveday in the enemy Magenta Baron. Once taken off, the planes roared to opposite sides of the horizon bisected by Cuffley Hoo – the top of which would be their main reference point for all their manoeuvres. The crowd came out and cheered at each turn and swoop, waving hands holding empty teacups. On the dot of five o'clock, the planes flew away from the manor in opposite directions, turned and started to fly directly at each other across the hill. To the spectators, it looked like they were going to hit each other as GloGlo intended.

Once both Tiger Moths attained top speed, they narrowly passed each other to the gasps of the crowd, and then climbed higher to start the GloGlo-choreographed dogfight with each plane diving at the enemy from behind. After two attacks each, GloGlo started her loop-the-loop before releasing a canister of grey smoke to show she had been hit and faked that she was going to crash in the woods behind Cuffley Hoo. She would safely land at the aerodrome while Charlie distracted the crowd by flying low over the house, releasing more red, white and blue victory smoke to the cheers of the spectators.

Loveday was enjoying herself acting her part as the gunner. Whenever Charlie and Reggie came into her sights, she screamed her head off while *rat-tat-tatting* on the wooden gun aiming for Reggie's head. She loved the rush as GloGlo dived down to gain enough speed to start the loop-the-loop. It seemed to take a long time to fly up to the top of the loop where the Tiger Moth floated gloriously in the air upside down before starting the descent.

Loveday could see the Hoo coming into her vision, when suddenly, there was a loud explosion. The biplane shook, the propellers stopped, Showgirl One shuddered and slowly began to corkscrew down to earth. Loveday turned to GloGlo, who, looking panicked, signalled for Loveday to jump. Loveday fumbled with her safety belt and screamed loudly. GloGlo leaned forward and, in one strong movement, released Loveday's buckle, and the centrifugal force of the corkscrew pulled her youngest sister out of the plane.

At the top of their loop, Charlie and Reggie floated briefly, and Reggie turned to see Loveday and GloGlo's loop. Seeing Showgirl One fall out of its loop and begin to corkscrew, Reggie signalled to Charlie, who had also turned around, and they both saw Loveday get sucked out of the plane and start to fall towards the ground. Charlie dove after them. Thank goodness Loveday's pink suit stuck out against the background of trees and fields.

***

GloGlo shrieked as she focused on gaining control of Showgirl One's plummet to earth and watching for Loveday to pull her parachute cord as per her safety instructions. GloGlo hung on to the Tiger Moth's stick, yanked it with all her strength and managed to level its descent. Time seemed to slow right down as she considered her options. She could jump, but without her at the controls, Showgirl One could crash into the spectators. The only alternative was to try to glide down to the ground. She used her feet and hands to adjust the ailerons and rudder to get a feel for how an engineless Showgirl One would respond. The altimeter taunted her, three thousand two hundred feet, three thousand one hundred feet… Showgirl One was descending too fast to glide.

***

Why wasn't Loveday's parachute opening? Reggie checked the altimeter. They were still at three thousand four hundred feet, so Loveday was getting close to the altitude when her parachute, if it opened, would no longer save her from crashing into the ground. She groaned, "Come on, Loveday!"

***

GloGlo realised she needed to reduce speed as much as possible and get rid of excess weight. Snatching a look at the ground to make sure she was over land and nowhere near the spectators, she threw out her tool kit, tuck box, and spare chocks. Three thousand feet, two thousand nine hundred feet. "Come on Showgirl One!" She glanced behind her to where she expected to see Loveday's parachute. There was nothing but a small magenta speck falling below her to the ground. Loveday's main parachute had not opened and neither had her reserve chute.

***

Reggie pleaded to the gods for Loveday's parachute to open but still it did not. Stricken, she alerted Charlie, released her safety belt, climbed up on to the seat and fuselage holding onto the wing. Then she assumed skydiving position, spotted the pink dot of Loveday far below and leapt away from Virgil, avoiding the tail, diving straight for her sister.

***

GloGlo could see the River Mimram glittering as it fed into Long Lake. Over a hundred metres in length and only a couple of feet deep, GloGlo figured her best bet was to aim for Long Lake and try to land on its surface by aquaplaning. If only she could gain more control. Then she had a brainwave. She could eject Showgirl One's undercarriage which would make the biplane much lighter and improve her chances of landing safely on water. She pulled on the lever to release the undercarriage, and Showgirl One immediately became more responsive. She was gliding.

***

Loveday was flailing like an errant hailstone in a storm. The ground was getting nearer and nearer. Suddenly a small metal box smacked her in the head causing her vision to blur. "Ow!" she moaned as something else hit her head and exploded in a brief whiff of pork pie.

***

Reggie shot like a bullet and willed herself to skydive as fast as she could towards Loveday. She could see the flash of the falling lunchbox and, more alarmingly, the undercarriage which momentarily blocked her view. Thank goodness for Loveday's magenta suit.

***

Loveday came to, looked down, looked up and screamed as the undercarriage swooshed past too close for comfort. She registered another object out of the corner of her eye but could not comprehend what it was before it crashed into her, sending all the air out of her lungs and pains shooting down her back. Just when the pain could not get any worse, her neck jerked upwards, and she found she was no longer hurtling to the ground but seemingly increasing in altitude. Confused; she thought perhaps this is what happens right before you die, your soul heads upwards to Heaven before it's even out of your body. The pain was intense and her chest was being crushed.

***

Reggie had been keenly aware she only had one chance to use her velocity to grab her sister and hold on to her before she could open her parachute. She collided with Loveday at full force, her tense body slamming into Loveday's back and wrapped her arms and legs around Loveday's torso. Squeezing Loveday into her chest, Reggie managed to pull her parachute cord. She barely had enough time to regain a double-handed grip on Loveday before her Union Jack parachute tugged them up into the sky.

Loveday hung limp, moaning and crying. Reggie couldn't see her altimeter but her gut feeling told her they were far too low to land without risk of injury. It couldn't be helped. She surveyed the horizon and the landscape, figured out her bearings and allowed herself a brief moment of relief as Cuffley Manor came into focus. She registered the tents of the fête and the glittering water of Long Lake which had been roped off from the crowds. The lake bisected a large grassy patch where they could land. If they ended up rolling into the lake, they would be safe, as it was barely waist deep.

Reggie yelled into her sister's ear, "Loveday! Get ready to hit the ground and roll like a stunt woman," and they landed in a tumbling heap on the grass next to Long Lake. Reggie ended up pinned under Loveday, unable to move. Relief washed over her, as she could tell Loveday was breathing heavily and hence still alive. Reggie cautiously moved her toes. Her feet and ankles were unscathed.

Loveday remained still with shock as the potential impact of what just happened coalesced in her mind. Reggie could feel a massive pain tsunami starting to swell over her whole body, telling herself it was just bruising, stressed muscles, shock and fear. When she realised she had just leapt out of a plane, skydived and parachuted down, the delayed stress caused her to burst into tears.

Loveday, becoming aware of someone shifting under her, rolled off, looked across at her sister sobbing, which made her cry even more, and managed to get some words out between sobs. "Reggie! You saved me, you saved me!"

Reggie sobbed back. "Of course I am going to save you, you scrawnbag of a chook! Every time. Are you injured? Can you move? I can't move my legs, but I think it might be you squishing me. Either that or I have broken my back."

Loveday bawled into Reggie's shoulder. "I had one job, be ballast! How hard is it to be ballast? I thought I was going to die!"

Reggie moved her free hand to stroke Loveday's hair, her brain switching into its usual, rational modus operandi. "Well, you didn't die, so get off me. We need to find out if GloGlo made it and get us both some medical attention. I did see Showgirl One start to glide towards the manor once her undercarriage had been released. You do know GloGlo nearly crowned you with Showgirl One's undercarriage, don't you?"

"Nonsense, it was miles away! Actually, she did crown me with her lunchbox and a pork pie," said Loveday, sighing as she rolled onto her back, relaxed her eyeballs and let them sink into their sockets, taking a long, slow, deep intake of breath. She turned her neck. Thank goodness for the helmet. Her entire body cried out in pain, and she noted her head was barely a foot away from the side of the lake. "Could have been worse, Reg, we might have ended up in the water. And look! My new nail polish survived unscathed."

Reggie stuck her little finger in her ear wiggling it about. "Stop screeching! What happened with your parachute by the way?"

Loveday looked askance, "I don't know, I tried to open it but nothing happened. I think I was too panicked and concussed to operate it correctly." A loud whooshing noise from above their heads caused them to look up to see a magenta biplane, minus its undercarriage, flying low over Cuffley Manor, heading straight for them.

Reggie immediately guessed exactly what GloGlo was trying to do. "Blimey, GloGlo's gliding. Her rudder must still be working as she is trying to land on Long Lake. We have to move. Loveday, quickly!" Reggie tried to stand but ended up in a crawl. She looked up at the plane, the manor and the crowds and began yelling. "Yikes! There's also a coach heading towards us. Oh, Good Lord, it's Ash in Bluebell. Either we go in Long Lake or Bluebell does."

Loveday quickly registered Bluebell was heading directly for them. Reggie glanced up and could see Showgirl One about to overshoot where they were. GloGlo was coming down but was still too high, and too fast, to aquaplane safely on to Long Lake. Loveday, however, was not focused on the sky, but on the ground as Bluebell rocketed towards them. "Reggie, we need to jump in the lake. Now!"

Reggie felt a strong tugging at her back as she tried to move. Looking behind her she saw her Union Jack parachute starting to catch the wind and drag her farther into the path of the coach. "Help me, Loveday, release the parachute, my hands aren't cooperating." Loveday grabbed the buckle, which released the parachute, pulled it and rolled them both forward into the lake. They came up spluttering to see the coach thunder past only a few feet from their noses. Bluebell ran over Reggie's parachute, catching some of the cords in its rear axle such that the coach was dragging a partially inflated Union Jack. By this time, Beaver had reached them, huffing after the fastest sprint he had ever made. He grabbed Reggie, lifted her out of the water and pulled Loveday up on to the grass. They could see the coach continuing towards the Hoo with GloGlo flying right above it.

"What is Ash doing? GloGlo isn't going to make it. She is going too fast to land on the lake and will crash into the trees," said Beaver alarmed. "Wait a minute." His voice dropped, as he realised what was happening. "She's not going to land on the lake, she is going to land on Bluebell!"

***

GloGlo glided over Cuffley Manor, realising she still had too much speed. Even if she didn't overshoot Long Lake, forty knots was much too fast to land on water without Showgirl One cartwheeling and sending her to a watery grave. She saw a blue flash on the ground to her left. Bluebell, with Ash driving, and the Jane Austen Appreciation Society waving out of the windows signalling for her to follow. She also caught a glimpse of a Union Jack parachute trailing behind the coach. Loveday must have landed.

Ashwariya had accelerated to pass GloGlo with all Bluebell's lights flashing, klaxon sounding and her arm waving out the driver's side window. All the tour group ladies had stuck their heads out of the windows, waving their handbags and copies of *Pride and Prejudice*, pointing upwards at the coach's roof. A head appeared through one of the skylights holding a book in each hand. It was Blessing's daughter, Vanessa the Maiden Combust village policewoman, taking command of the situation. GloGlo suddenly understood what Ash wanted her to do. "Yes, Ash, you amazing daredevil."

***

When she had seen GloGlo's plane start to corkscrew out of control, Ashwariya immediately revved up Bluebell to follow the falling Tiger Moth. Led by Vanessa, who was the youngest member of the Jane Austen Appreciation Society by two decades, the other society members leapt on board, instinctively feeling their favourite author was somehow telling them this was the time to show up to the party in the grounds of the house they believed was the model for Netherfield Hall in *Pride and Prejudice*.

Ash could see the plane was heading to the other side of the stately home and gave chase. Accelerating along Long Lake, she watched Reggie and Loveday land almost in front of her. Ashwariya swerved to avoid them as they rolled into the water. Over Bluebell's loudspeaker, she yelled, "Okay, ladies, tell me where the biplane is and when we are lined up directly underneath her." Vanessa pushed open Bluebell's skylight and clambered on top of two seat rests to enable her to shimmy her torso through the opening. Ashwariya accelerated to overtake GloGlo and expertly slowed Bluebell to match Showgirl One's speed, telling everyone on board to signal towards the coach's roof out their windows. Vanessa yelled down for the ladies to pass her two copies of *Pride and Prejudice*, one for each hand.

GloGlo tweaked Showgirl One's flaps, skipped a little to the left to lie directly above Bluebell and pushed her stick forward, eyes on Vanessa who, by this time, was more than half out of the coach's skylight with what looked like large orange, rectangular paddles in each hand, authoritatively acting as a landing marshal. Ashwariya yelled into her microphone. "Need an update, ladies. Where is the plane in relation to us?"

The Jane Austen Appreciation Society ladies yelled that GloGlo was right above them. "Her nose is at seat-12, and her rear is at seat-24. Now seat-14 ... seat-18. You are going too fast. Slow down a smidgeon, dear, easy does it."

Ashwariya slowed to forty miles an hour, and she saw Showgirl One's nose above her through the windscreen. "Too slow, too slow, speed up a tad, pet!" yelled the ladies. Ashwariya sped up. "Too fast, too fast, she's over the back, she's over the back!" Ashwariya slowed down a smidgeon as Showgirl One's belly flopped onto the coach's roof and Vanessa sank back into her seat.

Ashwariya could see Cuffley Hoo fast approaching. Her timing had to be perfect. Braking too quickly would send Showgirl One and GloGlo cannoning forward into a wall of rock. Braking too slowly and Bluebell would crash.

Through the steering wheel, Ashwariya could feel the coach's handling become less and less responsive. "Hang on, everybody, I am going to try to brake. Let me know exactly what is happening on the roof." Ashwariya pumped her brakes gingerly. She did not feel Showgirl One shift, so she braked harder and Showgirl One slid forwards. "She's pivoting on the roof, dear. She's twirling!" Ashwariya took her foot off the brake pedal and pumped it lightly once again. The rock face at the bottom of the Hoo loomed. Ashwariya steered into a turn and one of coach's front tyres burst, sending Bluebell into a long slow jackknife to the right which had the happy result of rebalancing Showgirl One before sending the vintage biplane too far to the left and start to skid down the coach's roof to the rear. "She's at the back dear, and she's askew!" Just as the Hoo was filling Ashwariya's windscreen, the coach finally slowed to an almost controlled stop.

Ashwariya leapt out of her driver's door. *Please let her be okay*. She looked up at the rear of the coach and there was Showgirl One definitely askew but safe, with no movement from the cockpit. Suddenly, she heard a familiar voice and burst into tears, as GloGlo's elbows appeared above Showgirl One's magenta fuselage.

GloGlo clambered out the biplane and onto Bluebell's roof. "You are a blooming genius, Ash! You saved us both! Thank you to whoever used *Pride and Prejudice* to guide me down! I even recognised the front cover!" And then she also burst into tears.

"Oh, my poor darling, I thought I'd lost you. Can you make your way forward so you can get down using the driver's door as a ladder?" GloGlo, not without pain, sidled past Showgirl One's fuselage and stumbled along the coach's roof to the front. With Ashwariya's help, she clambered down to the ground in front of the Jane Austen Appreciation Society. Vanessa, who had completed many first aid courses, encouraged her to sit down but GloGlo waved her away.

"Hello, ladies, thank you for flying with Lady Catherine de Bourgh Airlines today at a height of approximately ten feet. We hope you have enjoyed your trip," said GloGlo theatrically before she promptly fainted into Ashwariya's arms. The literary ladies broke out in spontaneous applause and brought out the contents of six thermoses, one each of tea, Bovril, Oxo, Marmite, Robinson's barley water and gin. These were all proffered to revive GloGlo, who came to, gazed into Ashwariya's eyes, kissed her on the lips and fainted again.

***

Joan escorted Reggie and Loveday in her Hillman Minx to Cuffley Manor's drawing room to be checked over by Doctor Otukile and fussed over by everyone else. Vanessa, who had summoned a police car to the crash scene, arrived with GloGlo and Ashwariya. All three MacGuffin sisters, while aching all over and visibly limping, were quick to move between tears, laughter and silence as the events of day weighed down on them, their minds going full tilt. For Reggie, as they hobbled into the house, the key question was whether what they had witnessed was an accident or sabotage, and if the latter, who was responsible?

Lying on separate sofas, alternately nattering and napping, making sense and making no sense, the sisters began to relax and fill everyone in on what had happened from their viewpoints. Charlie lit a fire in the big inglenook fireplace, and Joan and Blessing brought up pots of hot, strong tea, coffee and juice from the kitchen. Beaver turned up, looking shocked, with an armload of blankets and a bottle of brandy. Incredibly there seemed to be no broken bones. Ultimately Dr Otukile gave them all a clean bill of health, apart from multiple bruises, sprains, aches and pains for which he prescribed double-strength Anadin, rest and sleep.

Charlie looked as stricken as Beaver. "I am so sorry for everything that happened today. You are all perfectly marvellous. Hats off to each of you for being alive and barely injured. Even Showgirl One and Bluebell seemed to have survived with only a few scrapes."

Each sister had multiple layers of blankets tucked in so effectively by Beaver they could hardly move. GloGlo piped up from underneath her cocoon of wool, flannel and candlewick, "Charlie, we also must thank the Jane Austen Appreciation Society. And my dearest, Ash, of course. They were amazing. And here's to the Kitty Cadbury School for Girls Air Cadets program for ensuring we each received our flying, gliding, parachuting and skydiving badges at sixteen. Thankfully, Reggie has started brushing off her skydiving skills recently. I have no idea how Loveday managed to dredge up any muscle memory of this skill, however."

Loveday shrugged her shoulders and opened her hands in a 'me neither' gesture and winced in pain.

Blessing added, "And that was my Vanessa who flagged you down from the roof of the coach. I am so proud of her and her passion for great literature!"

Charlie smiled at them all. "You all have my undying admiration. What a squad! I wish I had gone to Kitty Cadbury's. Were all the pupils like you?"

Reggie, feeling the effects of tea and brandy seeping deep into her bones and brain, was getting back to her usual caustic self. "Of course they were, Charlie. Actually, all women are, in case you hadn't noticed."

Beaver laughed with relief. "Man, oh man, if Eighth Wonder Films gets to hear about your exploits, I think their stunt team might hire you. They are always looking for new ideas to up the ante in the next Dynamite McQueen film."

GloGlo grimaced as she hauled herself up onto her right elbow. "Oh, that would be marvellous. The flying circus would have a solid chance of taking off with that kind of publicity." She turned thoughtfully and whispered to her sisters. "Unless of course it was the film company who wanted to sabotage us."

Cliff, who had seen everything from the roof, made his way down to check on the commotion and arrived with the help of Vanessa who had been using the manor's telephone to organise transport to take the Jane Austen Appreciation Society members home. He was happy to no longer be the centre of attention but also horrified at what had happened, applauding each woman's high-flying, death-defying, daredevil skills. Apparently, the crowd thought everything was part of the display and was gobsmacked with glee at the stunts being performed in front of them. The fête's takings were the best ever.

Leaving the sisters to conk out under the collectively therapeutic, warming effects of the huge sofas, the weight of the blankets, the crackle of the fire and the heat of the drinks, Joan and Blessing retreated to the Aviatrix Arms to discuss next steps while Ash, Vanessa and Beaver disappeared to remove Showgirl One from Bluebell's roof and check over the coach for damage. Letting the other volunteers clean up after the fête, they also walked the grounds under where the flying display had gone horribly wrong, searching for Showgirl One's undercarriage, chocks and toolbox. They even found GloGlo's empty lunchbox before the sun set behind the trees.

***

In the pub, Blessing drained her double amontillado on the rocks. "Putting my analytical head on, I think we need to delve into the connection between the events of today, last week's bus attack and the MacGuffin sisters' unknown stalkers on the train, and last month's bomb blast at Ravenwood Studios."

"Go on," said Joan, instinctively feeling that Blessing

was on the right track.

"Well," said Blessing, "I have been considering all the pieces of the puzzle and how they might fit together. Let us return to Ravenwood Studios and last month's bomb blast. We suspect the one syndicate inner circle member who escaped the blast of being the instigator of the attack, which made him or her, the new syndicate leader. Why not stop there? Surely, a major goal was realised on that day. Why then follow the MacGuffin sisters of all people on the train? Why the bus attack and why try to down a plane with only two of the sisters in it at the fête? The clear reason, in my mind, is that the new syndicate leader wants to still carry out the plan to sabotage the World Cup Final to cement their status as leader, to bring Britain to its knees, and now I think I can add, kill the MacGuffin sisters and destroy WI-5. Let me tell you my reasoning: the new syndicate leader is not working alone. Yes, he or she still has syndicate minions following orders, but I think there is also a closer, unknown collaborator. Remember, Reggie saw two people following on the train earlier this week, a man and a woman. And don't forget, after the Ravenwood Studios bomb blast, one syndicate member escaped in a silver Rolls-Royce which had a driver. And you know, it almost worked perfectly, apart from WI-5 and film company chief, Babette Kohlrabi, witnessing the event and surviving the bomb blast, with Babette then disappearing. I think the new leader is seeking revenge for WI-5 messing with events at Ravenwood Studios and to eliminate us from being a spanner in the works of their planned attack on the World Cup Final. I think they now also want to kill

Reggie and GloGlo because somehow, they know it was Reggie who discovered the Ravenwood bomb and survived the blast, and it was GloGlo who flew the plane that saved her. After their failure of following the sisters on the train, their follow-up plan was the bus attack to knock out a whole swathe of WI-5 operatives, including Reggie, GloGlo and Loveday. However, I cannot for the life me explain what would they gain from killing GloGlo and Loveday at the fête, unless they thought Reggie was in the plane with GloGlo which, don't forget, was where she was meant to be. And that is as far as I have figured things out."

Joan thought through Blessing's logic and slowly nodded. Blessing, however, started to pick apart her own theory. "But what if we look through the telescope from the other end and surmise the reason for the bus attack was simply to stop it from driving on to the roof of the V&A. What if there is something on the roof of the V&A that our foes do not want anyone else to see! And what if, true to form, they had planted a bomb up there? After all it was their *modus operandi* for the Ravenwood Studios soundstage attack. If I wanted to take out WI-5, a huge bomb on the roof, timed to explode when the most people would be at work, would be the way to go. What do you think?"

Joan hugged her friend. "I think we need to call Morag."

"Before you do, if there is a bomb on the roof of the V&A, and it looks similar to the one which exploded at Ravenwood, I think we can surmise Crêpes Suzette,

Marquise of Disguise, Queen of Kaboom, is either the new head of the syndicate or his or her accomplice."

Ten minutes later, Joan came back from the phone box in the pub's car park and told Blessing that Morag was heading to the V&A Museum's roof with the bomb squad and Morag would telephone the same call box in an hour with the results.

Joan bought another couple of rounds and looked at her watch. "Almost time for Morag to call. Let us drain these glasses and get to the phone box."

Morag informed them about a huge pile of dynamite connected to a timer in a Melting Moments biscuit tin had been found on the roof of the V&A and was now safely defused. Blessing and Joan hugged and returned to the pub for a celebratory, relief-laden double sherry and a packet of pork scratchings. "So, Suzette and her accomplice are behind all this and are probably already here in Maiden Combust, or about to be here, in disguise. And you know what, one or both of them must be our mole in WI-5."

***

Both Showgirl One and Bluebell were deemed repairable and safely back in their respective hangars. After failed attempts to remove Showgirl One from Bluebell's roof using the local breakdown lorry, Beaver and Ashwariya decided the best plan was to leave Showgirl One up there and use the hangar's roof winch to safely lift her off. When inspecting the damage to Showgirl One, they were shocked to find two bullet holes clearly visible in her fuselage. It had been no accident. The undercarriage, still in one piece, was found hanging from a tree.

After being brought up to date with the news of the bomb on the V&A's roof and the bullet holes in Showgirl One, Loveday and Reggie were driven to Reggie's maisonette in Beaver's Sunbeam Rapier while Joan and Blessing drove Ashwariya and GloGlo to the control tower in the Minx. After hot baths, and with hot water bottles clutched to their bodies, Reggie, GloGlo and Loveday turned in to their respective beds and fell asleep as soon as their heads hit their pillows. They did not even have the energy to turn off their bedside lights. Ashwariya and Beaver sombrely checked on their charges, drew the curtains, turned off lights, straightened bedding and climbed in carefully, not wishing to disturb their comatose loved ones. They were relieved that everything had worked out, though it was evident how little distance separated life and death.

***

It was after nine o'clock on Sunday morning when Reggie woke up alone. She stretched and loudly exclaimed, "Oh man!" a habit she had picked up from Beaver, as all the aches and pains in her body woke up too. She managed to roll on her side and sit up on the edge of the bed, her head bent over, as she gathered herself to stand up and put on her dressing gown. Loveday was already in the loo when Reggie knocked on the locked door. "Loveday? How are you feeling?"

"Like I have been run over, but pretty good, considering I diced with death and won. How is my saviour?"

"Same, considering that landing knocked it out of me. I am pretty hungry, which I think is a good sign."

"I ate a whole afternoon tea yesterday as well as all the overcooked trimmings from the pork pies in the morning. Thank goodness, I did, as I think it is helping me regenerate my body as I speak." laughed Loveday through the door before groaning loudly as the laughing caused stabbing pains.

"The toilet door opened and Loveday gave her a sister a long hug, tears coming to her eyes as she whispered in her ear, "I am so glad you were born. Thank you for everything you did and do for me. I know you might not think it but I do notice what you do. In the past you could have so easily thrown me under a bus for some of the stunts I have pulled but you didn't and yesterday you were completely heroic. I want to make it up to you."

Reggie pulled away, embarrassed at her own tears. "I don't know what I would do without my haphazard little sister. Come on, let's totter downstairs like a couple of old ladies and get some tea on."

As Loveday was putting on Reggie's old dressing gown, Beaver called up the stairs, "I can bring tea up to you if you want to stay in bed."

"Don't worry, Beavie, we are awake, mobile and coming down. It takes more than nearly-plummeting-to-their-deaths to stop the MacGuffin sisters," Reggie responded, sounding more cheerful than she felt.

Beaver had lit the boiler early so the council flat was warm and toasty for once in the morning. He had also put the gas fire on in the living room. *Such luxury,* thought Reggie, as she and Loveday sat side by side on the put-you-up under a blanket, warming their feet by the fire and sipping their tea. Beaver stuck his head in the door and chirped "When you are ready, I can make you any breakfast you wish. I zipped out to the parade, so we have some fresh bread, Eccles cakes, bacon, Braughing sausages and the oven is on, so I can make cheesy eggs en cocotte."

Loveday looked happily surprised. "You can make eggs en cocotte, Beaver? Is there no end to your talents?"

Beaver looked half-pleased but also suspicious, a little unsure if Loveday was making fun. "Yes, we learned how to cook at lumberjack school by cooking eggs in a hot spring while being chased by bears." Without blinking, Reggie looked at Loveday who was nodding, and back at Beaver, enjoying the banter and knowing each was not quite getting the other.

"Well, I will have eggs en cocotte, a Braughing sausage and an Eccles cake, all cooked in a Hertford hot spring, and more tea please plus a bear hug," said Loveday cavalierly waving her mug.

"How many eggs would you like?"

"Two, please. I can't remember when someone other than me, Mum or Dad cooked me a breakfast."

"How about you, Babycakes? The usual?"

"Yes, please, Beavie, though I will take two eggs today as my poor old body is a spent force and needs building up."

Loveday looked over at Reggie. "But you don't like eggs."

"I do when Beaver cooks them and stirs in lots of cheese. They are divine. My favourite is your breakfast Yorkshires though. I had three last weekend. Goodness, that seems a long time ago," responded Reggie with an arched grin.

While the eggs and sausages were cooking, Beaver kept the tea coming, made toast and heated up the Eccles cakes so the sisters could get something immediately into their bodies.

"I could get used to this." grinned Loveday. "Thanks, Beavie."

"I am not so used to this that I don't appreciate it but it is lovely knowing I can get looked after when I need to be. I am happy to share Beaver on a split rota."

"I thought I would move in permanently."

"Dream away, Loveday. I am happy to share my bliss, not give it up entirely. Besides, don't forget you are here for a specific purpose. I might need you to move in up at the big house to keep a closer eye on things."

Loveday theatrically feigned offense. "Save my life one day and kick me out the next!" Reggie gave her a look, lips pressed together on the right side of her mouth. When the eggs, bacon and sausages were ready, both sisters moaned and groaned their way to the kitchen table.

"Beaver, these eggs are heaven. Thank you so much."

Between mouthfuls, Reggie shared her ruminations. "Firstly, bullet holes mean attempted murder and a bomb on the V&A roof means the destruction of WI-5 and the world's largest art and design museum. However, I don't think we can know who wanted who dead yesterday at the fête. GloGlo could have been the target, or Charlie, or me or even you Loveday. Perhaps Cliff, as no one could have known he wasn't going to be part of the display until the last minute. It could also have been the whole fête that was under attack. I don't think we can come to any firm conclusions at this point. Last night, darling Beaver telephoned Mum and Dad to update them on what was going on. Mum wasn't there, but he spoke to Dad who was happy we were all fine and tucked up in bed, but sounded extremely concerned about the possibility of accidents, let alone sabotage. Do not forget, we now know the V&A roof bomb was timed to explode on Monday when Dad would have been at work. So he could have been a target too, though I think it more likely that, whoever it was, wants WI-5 to be destroyed. I think we should call him once we have finished eating. Mum might be home and worried sick when she finds out what's happened."

***

Alfie picked up the phone as soon as Loveday finished dialling. "Hello, Dad, it's me. It's us actually, as Reggie is here as well. We are both fine and so is GloGlo who is coming round later. Just like Bluebell, we have a few dents in our coachwork but we are still roadworthy. It was very exciting. Reggie was a total hero, as was GloGlo. Beaver has been looking after us like the star he is. We are staying at home today, trying to pull back from the shock and figure out what might have gone on."

"Oh, Loveday, I haven't slept a wink since Beaver called. Your mother also called last night to say she has to stay at work throughout the weekend and the next week, so I had a terrible night. Also, did you know Morag found and dismantled a bomb on the roof of the Victoria and Albert Museum which she, Blessing and Joan believe was set by the syndicate agent who destroyed the Dynamite McQueen soundstage? They think the motive is revenge against WI-5, and somehow the three of you are being targeted. They believe the syndicate is now being led by Crêpes Suzette with help from an unknown co-conspirator. Their plan to sabotage the World Cup Final is still on and somehow centres on Cuffley Manor."

Loveday reassured her father. "Dad, we are all fine. But we are also worried about you as if you had been at work when that bomb went off, you would also have died, so this worrying goes both ways."

Alfie sighed. "This is getting far too dangerous, and I do not want any of you involved any more. I have been so worried about you, but I also want to see you all with my own eyes. I will get the train up this morning. Can Beaver meet me at Hertford North late morning in the Rapier?"

Beaver, who could hear Alfie's voice coming through the receiver, nodded. "Tell him, no problem. I will wait for Alfie to arrive before making lunch. Then we can all eat together. Hello, Alfie," he said loudly so Alfie would hear, "how does tomato soup, grilled cheese sandwiches, fruit cocktail and cookies for lunch sound?"

"Brilliant, the menu sounds just the tonic for dealing with all these shocks one after the other. I will phone from King's Cross when I know what train I will be catching. See you all in two ticks. And Loveday, I think we should put an end to all this nonsense especially for you right away. You should come back home with me tonight."

Loveday was about to protest when Reggie put her hand on her arm and shook her head. Reggie simply said, "We will see you later, Dad."

Reggie nodded at her sister. "Don't worry, Loveday, we will work on him together to allay his fears. I need you this week and next. You are not going anywhere."

Beaver ordered Loveday and Reggie to sit back down on the put-you-up. "You two are taking it easy today. I will call Ash and see if GloGlo is up to coming over for lunch so you can all talk with Alfie and convalesce together."

***

GloGlo and Ashwariya turned up for elevenses. Amazingly, GloGlo, who was not feeling as knocked about as Loveday and Reggie, had spent the morning with Ashwariya and Charlie supervising the safe removal of Showgirl One from Bluebell's roof. GloGlo recounted Charlie's report about Cliff being almost his usual self after a good night's sleep. Having a front row seat from the roof of the manor for all of yesterday's action had revived him no end.

Alfie called from King's Cross to say he would be arriving at Hertford North at noon. On his way to the station, Beaver stopped off at the parade and picked up the Sunday papers, tinned soup, tinned fruit, biscuits and chocolate bars (Mars bar for Alfie, jamboree bag for Reggie, coconut tobacco for Loveday, a Marathon bar for GloGlo and Caramac bars for himself and Ashwariya) as well as a big bottle of McMullen's Maxicola.

Over lunch, the four MacGuffins and Ashwariya were safely ensconced around the table, holding each other's hands, while Alfie gradually calmed down, listening to his daughters as Beaver made lunch and set the table.

"Oh my goodness, Beaver, the way you look after us is wonderful. Do you get this every day, Reggie, even when you haven't dodged death the day before?" asked Alfie admiringly.

Reggie grinned. "Actually, yes."

Alfie nodded. "Beaver, you are obviously one of the best decisions Reggie ever made, and she is known for sound decision-making. Now, girls, tell me again, everything that happened, detail by detail, leaving nothing out. This time I will make notes. Beaver, can you rustle me up some paper and a pen? Oh, thank you."

Reggie took the lead, filling Alfie in on the whole weekend, with Loveday and GloGlo chiming in as needed. There were no big revelations however. Feeling badly about making a joke of it the previous day, Reggie assured Loveday that she was not responsible for the suspected poisoning of Cliff. Beaver suggested it was possible the gun shots could have been accidental. It was the country after all but with the news of the bomb on the V&A roof, Reggie considered it unlikely. "Let's keep our options open," Alfie said. "Do you know if anyone has called in the local police?"

"Actually, Vanessa is a constable in the Hertfordshire constabulary, so I think they already know," said GloGlo. "She is also Blessing's daughter and Dr Innocent's sister, so there is nothing much that goes on around here that the Otukile family does not know about."

Reggie groaned, "I know there is nothing we can do about it but we do not need police swarming over Cuffley Manor this week, considering the film company's arrival next Tuesday and the WI-5 noose tightening around this place with all the activity that entails. However, Vanessa is so impressive, and I think if anyone can discover why we were shot at, she can."

Alfie nodded. "Today, I want you all to focus on resting and recuperating. But, with everything kicking up several gears, Reggie, GloGlo and Ashwariya, are you all going to be fit enough to survive the rigours of the week or does Morag need to cancel the whole operation?"

"Dad, we are all going to be fine," said GloGlo, as Reggie nodded.

"What about me?" pouted Loveday.

Alfie put down his soup spoon. "I don't want you involved any more. Reggie and Ash have the experience to work their way through this, and I trust GloGlo to keep her head down, but it's all new to you." Turning to the others, he said, "I want Loveday to come home with me tonight and stay there."

Loveday looked aghast. "You must be kidding, Dad. I can look after myself, thank you. You can trust me as well as them, you know." She crossed her arms over her chest like a recalcitrant child. "I am staying."

"Loveday, you are not staying. In case you haven't noticed, this is not your usual head-in-the-clouds flimflammery. This week's events are far too dangerous and close for comfort. Your mother and I are both worried and don't want you to take any more part in this." Alfie looked appealingly at Reggie. "Look, Reg, in her first week, Loveday has already faced three near-death experiences if we include the probably-tampered-with pork pie which Cliff ate by accident and could have been meant for her. I think Loveday has been deployed in the field too early."

Reggie looked her dad in the eyes. "Dad, I appreciate your concern. But we need Loveday here. Who would want to kill Loveday apart from you and Mum a month ago, ha, ha? Besides, Loveday is crucial to the mission, as she will be our lead contact with the film company inside the house and on the set. Her cooking skills are going to be on the front lines and she will have vital access the rest of us won't have. Please trust me to look after her."

Loveday put her hand on her father's arm. "No one knows me here anyway, so why would they want to kill me? I am only going to be the new cook who is going to bake her heart out and report to Reggie what I see and hear. The old cook, Mrs Gascoyne, has already given me her seal of approval."

GloGlo nodded with a serious look on her face. "Ash and I will also do our best to protect Loveday."

Facing down all three of his daughters and their united partners was not for the faint of heart for anyone, let alone a doting father. After a pause, he said, "Reggie, please be careful. Don't forget the most likely scenario is that yesterday some person or persons, unknown, attempted to kill your sisters."

Reggie sensed her dad was about to buckle. "I know it is risky, Dad, but it is a calculated risk. Don't forget that this week, our mission is going to come to a head. The film company is arriving to start production and then the World Cup Final happens. Loveday is central to our plans to conduct surveillance of the cast and crew to find out exactly what is going on. And apart from a collection of theories, we actually do not know what is going on so we need all hands on deck. Loveday will be under my tutelage and control all week, and a role has opened up which perfectly fits her skills and experience. I will also do my damnedest to keep her out of harm's way." Loveday nodded at both her sister and her father.

Reggie looked at her sister with what she thought were steely eyes. "Loveday, that means no planes, no buses, no London, no going off on your own without regularly reporting to me. And to get our bodies and minds ready for the week ahead, we are each having an ice bath tonight. Got it?"

"Roger, wilco Reg." nodded Loveday who then mouthed, "Ice bath?"

GloGlo leaned over and whispered, "Don't worry, it's not as bad as it sounds. We should have had one last night to jumpstart the healing process, but tonight, we probably need it more for our brains." Loveday remained unconvinced but stayed silent.

Alfie sighed deeply, knowing he was on a losing wicket, bested once again by his progeny. "Well, all right, one more week and then we will review the situation. To save my sanity, I am going to be here as well to keep a close eye on you all. Oh yes, I am! I have decided to implement Morag's idea to double check that no V&A artefacts remain at Cuffley Manor from when they were stored there during the War. I will bring Tolly with me as two heads are always better than one. He does have the next couple of weeks off, but I think the opportunity to drive the museum lorry will entice him back. I am also going to ask Morag for reinforcements. I don't know what your mother is going to say when she arrives home to an empty house and finds out we are all together having adventures without her in the wilds of Hertfordshire. Be warned."

All the World's a Stage

After a day of rest, Reggie had ordered everyone to meet in the kitchen at Cuffley Manor at nine o'clock Tuesday morning to receive preparation instructions for the arrival of the Eighth Wonder Film Company. Loveday was to focus on greeting the grocer's van which Reggie had organised to arrive with her shopping list of provisions. Loveday surprised herself by not feeling nervous about all the demands being placed on her by the impending arrival of the film company and the need to keep her eyes open while catering to the cast and crew's culinary needs. She could be who she was – a cook. She would be playing herself.

Reggie paired everyone else up to focus on specific tasks that needed to be completed, whether it was readying the aerodrome to receive the film company's cargo plane, putting flowers and installing listening devices in the four grand bedrooms and bathrooms where cast and crew would be staying, ensuring the attic recording equipment was installed correctly or confirming the crew transportation plan. Later that afternoon, Reggie, GloGlo and Loveday were going to be formally interviewed by Constable Vanessa Otukile about the shooting at the fête.

Once everyone had scattered, Loveday used all the ingredients she had on hand to start cooking and checked her lists for all the new grocery items that were to arrive. The WI ladies must have worked like demons to clean and clear everything up after the fête. She was both relieved and grateful to see the kitchen was in tip-top condition, and to have it to herself with hopefully no interference from Mrs Gascoyne. After the grocer's van arrived with the delivery, Loveday reviewed her to-do list, deciding that the film company's breakfasts were pretty well taken care of but more vegetarian lunch items were needed. As she moved around the kitchen, cooking up batches of ratatouille and stuffed marrow, all stiffness gradually disappeared from her body.

***

After Loveday returned to the kitchen from being interviewed by Vanessa, she heard buzzing from the tube post room. It was Reggie alerting Loveday that the Eighth Wonder Film Company Skyfreighter cargo plane was arriving in thirty minutes, an hour earlier than planned. Loveday double checked that everything was turned off, threw her apron over a chair, scraped her hair with a comb, grabbed an umbrella as it looked like rain and headed outside. After the horrific egos on display during the press call, she did not want to miss the arrival of the full cast and crew.

As she made her way gingerly through the woods to the aerodrome, Loveday could already hear the deep rumble of aircraft engines gaining in volume. This was a much louder sound than the insect buzz of the Tiger

Moth's engine and the guttural sewing machine noise made by the Brabazon Speedbird. When she emerged into the light, a huge silver aeroplane flew low over the trees with its undercarriage down, ready to land. She walked over to her sisters and the rest of the Cuffley Manor greeting party. Tansy, dressed as if for a Buckingham Palace garden party, looked blankly through her and turned to brush dust off of Cliff's aerodrome overalls.

Gazing at the aeroplane, GloGlo was in a heightened state of excitement. "That is the largest plane ever to land at Cuffley aerodrome, and thank goodness, the RAF had reinforced the landing strip with concrete during the war. It's a Brabazon Skyfreighter – an art deco beauty. And a local beauty too as it was manufactured up the road at Hatfield. Way before my time of course."

They watched the Skyfreighter make a smooth landing and taxi towards the main hangar. After rumbling to a stop, the large cargo door at the back swung down to form a long ramp and out walked fifty people followed by loud honking. The last few people jumped off the ramp as a long, low, silver rocket-on-wheels, seemingly made of mercury, motored slowly down.

"Blimey!" exclaimed GloGlo. "I didn't think I would ever see this in real life! That is the Thunderbolt Invicta, Brabazon's famed one-of-a-kind car built in the 1930s. Strike me, it is stunning. Two engineering marvels in one day! Be still, my beating heart!"

Loveday also stared with an open mouth. "Is it really a car? It looks like a plane without wings. I think the huge silver aeroplane gave birth to a little silver aeroplane."

"That is the point," responded GloGlo. "I heard about it when I apprenticed at Brabazon. It is the only car the Brabazon aircraft corporation ever deigned to design. I didn't know it still existed in real life. I thought the one in the films would be just a prop and wouldn't be able to move under its own steam. All those curves, not a straight line anywhere. Apparently, the designers used the actress playing Dynamite McQueen in the early films as inspiration. It looks pretty obvious when you see those bulbous headlights! And I think the radiator is meant to reflect the nose cone of a futuristic fighter plane. The body looks like molten metal, doesn't it? I don't know what it is made of but I know the patterns of rivets are mostly for effect. Look at the chevron-shaped aerofoil, twin tail fins and exhaust pipes. And the line of the gullwing doors with the windscreen wrapping around like a cockpit. Rumour has it, there is a real ejector seat. Those twin front axles have to be heavy enough to bear the weight of all the weaponry you see in the films. It is so utterly fab. I would love to see under the bonnet."

The low-slung Thunderbolt gingerly made its way over the lip of the ramp onto solid ground. Blessing's camera flashed. All eyes were on the car, as it came to a stop. Reggie had moved to Loveday's side, mouth also agape. "Oh my goodness, these film industry people know how to make an entrance."

A gullwing door opened on the opposite side of the car and a chauffeur appeared, dressed in a dazzling silver uniform, heavily sequinned cap, white fur collar, bushy moustache and large dark sunglasses. He came round to the side, facing the crowd, and opened an almost invisible gullwing passenger door which floated up to reveal the hem of a glittery dress, a slender ankle and a woman's silver shoe stepping out on to the ground. Behind this vision followed a man in an equally glittery suit and fur coat.

Nobby walked up and shepherded all the new arrivals to Bluebell, which was waiting by the hangar with Ashwariya, to drive them to the manor to divest luggage and then on to Hertford for a cast and crew dinner. Everyone else made their way to the manor along the footpath, with GloGlo staying behind to admire the car and strike up a conversation with the sequinned chauffeur.

Inside the main hall, Vesta Currie stood on the grand staircase and addressed everyone, "Welcome to our home for the next two weeks, the magnificent Cuffley Manor, the historic home of the Cuffley family. The executive team and lead cast members will be staying here in this grandest of grand houses, thanks to the hospitality of Lord Cuffley and his staff. For the rest of you, see Nobby for your accommodation allocations and call sheets."

Nobby took charge. "We will all be meeting for dinner at the Salisbury Arms in Hertford tonight. Make sure you are on the blue coach outside in half an hour. For those staying here, the coach will bring you back after dinner. For those staying at the Salisbury Arms and elsewhere, do not forget to take all your luggage with you. The coach will pick you up after breakfast tomorrow morning and bring you to the aerodrome, so we can unload the equipment. We have also arranged for a local taxi company to be on call if needed. Phoebe has maps and the list of which equipment and sets go where."

Phoebe waved her clipboard half-heartedly. Vesta leapt in. "I want you all fresh, so get a good night's sleep and watch your alcohol intake at dinner. I will be cracking the whip tomorrow, as we need the interior sets installed right away. While this is happening, I will be conducting a full-dress rehearsal of the garden scenes throughout the morning with filming in the afternoon. I would like to thank Lord Cuffley and his family for their generosity in letting us film here. I assure him, we will treat his family home and gardens as if they were our own. My lovely principal cast, please don't go anywhere, as the staff are ready to welcome you and show you to your rooms. Everyone else onto the coach in twenty minutes. Phoebe, make sure everyone gets on the bus!"

As they walked through the main hall, Fontaine bickered at Vesta. "This house looks appallingly dilapidated. My room had better be up to snuff. This light could not be more unflattering."

Reggie looked at Charlie, who looked at Cliff, who looked at Beaver, who looked at Joan, who looked at Blessing, who looked at Loveday, who did not look at Tansy. GloGlo came bounding in with a scowl and the news that Gaylord, the glittery chauffeur, disappointingly, was unimpressed by GloGlo's enthusiasm for the Thunderbolt and had brushed her off completely, as he was needed at the manor immediately to ensure Fontaine's apparently bottomless pit of needs was being met.

Behind a makeshift reception desk created the day

before by the ever-capable Beaver, Joan handed out room keys and instructions while Tansy stationed herself beside the desk to make eye contact with everyone she considered important. Beaver and Charlie showed the guests to their rooms.

After all the guests had left, Tansy handed out black and white maid's uniforms to Loveday, Blessing and Joan. "I have a gift for you, girls. I thought we would look more professional if we wore a uniform.

"And it would underline the fact that you are below stairs and the guests and myself are above," said Tansy, prodding Blessing with brim of her hat.

"What about your uniform, Tansy?" Loveday couldn't help herself asking. *What was Tansy even doing here?*

"I will not be serving guests, naturally. I will straddle between the guests and the staff as a personal hostess, a bon vivant dressed accordingly to my rank and class. Our guests are used to the best of London glamour, and our Hertfordshire country manners might be a little off-putting, so we must all be as professional as possible in our respective positions, right to our fingertips. Best foot forward, girls." Tansy turned on her heels and went upstairs with a self-important air to *fine tune the details until they achieve utter perfection.*

Returning to the hall and overhearing Tansy, Charlie saw the need to lighten the mood as Blessing and Joan pursed their lips as much by being called *girls* by a woman much younger than themselves as by having to wear a uniform. "You have all done such a marvellous job preparing everything. Your presence here is hugely important to me and my brother, and we can't thank you enough. The manor hasn't looked this good for years. That actress, Dynamite, was very complimentary. She seems to have her feet firmly on the ground. But Fontaine... dear Lord, under what rock did he crawl out from? If you have any trouble with him or with anyone, let me, or Reggie, know. Tomorrow, they will be out rehearsing in the morning in the gardens and then filming in the afternoon, so we won't see any of them between breakfast and dinner. Does that sound right, Reg?"

Reggie nodded. "Yes, I am happy. Tomorrow, I will be at the aerodrome the whole time."

Charlie maintained his perky mood. "And they are all off to Hertford for dinner tonight, so no one has to be on duty until tomorrow morning. How about we all retire to the Aviatrix Arms for dinner? Our treat. How about we head over on foot across the fields?"

"Oh, Clifford," said Tansy, suddenly appearing again. "How am I going to walk there in my heels? I might need Charles to carry me, *har har har*. What about the lovely new wine bar in Hertford, you know, the ritzy one in Parliament Square with the moody lighting?" Eyes wide, Cliff and Charlie slow-blinked, not saying a word.

Reggie stepped in. "We need some fresh air and a walk so the pub it is. I am sure you can rustle up a pair of wellingtons somewhere Tansy if you care to join us."

***

Everyone made it to the pub except for Tansy who wouldn't be seen dead in the Aviatrix Arms let alone in wellingtons, and Blessing, who was busy in the attic ensuring any conversations picked up by the listening devices were being recorded. Cliff smiled as they walked, happy to avoid Tansy. It had also been a long time since his brother had felt relaxed enough to go to the pub.

As they drained their first glasses, GloGlo updated them on Showgirl One's condition after having been dismantled and put back together. The two bullet holes in the engine casing had been easily plugged so Showgirl One's participation in the World Cup Final flypast need not be scuppered. Much to her relief, the undercarriage was undamaged. All the Tiger Moth needed was a new coat of magenta paint on her underside. Bluebell, the coach, had also been checked over. She had some dents in her roof, a couple of cracked skylights, and two already-replaced blown tyres, but nothing to stop the film crew from being transported between Hertford and Cuffley Manor over the next fortnight.

Cliff asked what many were thinking, "Does anyone know who shot at the plane?"

"Yes, why would someone want to shoot Loveday and/or GloGlo?" replied Charlie. "I think I should check in with the Hertford police and ask Constable Otukile to drop in tomorrow, so we can get an update. And I should also get Dr Otukile to check on Cliff again to make sure he is completely well. I know you didn't sleep well last night, Cliff."

"Actually, Dr Otukile causes quite a stir in these

parts," said Cliff, barely suppressing a giggle after having drunk a full pint of Country Best Bitter, all shyness gone. "Eh, Charlie?"

Charlie looked sheepish and quickly changed the subject. "However briefly the film company will be using the house, I have some hope the glory days of Cuffley Manor might not be completely behind it. Cliff and I never experienced those days first hand, but our dad talked about them a lot. Before the war, in the 1920s and 30s, it was full of servants and shenanigans. The army later made use of every inch of the place for troop training, equipment testing, as a convalescent home and for some secret operations which, if you knew about, Cliff, here, would have to shoot you." Rather alarmed at this, given the events of the weekend, Loveday looked at Cliff, who nodded enthusiastically, and then shook his head, his cheeks rosy-hued.

Reggie leaned in. "The history of the manor and your family is so interesting. Can you tell us more?"

Charlie registered he had everyone's attention. "Well, Dad confided in me that his upbringing here was pretty ghastly. He was afraid of our grandfather's dark moods and didn't go to proper school but had a succession of disinterested tutors and governesses which led to a somewhat patchy education. I think that is why he and Mum sent Cliff and I to the primary school in Maiden All Saints and the grammar school in Hertford, so we could be around other children. In 1939, when he was nineteen, Dad enlisted, happy to go to war, apparently a better option than his life here. His father had died right before the war so it was touch and go whether Dad would return to the house. While he was off fighting, Dad handed the place to the Ministry of Defence. Dad once told me that after the war, lots of people gave up their old lives and started new ones. He was also severely tempted to wipe the slate clean and start afresh. However, he did come back after the war to settle the family affairs with the intention of selling the estate. Obviously, he changed his mind. He told me that the manor was in a terrible state when he was demobbed. The army had left in a hurry, not fixing what they had altered and leaving a right mess. He didn't even have keys to everything but remembered his father used to hide spare keys in the underground icehouse in the garden, and the key to the icehouse was hidden in a tobacco tin behind one of the loose tiles which surround the fountain. He could not face living in the rotunda alone, so he camped out in the lodge and lived like a hermit there for a few months. The lodge was in much better repair than any other building on the estate, as the army had only used it as a kind of sentry office. No one in town bothered him or even remembered him. Most of the locals who worked at the house before the war and might have known him as a child, had long since died or moved on. He also looked quite different. War had changed him from an angelic-looking, skinny boy into a gloomy, battle-scarred recluse who looked a lot older than his years.

"Dad kept the proverbial wolf from the door by using his old cheque book which he came across in a desk drawer and discovering, although there was not much in the account when he had left, it had grown because of the deposits his deceased father's solicitors had made as they sorted through his estate. Hence, he had money to buy food and didn't need to find a job right away. He dilly-dallied about meeting with the family solicitors to finalise his father's probate, as he understood once he was the official owner and became Lord Cuffley, there was no turning back and he might be overwhelmed by the same dark forces which overwhelmed his father. As you all know, Cuffley Manor was built for a different time and set of values. What was so good about owning a big house, reams of land and a battered aerodrome if there was no significant money coming in to maintain it? Are you sure this isn't boring you all? Cliff looks like he has fallen asleep. Shall I get another round in?"

Beaver signalled to him to sit down. "Charlie, this is very interesting. I will get the next round in and also some food. What does everyone want?"

After Beaver returned with the drinks and food was ordered, Charlie carried on, "While Dad was lying low, I think he was also grieving for his father but would never admit it. He spent those months after being demobbed, barely existing, avoiding the ghosts. Once spring came, I think the worst of his depression was starting to lift. He gradually explored the estate and began to notice daily changes as shoots appeared, leaves unfurled, flowers blossomed and the colour palate changed from brown to green, to yellow, to white, to pink and to purple. Rabbits, foxes, birds, squirrels, mice and deer all appeared. I think seeing the grounds come back to life brought him back to life too. Eventually, he plucked up the courage to go back into the manor and live there. In the hangar, he found his father's old motorbike which he managed to get going, so he was able to explore the countryside he had once known so well and from which he felt strangely disconnected. Then, he made a big decision which directly led to him meeting our mum. But I am getting ahead of myself. Ah, the food's arrived, wonderful. Tuck in, everyone."

They all ate, enraptured. Cliff was especially attentive once he had hot food in his stomach. He always loved hearing family stories and Charlie always told them well. However, he wasn't used to Charlie being so open about their father. Joan sprang for the next round and everyone settled back in their seats, happily sozzled. Fortified by another pint of McMullen's AK, Charlie finished his story.

"Let's see. Oh, yes. Dad's big decision. Dad got in touch with a couple of old friends he had met during the war. He had their address in London, wrote and invited them to come and camp with him in the lodge for a weekend. He wanted their help and advice to answer the question: 'Do I stay at Cuffley Manor and grasp a nettle which could sting me very badly, or do I sell up, walk away and start a new life?' Apparently, the three friends spent the whole weekend walking around the estate and talking through all the options. If Dad stayed, he knew he would have to dedicate his life to bringing the manor back from the dead, come what may, with no half measures. If he left, it would be a new start and a new identity.

"As you can see, Dad decided to stay. His friends were enthusiastic, and Dad could see the place afresh through their eyes. They discussed how the estate could start generating income. As he had been a pilot during the war and he had decent maintenance skills, it seemed natural to focus on the aerodrome at first. He thought pilots from Hertford and the surrounding villages might want to use the aerodrome because the nearest airfield was in Hatfield next to the Brabazon factory. A month later, his two friends came back to help out with the clean-up, and this time, they brought a friend with them, and this friend became our mum."

Charlie sat back as though finished. He took a drink, looked at his watch and said, "Should we all head home? It is getting late."

Joan looked flabbergasted. "Charlie, can't you see you have everyone in the palm of your hand? Do get on with telling them what happened next. They are hanging onto your every word."

Charlie's eyes twinkled. He was enjoying himself enormously. "Mum and Dad were married not long after they met. Dad focused on the aerodrome; Mum focused on the house. Slowly, the aerodrome became solvent while the house was updated. To have some regular money coming in, Mum worked in Hertford, in the Addis toothbrush factory, in the offices. Everyone made a big fuss about Lady Cuffley working at the factory but that was Mum all over. No airs nor graces. Then we both came along, almost exactly nine months later. Cliff is older than me by fifteen minutes, so he is Lord Cuffley and I can be the ne'er-do-well younger son." Charlie laughed at this, as Cliff blushed and rolled his eyes. "We lived in the lodge until things picked up. When Aunt Elsie was hired as housekeeper and nanny, we moved into the rotunda and Aunt Elsie settled in the lodge. Actually, she is not really our aunt but we always called her Aunt Elsie. Then Mum died quite suddenly. We were still young boys. Afterwards, Aunt Elsie became more of a grandmother to us. She took us to school every morning, marshalled us on our annual school uniform buying trips and came along to parents' evenings. She also cooked for Dad and us, and kept the rooms we used in the house clean. Other than us, we never knew her to have any other family. I remember hearing a rumour that she once had had a child of her own, a son I think it was, but he must have died in the war. I do think looking after Cliff and I helped her get over the grief, as she treated us as if we were her own children. We were always over at the lodge to spend our free time with her. We do owe her a lot. I am not sure how we can repay her kindness other than letting her live in the lodge for free and visiting her regularly."

Charlie looked at their enthralled faces. "Sorry if I have monopolised the conversation. It doesn't happen often. You know I think we should end it there. A tipsy film company will be returning imminently at the house, members of which may not be in a fit state to find their rooms on their own, so Cliff and I should be on hand to help."

Looking pointedly at Joan, Blessing and Loveday, Beaver said with a wicked grin, "And tomorrow, don't forget your uniforms, otherwise Tansy will be after you."

Charlie, stood up and sat down again with a start. "Cliff, I just remembered that, with all this talk about Aunt

Elsie, she was going to come and look after you during the afternoon of the fête when you were convalescing. Did she stay long? I haven't seen her since, have you?"

Cliff looked awkward and shook his head. "I didn't see her on Saturday. She never turned up, and I haven't seen her since either."

The Body in the Shrubbery

Two rather fragile brothers sat in the kitchen early the next day, nursing hangovers and mugs of tea. "I hope we are not going to regret fraternizing with the film company people," moaned Cliff thinking this was highly likely.

"Well, you know these actors," said Charlie sagely, having never met an actor in his life before last week. "But they will only be here for a short time and are paying handsomely for all the upheaval. Reggie will come down on them like a ton of bricks if they don't keep to their part of the bargain. Besides, they gave us a fat cheque upfront which will get our heads above water. Loveday, Blessing and Joan are looking after their stomachs, and Beaver is looking after everything else. Fingers crossed, the extra load on our ancient pipes and wiring won't result in anything exploding. GloGlo will smooth over any ructions at the aerodrome, so I reckon the team can deal with anything. And don't forget Tansy can 'straddle' if needed," said Charlie with a big grin while Cliff held his head in his hands.

Loveday rushed in, wearing her maid's uniform and a don't-mess-with-me expression. Both Charlie and Cliff's moods lifted when they saw her. "Oh, Loveday," said Charlie. "How are you feeling about all this? I am so sorry about Tansy's uniform idea. You do not have to go along with it you know."

"Oh, it's all right. Joan, Blessing and I have decided to play along and are having a fun time practicing our curtseying, bowing, scraping, wiggling our epaulettes and wondering what or whom Tansy will straddle next." Both Cliff and Charlie laughed aloud.

Loveday continued, "Blessing is kicking herself about why she did not think of coming up with the idea of uniforms herself. As she says, even though Tansy might be a complete idiot, she is trying her best, and Blessing thinks the uniforms are hand-made to a very high standard. Better than anything she could rustle up. We did suggest Tansy take on the high-profile job of personally handling Fontaine de Havilland, which would have the double benefit of less Tansy in our midst and less us having to be in close proximity to that Max-Factored ogre. Tansy will be worth her weight in gold if she can pull it off, and she sparkled at our praise and suggestion. I have a feeling that, like me, Tansy finds herself always on the outside looking in, and sometimes handles it rather badly."

"Oh, Loveday," said Cliff earnestly, "I hope you don't feel the same about us. We want you to always be comfortable on the inside, where it is warm, and not out there in the cold, lonely world."

Loveday smiled and wiggled her epaulettes for effect. "Actually, for once, I do feel like I am on the inside with you and everyone else. I am quite enjoying myself, even though I have almost been murdered. In terms of my cooking duties, Reggie has all the details nailed down in the contract. Any deviations, and she gets to charge them more. And I got a good head start yesterday. Besides, their regular catering company is feeding all the crew and background players, so it won't be so onerous. Apparently, there will be extras bussed in today for the background of the garden scenes, and the dancers have arrived to be briefed for tomorrow's interior scenes. Thank goodness, I do not have to feed them all! Apart from breakfast and dinner, I am only cooking special snacks for Vesta, Dynamite and Fontaine. How bad can it be? Dynamite just needs a hot daily soup, and somewhat unexpectedly, dear old Fonty has requested a selection of high-calorie treats throughout the day for his snack attacks. His only redeeming feature to me seems to be the amount he eats and what he likes. Pork pies, jam roly-poly and cheese and pickle fancies with extra onion, so at least his appetite is healthy even if nothing else about him is. If he crosses you, let me know, and I will spit in a cheese and pickle fancy. Sorry, boys, I have to fly, I left Blessing and Joan ready to do battle with Tansy and whoever comes down first. I am expecting a breakfast Armageddon and want to get a front row seat."

***

Breakfast did not live up to Loveday's dramatic expectations. It went disappointingly smoothly without frayed nerves or escalated tensions, although Dynamite came in favouring her ankle saying she had twisted it on the way down. There was a buffet of toast, butter, jam, marmalade, Bovril and fresh fruit for people to help themselves. Loveday had cooked up a large batch of sausages, bacon, spam and kidneys in advance and prepared eggs to order. Joan took the orders, Blessing helped in the kitchen, while Tansy walked around the table snapping her fingers for service. After half an hour of being snapped at, Joan grumbled how she wanted to tear her epaulettes off and shove them down Tansy's throat. Blessing took over serving duties to let Joan cool down. The guests were all subdued and silent, studying their scripts and notes. No one lingered, although Nobby, who was the last to leave, said, "Thank you, on everyone else's behalf," as Loveday handed him Fontaine's morning snacking basket. She hoped Nobby would be receiving extra pay, as she imagined feeding Fontaine must be like duelling with a recalcitrant bronzed crocodile. One moment of inattention and you could lose a hand.

Once everyone had departed and she had cleaned up, Loveday made a thermos of soup for Dynamite and another picnic basket of snack goodies for Fontaine. However, when Loveday headed over to the great lawn to deliver the food to the set, the place was empty apart from Phoebe, who was scurrying around ticking things off on her clipboard. Loveday didn't want to scare her, so she stood to one side until suddenly Phoebe scurried backwards right into her. "Excuse me, it's Phoebe, isn't it?" asked Loveday tentatively. "I'm Loveday, the house cook. I have a few snacks for Dynamite and Fontaine which I am meant to give to Nobby. Do you know where I can find him?"

Phoebe jumped and looked alarmed on seeing

Loveday, but even more so as someone was actually talking to her and asking her a question rather than giving her an order. She soon regained her composure. In a pinched whisper, she explained to Loveday that as the garden rehearsals were now over, Vesta was giving the cast notes in the drawing room, and she would be happy to escort Loveday there.

In the drawing room, the cast faced Vesta, who was the only one standing. Vesta, befitting a much-hyphenated producer-director-lyricist-choreographer, was resplendent in a shimmery leopard-print, leotard-culotte combination. "Everybody, everybody, thank you, can I get your attention? Settle down. Oh there you are, Phoebe. Stop wandering off. Settle DOWN. Fontaine, I am looking at you. Don't make me come over there. My darlings, it was a lovely rehearsal today – sublime. But before we break for lunch, I have a few notes. Phoebe, my stool. I don't want to have to ask again."

The stool appeared and Vesta shuffled her buttocks to get comfortable. "Much better. Where is the star of my firmament, my beloved Yazmine, Dynamite McQueen? That bikini fits you perfectly. It matches your hair tone beautifully, but I want to focus on your delivery. I don't want to say the word 'hopeless' because I am saving it for Fontaine, but I think in this sequence we do need to feel your hopelessness, as this song and dance number represents Dynamite hallucinating about her one true love while strapped to the undercarriage of a plane about to crash into central London. When you declare your unspoken love for darling Fontaine, I mean, Hesketh, of course, I think we need a bit less pushing Hamlet through a sieve and a bit more *joie de vivre. Comprendito?* Are we on the same bus to Smethwick? The feeling I want to see in your eyes relates specifically to communicating directly to the audience's collective hearts, via their collective eyes, larynx and oesophagus, the feeling that lady luck has dealt you a joker and now you are dicing with death and *blah blah, Bridget the Midget Queen of the Blues*, how am I going to get out of a scrape this time? *Comprendolez?* Consider fingering your harness with an insolent 'I may be about to die, but I am still chipper in my gold bikini', *blah blah fishcakes* grin while you fantasise about Fontaine, I mean Hesketh. I know we are dealing with Fontaine here, my darling. We can only slap on so much makeup, coat the lens in Vaseline and put the lights behind him. My advice to you is to focus on him as he was twenty years ago (I think I have a photograph in my glove compartment), react and try not to think about the poor dear sad old carcass you see in real life. Fontaine, darling, don't interrupt me when I am plundering for motivation.

"Now, onto the dance sequence itself. Yazmine, darling, how severely did you twist your ankle? Do you think Busby Berkeley wouldn't make you carry on? Remember, it is a fantasy sequence, so I want a bit less I-am-stuck-in-an-open-prison-taking-tap-lessons-from-a-talentless-inmate-with-a-mascara-fetish and a bit more *razzmatazz*, can-can, here-I-come-Broadway, knickers or no knickers. Let us hope on the stethoscopes of Doctors Kildare, Finley, Zhivago and Who that you are truly healed and revitalised for tomorrow because your stand-in is stuck in Cockfosters with a colicky toddler. Phoebe, if you cannot find a replacement, I may need you to stand-in for the stand-in. Also, I want any close-ups with Dynamite and Hesketh to be from the waist up. I fear he has been noshing on snacks all morning and the camera picks up everything. Yazmine, the love in your eyes cannot show any ripples of anxiety when he gets close. I know it is your last Dynamite McQueen film, so let's give it more Natalie Wood and a bit less Ed Wood.

"Darling Fontaine, lovely emoting-to-the-gods Fontaine. You have my complete attention. All about you for once, my darling, as I don't want your enormous talent to be wasted, but in order for that to happen you have to bring a big old suitcase full of it with you. Do you get my drift? Remember Hesketh is on the plane, in a coma, knocked out by Dynamite's kidnappers. By the end of the sequence, the audience needs to believe that you remain in love with Dynamite, and this leads you to awaken from your coma and declare her to be your one true love. Then you search for Dynamite in a frenzy, ultimately finding her strapped to the undercarriage and *blah blah rissoles*, you knock out the enemy, put on that lovely glittery helmet and gold lamé parachute, leap out of the plane, skydive to the front wheels to free Dynamite and leap clear before the plane crashes.

"And dancers! Blithe on your feet. Wispy as a cloud but sharp as lightning. More Cyd Charisse, less Sid James, *compretaporter*? So that is it everyone. Time for lunch, and next we head to the aerodrome to strap Dynamite to the Skyfreighter's front wheel for the rest of the afternoon.

Fontaine, would you mind if we squeeze in a little work on your solo dance number to get the camera angles right? *Hmm*? Phoebe, rustle up some healthy snacks for Fontaine, and three eclairs, a game pie and a bag of hula hoops for me, and meet us on the lawn behind the house with everyone I might need. And also, when I say I want strawberry milkshake, I want Nesquik, not that cocktail of diarrhoea mixture and nail varnish you rustled up last week. *Compostez*?"

Loveday intercepted Phoebe who was trotting forlornly towards the catering table. "Phoebe, remember I have all of Fontaine's snacking treats in my basket here. I heard Vesta's instructions and think I can provide most of it. Shall I grab what Vesta needs and help you carry them over? I can also lay my hands on some Nesquik." Phoebe nodded with grateful eyes. Loveday ended up fetching all the requested food by herself, as Phoebe was soon overwhelmed by the demands of Vesta working on a new scene through lunch. Loveday stationed herself under a tent in the garden and watched while Vesta briefed Fontaine, Phoebe hovering in the background with her faithful clipboard. The lighting was being reset by a crew looking less than thrilled to not be enjoying their lunch.

"Fontaine, I want your Ruby Keeler not Christine Keeler. Phoebe, where are my eclairs?"

Phoebe pointed at Loveday who waved back and pointed at her baskets of food. Fontaine mouthed a long line of expletives which Loveday interpreted as *Can't the bleeding snacks come to me?* and answered in her mind, *No, they bleeding can't*, and stayed where she was.

Fontaine had a quick one-sided tête-à-tête with Vesta, who called over make-up to wrap him in a large, shapeless, floor-length grey smock, much to Loveday's amused delight. He bounded over to Loveday ready to thunderclap. "How does that cockroach-in-culottes expect me to work when I am half-starved. What do you have for me?"

Loveday replied, "Two Cornish pasties, four mini pork pies, jam roly-poly, hot custard and your uneaten cheese and pickle fancies with extra onion from this morning."

"Have you ever tried singing and dancing for hours on an empty stomach? Most cannot do it but I can. I will just take a pasty, two pork pies and a cheese and pickle fancy. Delicious, by the way. I don't know what you put into it to make a pasty taste so good, but I approve. Do you have my Irn Bru? I wish you had something stronger for me to deal with that helmet-haired, horned beetle of a harpy director."

Loveday swallowed a guffaw at his unintentional, uncannily accurate description of Vesta and handed over a bright orange bottle. "Here it is, don't guzzle it all at once, as there is not an unlimited supply. You know, I am fascinated about this surreal world where a stately home, a plane crash and the Hanging Gardens of Babylon all belong in one story. Are you Scottish by any chance?"

Fontaine thawed a smidgeon, as he caught the end of Loveday's guffaw, swigged from the bottle of Irn Bru and downed a pork pie in one bite. "Okay, much better, the performing seal is ready to perform. Actually, the pork pie was really rather good. Sorry, what did you say?"

"I asked if you were from Scotland… because of the

Irn Bru. It was tough to find here. Thank goodness someone found some at the Hertford Fine Fare stuffed in the back near the Maxicola."

Fontaine, a little stunned at Loveday's gumption and confidence, looked at her quizzically, wondering why she wasn't cowering like most underlings he was forced to deal with. He couldn't think of a pithy retort and was surprised to find himself speaking naturally. "Actually, I don't like it much, I am more of a cream soda man. However, my agent says it is good to have some complicated personal demands to keep the producers on their toes. Normally, I get fobbed off with Tizer or Vimto, so thanks for going the extra mile. On the last picture, I asked for Cromer crab and bonbons and got bloater paste and a sherbet dibdab. Christ Almighty, here comes our incandescently displeased swamp viper. Can you leave the basket here? I will eat the rest of it when she is done with me, if I am still alive. What is your name by the way?"

"Loveday."

"Memorable anyway, or it should be if I didn't have an ever-changing script and a feral scorpion in slingbacks to deal with. Thanks for all the grub."

Loveday nodded and moved to station herself in an empty director's chair to watch the performance. While Phoebe scribbled on the clapperboard, Fontaine took his position. Waiting for his cue, he looked over at Loveday, cracked an infinitesimal smile and nodded. Loveday blushed slightly and then more fully, blushing at having blushed. Why can a handsome man get away with being rude? With unexpected amplitude, Phoebe suddenly leapt in front of the camera with the clapperboard saying in a surprisingly commanding voice, "Scene forty-two, take one." She was her mother's daughter after all.

Fifteen minutes later, Vesta was finishing her third éclair, dropping crumbs down her leotard. "Cut. Beautiful job, Fontaine. Let us reset and go again with more *je ne sais croissant* this time. Give it more breakfast-at-the-Plaza and less bacon-baps-at-Butlins. Phoebe, there's cream on my leotard. Vim! Now!"

***

Bored after watching thirteen takes, Loveday headed back to the kitchen to heat up more soup for Dynamite, thinking that the poor woman being strapped to the open-to-the-air undercarriage of the Skyfreighter in a bikini for four hours would require something hot and fortifying. She hoped the actress's pay was worth it. Later in the afternoon, at the aerodrome and wrapped in a blanket, a fur coat and wearing fur-lined boots and hugging a hot water bottle, Dynamite McQueen thanked her. "The soup was excellent, thank you so much. What was in it?"

Loveday smiled at her warmly. "Lentils, onions, sage from the garden and homemade chicken stock. I thought you would need reviving. Do you want some more? You look so cold. Don't you love the English summertime? I can also get you some hot tea or coffee and can boil a kettle for the hot water bottle if you need more warmth."

"That is kind of you, but no, thank you. I need to get back under the aeroplane soon once they have finished fiddling with the set-up. I'm Yazmine by the way."

"Nice to meet you, Yazmine. I am Loveday. They never include your real name in any credits, so I am happy to know there's a real person behind the Dynamite McQueen façade."

"Yes, it is a ridiculous marketing conceit the producers have used to keep continuity since the beginning. It also keeps the actors on their toes, as we feel even more disposable than usual. They have been making Dynamite McQueen films for thirty years and it is pretty clear the films are bigger than any one actor. I think the first actress who played Dynamite might have been French or something. I am the sixth actress to play her and this is my last film, thank goodness! You might not guess it but I am Royal Shakespeare Company-trained. It was either scream in a bikini and pay the mortgage, or carry a spear and go on the dole. Thank goodness, I can sink my teeth into the scenes where Dynamite reverts to her alter ego, Penelope Knickerbocker. At least Penelope has some subtext I can play."

Loveday warmed to Yazmine. "Actually, I am named after you, or rather my middle name is. It's Penelope. My father is a huge fan of Dynamite McQueen. He should be here sometime this week and would love to meet you if it is at all possible. Thank goodness, my parents didn't call me Dynamite, although my second middle name is even worse. Mundesley, if you can believe it, named after a town on the Norfolk coast."

"Oh, Mundesley-By-The-Sea? I have been there with Nobby and our children. I remember a long beach and it being as blustery as all get out."

"Everyone remembers the wind and only the wind. Wait, Nobby? Children?"

"Oh, yes, that is why I do this job and put up with all the behind-the-scenes drama which sometimes is a lot more convincing than what happens when my co-star is in front of the camera, if you ask me. It's fine, as I get paid well and have a nanny included in my contract. Nobby and I have been married for five years and we have two children. Didn't you know? We keep it quiet as the publicity department prefers Dynamite to be single. As he and I are both in the film business, the money is good but never regular, so we have to make hay while the sun shines to keep a roof over our heads and food on the table. I am getting a bit old for Dynamite – so they keep telling me! They are going to recast her for the next film, but she has been very good to me for over ten years. This job has paid all my debts and our house is mortgage-free, so I am happy. I can even put up with gold bikinis and toxic fools like Fontaine for the long-term financial stability of my family. However, it is taking its toll on my body. The part is physically challenging. I twisted my ankle on those stairs and it is starting to swell up into something awful. I also twisted it earlier in the shoot at the studio the day of the fire and it has not been completely right ever since. I don't know if you know the main stage we use, at Ravenwood Studios, burnt down? It shook me up. Apparently, it was arson."

"Let me get you some ice for your ankle and more soup."

***

Once Loveday was back in the kitchen after her deliveries to the set, she picked up a tube mail message from Reggie that said, 'BIG NEWS'. Reggie arrived in a rush five minutes later. "Constable Otukile found a body on Cuffley Hoo last night. Yesterday, I gave the constable a list of names of everyone I could think of who was near Cuffley Manor and the aerodrome during the fête. Vanessa, that is Constable Otukile, has already interviewed almost the whole list about what and who they saw during the afternoon. The only person she was not able to find was Aunt Elsie, I mean Mrs Gascoyne. The last time I saw her was on the morning of the fête, in the kitchen with you and the sandwich makers. Charlie said he spoke to her in the early afternoon at the lodge but it was by telephone. Well, it is all for nought. You see, the body they found is Mrs Gascoyne's, and they found her right on the top of Cuffley Hoo!"

"Mrs Gascoyne! Elsie? On top of the Hoo? What on Earth was she doing up there? How did she even get there with her heart? When did it happen? Oh, those poor boys!" lamented Loveday.

"I don't know any of the details yet. Vanessa met with GloGlo and me at the aerodrome on Monday afternoon to walk through the flying display and where it all went wrong. Blessing, Joan and GloGlo helped work out the geometry of where the plane would have been when you and GloGlo were shot at and when you fell out. And guess what? They calculated that it would have happened right above Cuffley Hoo, which, due to its height they agreed, was also the best place to shoot at the plane with any degree of accuracy. Vanessa climbed the Hoo yesterday evening looking for evidence and found two empty gun cartridges and some recently flattened ferns. Then, she found Mrs Gascoyne's body in nearby shrubbery with a shotgun right beside her. The body has now been carted off to Hertford coroner's office. Vanessa telephoned me to say the cartridges and fingerprints match. It's incredible, but it looks like Mrs Gascoyne shot at you and GloGlo!"

The Prince and the Showgirl

Loveday's joints and muscles were feeling completely back to normal as she distractedly cooked breakfast and brought it into the manor's dining room. Her head was full of why Mrs Gascoyne would want to shoot at her and GloGlo and the mystery of how she had died. Thus far, no one had any theories which satisfied her. So absorbed was Loveday in her thoughts, that she didn't flinch when Tansy arrived in full Badminton Horse Trials regalia, snapped her fingers and brayed to the practically empty room. "Ladies and gentlemen, there is a full English breakfast here on these rather common looking hotplates. I was expecting sterling silver not CorningWare. If you need anything else, ask my staff, and I will make sure it happens post haste."

Vesta came into the room, demanding, "I will have a bowl of banana-flavoured Angel Delight, two Findus ham and cheese crispy pancakes, twelve Iced Gems (no green ones) and a pink gin." Luckily, Loveday had been forewarned. Tansy snapped her fingers as Loveday curtseyed and went into the kitchen.

Yazmine, completely transformed out of costume, came down next, limping gingerly. Loveday, returning with a fresh batch of kidneys and Vesta's morning repast, saw her limp. "Oh, Yazmine, your ankle does not look good. It is so swollen. Sit yourself down, and I will put a plate together."

"Oh, hello, Loveday, how are you this morning? Can I get some coffee and a bag of ice? You are right. This ankle is not going to hold up to any punishment today. Vesta, darling, I have to break the bad news. There is no way this ankle can cope with rehearsing the stairway dance sequence today. Can you get the stand-in?"

Vesta looked up over a tablespoon of Angel Delight. "Yazmine, darling, you have to be a trouper. The stand-in is still in Cockfosters with a croupy sprog and there is no one else."

Yazmine grimaced. "Are you sure? They only need to have size-six feet and fit the cozzie. Why not concentrate on Fontaine's close-ups and the long shots for today? I will be right as rain tomorrow. Are you sure you cannot rustle someone up at short notice? You do know everybody in the business after all. Say what you will about his appalling personality but Fontaine is a strong dance lead. He could throw a sack of potatoes around and make it keep time and look elegant."

"Oh, I don't know," said Vesta. "We're already so far behind. Last week, we lost three chorus dancers to injuries and quickly trained up three replacements. Can't do that today, not enough time to find a replacement and we cannot use a chorus member to replace Yazmine as they are too tall."

Yazmine pointed at Loveday. "What about Loveday, she looks roughly the right height?"

Tansy marched towards Vesta, knocking Loveday out of the way with her riding hat which she was holding in the crook of her arm. "I am a member of the Home Counties North ballroom dancing team and have gilded the dance floors of Fleetwood, Cleveleys, Lytham St Annes and the Blackpool Tower Ballroom. I am the perfect person to stand in for Dynamite McQueen. How lucky it is that I am here."

Vesta looked Tansy up and down with an unimpressed scowl. "Just in case my backup needs a backup, you may do, although you are too tall and angular." She turned to Loveday. "However, Angel-Delight-eclair girl, you might do. I like your attitude. Can you dance?"

Loveday looked alarmed. "*Err*, yes, but never on camera," she stuttered, horrified but also excited at the prospect.

Vesta fixed her eyes on Loveday, looking her up and down. "Never let it be said that Vesta Currie cannot turn water into wine. My mind is made up. You are the perfect size and shape, and you have that *je ne sais quoi* energy. We can get you a wig to cover your unruly mop. Yazmine will help you out with the choreography and the steps, won't you, darling? We can also rope in Fontaine like a truculent, over-moisturised, Pamplona bull. Don't worry, darling, his ego will kick in when he realises it might mean more camera time."

Tansy huffed like a filly in the cold and put her riding hat back on with a sharp smack, turned on her heel and fairly cantered out of the room. Just as the rising fear of what she was about to agree to almost led to her backing out, Loveday realised this would be the perfect opportunity to embed herself further in the company and WI-5's mission. Reggie would be so pleased as, thus far, the listening devices had not picked up any conversations of interest, confirming Reggie's thoughts that the cast and crew members staying at the manor were highly unlikely to be syndicate agents. "I would be happy to give it go if I can get help from the real Dynamite McQueen, I mean Yazmine."

A man Loveday did not recognise came into the room. "Where's breakfast? I am starving. Yes, Yazmine already told me her ankle was too painful to do the scene today, so I am assuming I get the morning off too?" With a shock, Loveday realised it was Fontaine looking quite normal in jeans and a t-shirt, unslathered in his usual makeup and sequins.

"Dream on, Fonty darling, the show must go on. We have a new stand-in for you to drag about, and you will make it work."

Fontaine lifted the lids of the hotplates and smashed each one down with a crash. "You have to be joking. I am not carrying some amateur never-was princess through her paces. I can only put up with so much. You know I have been with the Dynamite McQueen films longer than anyone else. My name should be above the title and not arsecheeking around with some no-name, no-talent, non-entity. That would be my worst nightmare. Have I made myself clear?"

"Perfectly," said Loveday.

"Sorry, Fontaine, it is in your contract, so do as I say and get your scrag end down to makeup. Don't keep everyone waiting. By the way, Fonty, meet your no-name, no-talent, non-entity," commanded Vesta.

Loveday stared him down. "I believe I am your worst nightmare. Care to make something of it?"

"Now, that is what I like. Finally some balls," said Vesta, as Fontaine's face registered surprise but not distaste. "Miss MacGuffin, Yazmine and I will take you to the ballroom to rehearse and put you through your paces. Then, I'll get Nobby to take you to hair, makeup and wardrobe. Then we will walk through everything on the ballroom set until it has been drilled into your brain. Hopefully that dreadful nag of a woman dressed for the Grand National will release you from your breakfast duties without me having to throw her over Becher's Brook and boil her up for glue."

"Everything is already cooked, and perhaps Joan and Blessing here can both serve and refill tea and coffee," said Loveday, looking at them both as they nodded enthusiastically.

"You will slay them, no question" said Vesta, as she gave Loveday a hug.

***

A huge staircase and circular dance floor had been built in the manor's ballroom, doing its best impression of the Hanging Gardens of Babylon, with reams of fake mauve and white wisteria draping over its follies. After two hours of intense rehearsal with Vesta acting as Fontaine and Yazmine giving advice, sitting, with her leg up on another chair, Loveday was exhausted, and her mind whirled with the complex choreography she needed to master. Every Dynamite McQueen film incorporated the old songs, and Loveday was buoyed by already knowing by heart the song they were dancing and singing to. It was *She's The Bee's Knees* which Alfie had on record. After an hour in makeup (at least she was sitting), the application of the blonde wig and being squeezed into Dynamite's white satin sheath dress and gold strappy heels, Yazmine asked "Do you want me here for moral support, or is it better for you if I go?"

"I think you should go back to your room, pack some more ice on your ankle and rest up," said Loveday. "You can find more ice in the kitchen. There is a big bag of it in the bottom of the freezer. You'll find it through the doorway opposite the stove."

Phoebe had appeared and helped Yazmine find the ice and get settled in her room, while Vesta escorted Loveday over to the set. "Thank you, Loveday, you look just the ticket by the way, and I think you are going to be fine. Fontaine may have the personality of napalm but he is a strong lead and will drag you to where he needs you to go. Don't fight his lead too much and all will be well."

Vesta fixed her eyes on her new protégé. "Now, Loveday, trust me. You are in my comfort zone, my firmament, in the hands of a complete professional. We will do a walk-through first. Do not use up all your energy on take one. I am going to want at least eight takes so keep some stamina for later. We will replace any close-ups of you with Yazmine when she is back in the land of the upright. Fake it until you make it, darling. And there speaks an old trouper who used it all up in 1944 and has been faking it ever since."

Twenty dancers arrived chattering and dressed head to toe in gold lamé. Vesta took them to one side, filled them in on the situation and gave them their orders. Some of them came over to Loveday and told her to not sweat it, they would look after her, guide her, keep her moving in the right direction and to not take any guff from Fontaine. Three of the female dancers winked conspiratorially at Loveday, and she recognised them as April, May and June from Morag's operations room. Morag had despatched more of WI-5's Showgirl Squadron to infiltrate the chorus. Loveday immediately felt she was in safe hands.

Fontaine arrived looking mightily annoyed and uncomfortable in his white tie and tails, bright orange skin and enough eyelashes and mascara to stop a bullet. He walked over to Vesta and threw some side-eye at Loveday. "Mutton dressed as mutton, I see. Well, I don't hold out a lot of hope for a borderline passable cook who suddenly claims to dance at a professional level. Shall we get this show on the road, Vesta?"

The whole troupe walked through the dance sequence first to get the camera angles right. *Thank goodness the choreography is repetitive*, Loveday thought, and the chorus dancers had much more complicated moves. Although being pressed against Fontaine and his intense cologne was repellent in the extreme, Vesta was right, he knew how to lead. Fontaine kept a firm double hold on Loveday, indicating clearly where she needed to go a microsecond before she needed to move. They walked through it again, faster this time, with Vesta clapping time. Loveday breathed a sigh of relief whenever someone else was the subject of Vesta's notes, especially when it was Fontaine who was getting angrier and angrier as Vesta picked on him.

Vesta finally called, "Places everyone."

Phoebe leapt in front of the camera with her clapperboard. "Scene forty-eight, take one."

Fontaine looked like thunder and muttered, 'Complete frightful farrago,' as Vesta yelled, "Action."

At the top of a grand staircase leading to the Hanging Gardens of Babylon, Fontaine de Havilland triumphantly stared at Loveday. Knowing the camerawoman was taking a close up of only his eyes, he whispered, "How I loathe this, let me count the ways."

With her back to the camera, Loveday stared into Fontaine's herbaceous border eyelashes, raised her right eyebrow and pursed her lips for emphasis. "You are a narcissistic, poisonous, manic-depressive, undescended testicle." The overture to "She's the Bee's Knees" started to swell out of the speakers as Fontaine fell to his knees. He looked up to one side, found his true love, the camera lens, and began to lip-synch.

Women have changed!
And men have received a shock,
Darning their own socks,
Winding their own clocks.

A second camera swooped down as Fontaine, still on

knees, rolled his eyes with delirium, as he held the satin skirt of Loveday's dress to his nose.

Men must change.
If a woman is hot to trot,
She don't need a sop
For her cherry to pop.

The music sped up and the melody began. Fontaine stood up and twirled Loveday around and back into his chest, before dropping her into an aggressive lunge.

In days of yore,
A flash of ankle
Was sure to make a fella rankle
And decree,
She's the bee's knees.

Loveday held her pose, and tried to remember her first of two sets of lyrics while blocking the pain from Fontaine crushing her hands. She mouthed:

Modern women who
Used to need saving,
Now demand that men go caving
Into their needs,
I'm sure you will agree,
That I'm the bee's knees.

Loveday stayed in her lunge, happy she had not

flubbed her lines. Feeling waves of coldness coming off of Fontaine while her character was in the spotlight, Loveday almost received whiplash, as he forcefully yanked her upright with her back to the camera and they quickstepped down the staircase. "You cannot move, you cannot act and your barely serviceable cooking does not have any star quality," gritted Fontaine while maintaining his gleaming grin for the cameras.

Loveday spat back. "I am doing everything you do, backwards and in heels, you pathetic, sociopathic, gaslighting waxwork." Fontaine emoted into the closest camera; a genuine gleam of pleasure apparent as he was enjoying this antagonistic banter.

If pleasing women is a thing for you,
Knicker elastic wants to ping for you.
Get on your knees
Until she's pleased.
To be the bee's knees.

Loveday did her best to gaze adoringly up at Fontaine, as she held his hands. "So, this is what acting feels like, it's easy-peasy! Why, anyone can do it." She whipped her head around, fixed her gaze on the nearest camera and resumed lip-synching.

Make sure you are clear,
What a man can do for you,
Train them, pain them,
To do the do for you,

And they will agree,
You're the bee's knees.

Loveday was settling into her role and managed to throw a conspiratorial look at the camera, as she leaned back against Fontaine's chest. Dancers holding torches slid down the lit-from-the-inside bannisters on either side of the staircase. At the bottom, Fontaine led Loveday in his signature twirl and spin. The remaining dancers danced down the staircase until they reached Loveday and Fontaine and leaned in, hands on chins while foamy, bubbly water gushed up from hidden fountains.

Throughout the seasons,
Create a reason,
To keep her wheezin',
Brazenly,
She's the bee's knees.

Led by Loveday and Fontaine, all the dancers descended, in pairs, to a circular dance floor and into their elaborate positions.

Women are in the driver's seat now,
Dynamite McQueen says rinse and repeat now.
By some degree,
She's the bee's knees.

Once she has
Saved the day for you,

She will surely
Pave the way for you,
To meet her needs,
From A, B, C,
To the highest degree,
You will agree.
She's the bee's knees.

Then two dancers leaned in and ripped off Loveday's dress and Fontaine's suit, revealing matching gold jitterbug outfits. The music cranked up to rock 'n' roll speed, and ten pairs of dancers formed a large double circle around Loveday and Fontaine, and started to jive, changing partners as they went. Once the original partners had been reunited, every second couple, along with Loveday and Fontaine, leapt on to an inner platform which rose in the air as they continued the dance. Then, both platforms moved slowly in opposite directions with couples continuing to change partners in new double circles. Once partners had been reunited for the second time, Loveday and Fontaine leapt onto a small central platform, continuing to dance as they were raised into the air, beaming from ear to ear and holding their final pose.

Vesta was pleased. "Cut, reset. Let us go again in fifteen. Loveday – excellent – I knew you could do it. Welcome to Home Counties Hollywood North." Fifteen minutes flew by and they did it all again and again, six more times. Loveday was punch drunk by the end, sustaining herself on nerves alone. Once she had changed out of the wig and costume, she ambled in a daze to the kitchen and fell asleep at the table.

***

Two hours later, Blessing and Joan arrived to find Loveday asleep when she needed to be preparing for the evening's dinner service. Waking up abruptly, thinking in horror that it was the middle of the night but realising she still had over an hour before the film company, and more crucially, Tansy, would arrive for the dinner service, Loveday dusted herself off and put previously prepared fish pies in the oven to heat up, and tomato rosemary soup on the stove to warm. Blessing made two big bowls of salad and pulled out of the fridge two big bowls of trifle. They had just finished laying the table as Yazmine, Nobby, Vesta, Fontaine and Phoebe arrived. Tansy came in seemingly dressed for a Dynamite McQueen lookalike competition. With a ruler, she measured and adjusted the cutlery at each table, which was somewhat surprising to the diners, as they were sitting there while she was doing it. Loveday ladled the piping hot soup into bowls.

"Good job today, Loveday. I hear everyone was mightily impressed with you, well nearly everyone, and your food is so much better than the gruel we normally have to put up with. You are an absolute natural on the set and in the kitchen," said Yazmine.

"Phoebe, my bounty bars!" ordered Vesta. Phoebe looked up, her soup spoon almost at her lips.

"Oh, Phoebe," said Loveday reassuringly. "Do not worry, as I have a secret stash ready to go. Would you like any bread and butter to dunk in your soup?"

Phoebe managed a timid smile at Loveday while Vesta frowned. "Thank you so much, Loveday, for looking after my little foibles when Phoebe is not in a position to do so. I am a chocolate-dependent asthmatic with an irregular heartbeat and piles, so I am used to being a burden to others as well as myself. My high standards of perfection, creativity and artistic temperament mean that I am constantly being tested and tortured. How about you, Fonty, what tortures you?" Fontaine looked annoyed and didn't say anything. Vesta continued, "Loveday, you did marvellously today, absolutely marvellous. Fontaine too, darling, you managed to get through, looking like you were almost enjoying yourself although I know you never do. I agree with Yazmine. Loveday, you are a natural, and I should know being a natural myself, from my cerebral cortex to my tippy toes. Do you know who told me I was a natural? It is imprinted on my memory as if it were yesterday." Vesta went quiet trying to remember. "Phoebe, do you recollect?"

"Was it Boris Karloff?" offered Phoebe, and the whole table erupted at the first joke Phoebe had ever told that landed with an audience. Once they were tucking into fish pie and the trifle was on the table, Loveday, happy to leave the theatrical fishbowl, left them to their own devices and went to update the Cuffley boys on all the goings-on of the day. Charlie and Cliff were aghast at the amount of effort she had had to expend.

"My goodness, Loveday, what a stressful day you have had. What you did was above and beyond. You have also added to the services provided to the film crew so Reggie should charge them vast amounts more and get you a million-pound contract with the film company. Let us wait on you for once." Loveday happily sank into a chair while Charlie made her a sandwich and poured some tea. She fell asleep in less than a minute and only woke up when Reggie came to find her so they could head home together.

While Loveday had been tripping the light fantastic, Alfie had telephoned Reggie with his plan to arrive the next day in the V&A lorry with Tolly in tow. He asked if he could stay in her flat on the sofa, while Tolly stayed with friends in Maiden St Irene. As the listening devices had not picked up any evidence that anyone was not who they said they were, Reggie hoped the arrival of Alfie and Tolly might provide the break they needed. The World Cup Final was only two days away.

Those Magnificent Women in Their Flying Machines

On Friday, Dynamite was only needed for filming a couple of static scenes, so Yazmine could handle those with aplomb and a bandaged ankle. After her triumph on the set the day before, Loveday was a little disappointed not to be needed. After the breakfast service was complete, she spent the morning making fresh soup for Yazmine and a big batch of cheese and pickle fancies and pork pies for Fontaine, along with more jam roly-poly (don't forget the custard) and delivered the basket to the film set before sprinting back to the manor to be in time for the arrival of Alfie and Tolly in the museum's lorry. She had doubled the recipe for the jam roly-poly and the pork pies, so Alfie and Tolly would also have something sturdy in their bellies to help them clamber through the attics and the chalk pits.

A few minutes after returning, Loveday heard a loud engine chug along the drive and come to a stop on the gravel outside the kitchen. She alerted Reggie via tube post that Alfie and Tolly had arrived, and lunch would be ready in the kitchen at noon. She ran out to see them opening up the lorry's rear doors in matching overalls and caps with 'Victoria and Albert Museum' printed on their backs and a picture of Michelangelo's David on their chests. Alfie held a large clipboard with several sheets of closely typed items firmly fixed under the bulldog clip. Tolly winked at her which made her smile. He opened the back of the lorry and crawled inside.

"Hello, Dad!" yelled Loveday, as she ran to greet Alfie. "Nice outfit."

Alfie strutted in his overalls, giving it his best Twiggy-on-the-catwalk impression. "Hello, Loveday. Yes, they're new. Do they make my bum look big? How have you been, stuck in this draughty old barn of a place? I have not darkened these doorsteps in decades, but you brighten everything up. Lovely to see you alive – kicking and cooking. I am really nervous being here and I have been so worried thinking about you."

"Actually, Dad, despite having been shot at, thrown out of a plane and starring in a film, things have been quiet. How about you? By the way, whenever you are ready, I have made lunch. I will let Lord Cuffley, known as Cliff to the rest of us, his brother, Charlie, Reggie, Ash and Beaver know they can come over and meet you both. Unfortunately, GloGlo is away for most of the day. Have you heard about what she is up to?"

"Oh, yes, practicing for the World Cup Final pre-match flypast. Reggie kept me informed of all the goings on. Your mother and I are not happy about GloGlo being back in the air so soon after last weekend, but I guess she knows best," gurned Alfie.

"Don't worry, she will be fine. Nothing is going to happen at the World Cup Final other than football. The security is too tight…" turning to a whisper, "…and we haven't picked up anything on the listening devices, so I think they might be just be actors and crew making a film here. So don't worry about GloGlo. Today she is flying to Duxford for rehearsals and there will be safety in numbers, as a whole squadron of Tiger Moths is taking part, not only GloGlo and Showgirl One. We have no idea when she will be home, but it is great you are staying the night so you will see her at some point."

Alfie gave his youngest daughter a big hug. "I think it would be helpful if, before lunch, we went over the V&A artefact list with Lord Cuffley and his brother, and they can help us figure out where best to start. My goodness, I remember the manor being big, but I didn't realise it was so huge. This could take days. Are you okay with me staying at Reggie's flat on the sofa? It won't cramp your style?"

Loveday rolled her eyes. "What style, Dad? All the exciting stuff happens here at the manor. Reggie's flat is for sleeping and eating Beaver's cooking."

Tolly, still in the back of the lorry, heard the rumble of conversation and laughter between Alfie and Loveday. He had removed two wooden planks from the back of the lorry to make a ramp and wheeled out the big iron dolly which would bear most of the weight of anything large they needed to move. "Hello, Loveday, sorry to hear about all your near-death experiences. Stuff really happens to you, doesn't it? I am looking forward to trying your food. I have heard so much about your culinary abilities from your dad."

"You look pretty good in your matching overalls,"

muttered Loveday to Tolly, as they entered the house. Tolly grinned at her, as Loveday led them both into the house to find Charlie and Cliff.

"So pleased to meet you, Mr MacGuffin," said Charlie. "I cannot tell you how much your daughters are proving to be a boon to the resurrection of Cuffley Manor. We are so happy that they are here spreading their magic, aren't we, Cliff?" Cliff shyly nodded but shook Alfie's hand firmly.

"Likewise, and please call me, Alfie."

"Only if you will call us Charlie and Cliff, Alfie."

"Really good to meet you too, Cliff. Let me also introduce to you my apprentice, Tolliver."

"Tolly, please. Your home is magnificent."

They all sat down at the kitchen table in the extra chairs Loveday had already placed. She puttered in the background, preparing lunch, hoping Tolly was watching her as Charlie and Cliff cast their eyes over Alfie's list. Nothing obvious twigged for them, but they thought smaller items could be in any of the many attic rooms while the larger artefacts would be in the tunnels of the old chalk pits. Charlie gave Alfie his bunch of master keys and explained to him how to get up to the attics via the servants' stairs.

Alfie and Tolly had a quick look in the first attic room they managed to unlock but found nothing on Morag's list. Seeing the number and size of attic rooms, they realised they would need the rest of the day to go through them. The chalk pits would have to wait for tomorrow. Even though they had only been in the one room, Alfie and

Tolly's overalls were quite dusty by the time they returned downstairs for lunch, which Charlie, Cliff, Reggie, Beaver and Ashwariya were already tucking into.

Charlie was in the middle of reporting that Constable Vanessa did not yet have any new information to impart after investigating the shooting and the discovery of Aunt Elsie's body. Charlie had let Vanessa into the lodge during the morning to see if anything could shed a light on Elsie's motivations but it was to no avail. Reggie thought it might be worth Charlie and Cliff taking a second look at the lodge and see if anything looked out of place or surprised them.

After lunch, Loveday stayed to the kitchen to prepare dinner for the film crew. Tolly and Alfie spent the rest of the day with Charlie's keys, letting themselves into more attic rooms and wiggling into corners, under furniture and behind cupboards. Although the rooms were full of furniture, boxes and family bric-a-brac, they did not find anything they were looking for.

Later that afternoon, Tolly drove the van to Maiden St Irene to see his friends, while Alfie and Loveday ambled to the aerodrome to find Reggie and Beaver. They had all been invited by Ashwariya to a family dinner at the control tower to greet GloGlo after a hopefully successful World Cup Final flypast rehearsal with her favourite feast, an Indian Railway dinner.

***

Alfie, Loveday and Reggie sat around the control tower

marvelling at Ash and GloGlo's do-it-yourself interior design skills, enjoying the smells coming from the makeshift kitchen and supping homemade sparkling cardamom wine. As they rehashed the aftermath of the fête, the diffusal of the bomb on the V&A roof and the shocking finding of Aunt Elsie's body on the Hoo and her possible motivations, their conversation was drowned out by the sound of Showgirl One flying low over the control tower. GloGlo was home. Bringing their wine glasses with them, they walked across the landing strip to wave her in.

"Welcome home, my lovely," greeted Ashwariya, as she gave GloGlo a big kiss. "How did it all go? Here's some cardamom bubbly for you."

GloGlo looked exhausted but happy. "Oh what a day! I was early if you can believe it, one of the first to arrive. For the next hour, we all gathered in one of the hangars waiting for everyone to turn up. They had a big tea urn and a lovely woman looking after us with homemade iced buns... *yum*. Over the next hour, another twenty Tiger Moths arrived, followed by a couple of Bristol Bombers, four Brabazon Skyfighters, three Spitfires and two Mosquitos. Then we were gathered all together and informed about the plan for the day." Pointing at the metal wing-walking structures on Showgirl One's upper wing, GloGlo said, "I'll explain those later."

Ashwariya interrupted her with another hug. "You know, GloGlo, we have cooked a big feast to celebrate your success. Why don't we head to the control tower and start noshing while you tell us all about it? Loveday, are you up for carving the tandoori turkey?"

"Before we head home, I need a volunteer to carry this box for me," said GloGlo grinning, as she stood next to Showgirl One's lower wing and reached into the front seat. Hearing GloGlo's plane land, Beaver had arrived and carried the large square box to the control tower.

Loveday walked with Alfie and took the plunge, pre-empting his concerns. "Dad, I know you and Mum are worried about me, but I want to see this through. You and Mum have always been on my case about not finishing things, so finally I have something I want to see through. Reggie and the rest of the team need me here. And, Dad, I am doing a good job and not only with the cooking."

Alfie looked at his daughter. "I know, my little scrawnbag of a chook. It is a bit much, that's all, to have all three daughters at Cuffley Manor mixed up in WI-5 activities."

Back at the control tower, Loveday attacked the turkey and everyone waited for Ash to load up the serving dishes with shrimp cocktails, carrot, coconut and onion salad, cucumber mint raita, curried devilled eggs, Branston pickle and paneer bhajis, lamb korma vol-au-vents, the tandooried turkey, pea and jeera rice stuffing, garlic masala spiced roast potatoes, butter sauce gravy and Ashwariya's mum's aloo gobi and gulab jamun.

"Crikey, Ash!" Loveday exclaimed. "What a feast! You must share your recipes with me."

Everyone was silent while eating. GloGlo cleaned her plate and sat back in her chair. "Oh, I do feel better. "I only had a gallon of tea, two iced buns and four ham and margarine rolls from a vending machine, which were a lifesaver at the time. We cleared the vending machine out, so I am hoping it gets refilled tomorrow. It doesn't look like there are going to be many leftovers from here for me to take!

"Anyhow, tomorrow, so exciting, only twenty-four hours to go! The footie starts at half past seven in the evening on the dot. The welcoming ceremony gets going an hour beforehand, at half past six. To get the crowd's attention, the Red Arrows will roar over the stadium, trailing red, white and blue smoke. Then the Brabazon Skyfighters and Bristol Bombers fly over, then the Spitfires and Mosquitos and finally a whole swarm of us Tiger Moths."

GloGlo explained the top-secret part of the ceremony would be the Beatles parachuting into the stadium and playing a couple of songs. "Of course, the real Beatles would not be parachuting in. Imagine if they sprained something! They have four experienced female skydivers dressed as the Beatles in moptop wigs and mod suits leaping from the wings of a Tiger Moth. After landing on the pitch, they will run behind the stage, so it will look like the real Beatles had parachuted in. The idea of famous people parachuting into the stadium before the match is why Showgirl One is fitted out with wing-walking gear."

Loveday went wide-eyed. "Golly, GloGlo, can you imagine if it was actually the Beatles leaping off Showgirl One?"

"Actually, no," said GloGlo, "one of the other Tiger Moths is handling the Beatles. However, I am going to be handling the only people in the world who are possibly more famous than the Beatles, the Royal Family! Once all the Tiger Moths have circled Wembley Stadium, they all fly directly back to Duxford except two of them. The first will be the Tiger Moth carrying the fake Beatles which, after circling the stadium, will fly high enough to allow the skydivers to leap off the plane, land in the middle of the pitch and run under the stage. Then the queen and Prince Philip will parachute in from Showgirl One. Well, two skydivers dressed like them at least, who then run under the stands, just before the real Queen Elizabeth and Prince Philip take their seats. *God Save The Queen* is played, the Beatles play two songs and the crowd goes wild as the footballers come onto the field. Of course, this is top-secret. You all cannot say anything about this until after it is all over tomorrow. Otherwise, Buckingham Palace and the full force of the firm will come after you. It's Princess Anne I would be most scared of."

"Wow," said Alfie, "I cannot wait to watch it on television."

"And I cannot wait to watch it in person," said Ashwariya.

"How come you have tickets, Ash?" asked Beaver.

"Well, I am ferrying members of the Jane Austen Appreciation Society to the game. They won tickets in the lottery and gave me one as they want me to not only ferry them to Wembley but also bring me home again. And so I will get to see the Showgirl Squadron Flying Circus in its inaugural event, and what an event," said Ash happily. "When did they spring the royal family's entrance on you, GloGlo?"

"I only found out about it today," said GloGlo with a grin and a mouthful of gulab jamun. "The parachutists playing the Beatles did a practice in full Beatles regalia. It looked so good; we all cheered as if the real Beatles were arriving. Next, the organisers told us the other top-secret part of the ceremonies. They had been organising it with Buckingham Palace for months, working with their dressers to make a copy of the outfits the queen and Prince Philip will be wearing. One of the other Tiger Moths was all ready to take the part when mechanical trouble reared its head this week, so it couldn't be there today for the rehearsal. And guess who volunteered as a replacement? Yes, I did! A new business cannot turn down work, you know. Anyhow, a couple of the Duxford mechanics bolted wing-walking frames to Showgirl One's top wing and attached the footholds, waist and chest belts, and harnesses, and I took two of the Beatles parachutists up for a test run to see how Showgirl One handled with the new equipment. She was fine, just as I thought. I was in the air for over an hour practicing various manoeuvres before heading up to three thousand feet for the skydivers to release themselves, leap into the air and parachute down."

"Oh my golly gosh. I cannot believe it. Amazing, GloGlo!" exclaimed Ashwariya.

"Oh, GloGlo, how exciting. You will be so easy to spot on the telly," said Alfie clapping his hands.

"Great advertising for the Flying Circus," said Reggie.

"And that is not all. Wait until you hear this bit. They asked me whether I could find experienced wing-walkers to play the royals. Of course, as lead pilot of the Showgirl Squadron Flying Circus, I said yes. I was thinking about Reggie and Beaver having the wing-walking, parachuting and skydiving skills to be the fake queen and prince!" Reggie and Beaver almost spat out their curried devilled egg and tandoori turkey meat respectively. "Don't you worry, it will be quite simple. I take you up, and you leap off when I give you the signal. You've done this before. And it's not a small target. You can't miss Wembley Stadium, it is huge. Aim for the big patch of green, and don't worry, don't look like that, Reg, there will be a long day of rehearsals tomorrow, so you can get over your jitters. So, what do you say? Do you both want to run away and join the Flying Circus?"

Taking a deep breath, Beaver said, "Okay, I'm in if Reggie is."

Beaver looked at Reggie. "What do you say, my little Nanaimo bar?"

"Hang on, my little custard cream, is what I say," said Reggie. "It is not much notice, GloGlo. And do we look enough like them? I don't think so."

"It's all about the costuming," said GloGlo. "They have professionally made outfits matching what Liz and Phil will be wearing tomorrow. The costumes are oversized, so you can fit them over your flying suits. You will still wear your own helmet, Beaver, though yours, Reggie, is a special one with a huge glittery tiara attached. And voila, here it is!" GloGlo handed her the large square box she had brought with her. Reggie opened it to reveal the helmet-tiara-wig creation.

"Blimey, look at this thing!" said Reggie with eyes wide as she gazed at the bedazzled helmet. "I haven't said I am doing it yet. Will there be enough time to rehearse tomorrow? It sounds like the fake Beatles practiced their jumps at least twice today."

"Well," said GloGlo, "tomorrow morning, the plan is you two will fly with me to Duxford. One of you will have to get strapped onto the wings and the other one could have the passenger seat. At Duxford, the plan is for multiple rehearsals for the flypast and the parachute drops in full costume."

"I don't think I can do it; I have such a lot to do," said Reggie nervously. "Who is going to look after the film company?"

"I will!" said Loveday. "I can look after them, with Joan and Blessing's help, of course, and Cliff and Charlie will look after me. There is no filming or rehearsing planned this weekend as they have been given time off for the World Cup. So what could go wrong?"

"Not the right question to ask GloGlo," said Reggie, "Well, I guess I could be spared. But what would Joan and Blessing say? I cannot just up sticks and leave my post."

"Well, actually," said GloGlo slyly, "I phoned Joan from Duxford, and she thinks it is a great idea to get someone into the inside of Wembley Stadium in case the syndicate makes its move during the game. So she has given the 'ok'."

"Come on, Babycakes," joshed Beaver, "England has made the final of the World Cup, just think! We might go down in history together."

Reggie looked rueful. "I am not sure I like your turn of phrase to 'go down' in history. I am okay with the wing-walking bit, but I want dibs on the passenger seat during the flight to Duxford tomorrow. I also will need more skydiving practice there. Okay, I'll do it, but only if the rehearsal goes well. Too many of us have either nearly died or been injured this week. I want that to stop."

"With Elsie Gascoyne's body found and the mystery of the shooter's identity solved, my guess is no one is going to be shooting at biplanes any more. Especially with all those people watching," said GloGlo, full of proverbial beans.

"Mrs Gascoyne's body doesn't explain everything. We do not yet know her motive," retorted Reggie.

"Oh come on, Reggie, you are a very safe parachutist, this won't be dangerous. Also, the security at the game will be as tight as Fontaine's trousers. Everything is going to be checked and rechecked."

Reggie looked sceptical. "I haven't been wing-walking since my little adventure at Ravenwood Studios. I especially don't want to have to climb onto the wing from the cockpit."

"You wouldn't have to. I will strap you both into the wing-walking apparatus at Duxford, and we will be able to do lots of rehearsing tomorrow morning there. We can go early if it would make you feel better," urged GloGlo, as she could see Reggie was wavering.

"Come on, Reg, it's a once in a lifetime opportunity. In for a penny, in for a pound, in for a cent, in for a dollar," said Beaver. "But I do have one pertinent question,

GloGlo, that I am surprised Reggie has not yet asked: how will we get home from Wembley?"

"I have already figured it out," said GloGlo. "You will be brought back here in a hire car. The driver will pick you up immediately after you land, and you might be able to get back to Cuffley Manor in enough time to watch the end of the match, as Charlie and Cliff are organizing a viewing party for the film company."

Reggie threw up her hands as she looked at both Beaver and GloGlo. "Okay, you two daredevils. I am only doing this because of my trust in you both. In this getup, Britannia will rule the skies as well as the waves!"

Kidnapped

On the morning of the World Cup Final, GloGlo, Reggie and Beaver met early at the aerodrome to review their plan for the day and check Showgirl One. They donned their flying suits and goggles and took off early for the thirty-minute flight north to Duxford airfield to join the squadron of historic planes. While GloGlo strapped a deliriously happy Beaver onto the wing, Reggie was relieved she could sit in the passenger seat with the queen's tiara helmet strapped firmly down on her lap.

A bleary trio of Loveday, Ashwariya and Alfie waved them off, wielding mugs of tea and wishing them the best of luck. Loveday gave them each a bag of bacon and sausage butties to keep them going, in case the Duxford vending machines came up short. Loveday and Alfie promised that they would be watching the pre-game ceremonies as well as the match itself from Cuffley Manor with Charlie and Cliff.

Beaver didn't stop grinning, whooping and yelping the whole flight, especially when GloGlo flew upside down over Hertford. The Showgirl Squadron Flying Circus was well and truly off the ground once again.

Reggie gritted her teeth and hung on to the crown. Why was she doing this again? Oh yes, for the screaming idiot standing on the wing who she was beginning to love more than anything.

Ashwariya left to clean Bluebell inside and out, ready to take the Jane Austen Appreciation Society to Wembley Stadium. Alfie and Loveday checked in with Charlie and Cliff before Loveday headed to the kitchen to wrangle the film crew's breakfast with Joan and Blessing. Alfie waited for Tolly to turn up in the lorry before they carried on searching the rest of the attic rooms and investigating the chalk pits.

The film crew's breakfast went off without incident. Tansy did not turn up, so feathers remained unruffled. Because of the World Cup, the crew had negotiated a break from filming for the weekend, so they and the actors headed out for the day, either shopping or going for a walk in the countryside, before congregating at Cuffley Manor, the Salisbury Arms or the Aviatrix Arms to watch the match.

As it was going to be a decent Saturday weatherwise and with Reggie and GloGlo gone for the day, and no filming, Loveday liked the idea of walking in the fresh air to settle herself after all the excitement of the week. Once she had cleaned up after breakfast, she got a head start on the film crew's dinner by laying the table, putting the previously frozen coconut curry soup out on the counter to thaw, washing the cockles, whelks and limpets for her East Anglia low-tide lasagne and making the fruit salad, before changing into walking clothes. She decided to explore the grounds, climb Cuffley Hoo and go over in her mind what had happened at the fête, which was only a week ago but seemed like ages given everything else that had occurred, and the subsequent finding of Mrs Gascoyne's body. She took an old golf club she had found in a cupboard to poke through the undergrowth. Why had Mrs Gascoyne shot at them? And how did Mrs Gascoyne die? Was it her heart which was why she had been in hospital in the first place? Loveday's brain suddenly took flight with of all sorts of unanswered questions.

***

GloGlo had been asked to ensure Beaver and Reggie arrived at Duxford earlier than the other Tiger Moths so they could be fitted into their Queen Elizabeth and Prince Philip costumes which had been specially designed with camouflaged parachutes. A floor-length white dress with a blue sash for Reggie and a formal naval uniform with a matching blue sash for Beaver. While they were getting ready, the four female parachutists playing the Beatles were also getting kitted out.

***

With no filming occurring and little activity at the aerodrome, Charlie relaxed for the first time in weeks. In the main hangar, he took time to check on the aerodrome's paperwork, review the mercifully small, outstanding bill pile and the latest bank statements. He also skimmed through Reggie's ledger, detailing how up to date each aerodrome tenant was with monthly payments and maintenance fees. Happily, he found no surprises. Reggie ran a tight ship. He cleaned up the workshop benches, the tool room and the spares room and chatted to the handful of fliers who were tending to their beloved aircraft. The grass on and around the landing strip needed cutting, but it could wait, as it could only be done in the early hours before the landing strip opened at eight o'clock in the morning. Charlie thought it was time to replace the hanging baskets and refresh the plants in the window boxes. He wondered if he could rig up some sort of automatic watering system as the sun, when it was out, blazed down upon the hangars. He couldn't remember the last time the gutters were cleaned out and all the windows looked filthy. The CUFFLEY sign was also looking in need of a repaint – one thing at a time.

Cliff had been put in charge of setting up the formal drawing room for showing the match, which meant putting out more chairs. When Cliff had not yet appeared at the aerodrome by ten, Charlie made coffee and sent him a message by tube post to bring the makings of a sandwich lunch. The hangar's buzzer sounded less than half an hour later. Cliff was on his way.

While waiting for him, Charlie put his feet up and reflected on how far they had come. This time last year, his father had been alive but becoming increasingly unreliable. For the few years before he died, they never were told in advance when he was going away or where he was. Then he would turn up, briefly, as if everything was all right. He was always so impatient with the boys. They never understood what they were doing wrong to make their father so touchy. The good thing was, Dad had had no problem handing over the running of the manor and aerodrome to Charlie and Cliff. In fact, for the past couple of years, Dad had not been around that much. He was often away in London. Aunt Elsie looked after the cooking and keeping the few rooms they used in the house, but she was starting to slow down even then. Poor Aunt Elsie. What must have happened? She probably knew where the old shotgun was kept, for safety reasons, to make sure the boys' inquisitiveness never got the better of them, but where did she gain the knowledge on how to load a gun let alone use one? He thought that only he and Cliff knew their father kept the gun cabinet key inside the cover of Charlie's childhood copy of *The Prince and the Pauper* in the library.

Since their father's death, Charlie's main wish was for him to get things organised enough so Cliff's life as Lord Cuffley could be as happy and stress-free as possible. Beyond having made a will, the last good decision his father made was to hire GloGlo a year ago. Her aeroplane maintenance skills had enabled him to travel more and more. She had helped the aerodrome business gain traction and taught both sons about engine maintenance, something their father had never done. It was GloGlo who had recommended hiring Reggie to help with bookkeeping and financial planning – another thing their father had been terrible at. It had come as a real shock to both Charlie and Cliff that he had left things in such a mess when he died. This contract with the film company would help them get the manor finances into the black, enabling some much-needed repairs and help with long-term self-sufficiency.

Charlie sighed contentedly. He earnestly hoped all three MacGuffin sisters would stick around and continue to turn Cuffley Manor water into wine. With the flying circus taking off and Bluebell booked solid, GloGlo and Ashwariya would surely stay forever. Reggie seemed to be a person who liked to make order out of chaos and move on sharply once the job was done. But Beaver loved this place, and Reggie clearly loved Beaver. And Loveday? She had been here such a short amount of time, but already she was adding a spark. And her food was so good! With Aunt Elsie gone, they needed her.

***

From the top of Cuffley Hoo, Loveday surveyed a large chunk of Hertfordshire in all directions. There was an especially lovely view of Cuffley Manor, the grounds and surrounding fields and woods. She could see the spires of St Andrews and All Saints churches in Hertford and the dome at Haileybury School. Her eye followed the River Mimram and the railway line, as they moved around small clutches of houses and spires, which must be the Maiden villages. Her heart was beating quite fast, as the climb up had been surprisingly arduous. The direct path to the top zigzagged tightly up the rear of the Hoo, away from the house. Mrs Gascoyne must have been knocked out by the climb, and she had been carrying a heavy shotgun and walking with a cane. Loveday also explored all the side paths from the bottom of the Hoo which ended at several white painted follies facing the house. From the top, she looked down and could see two vehicles driving slowly along the drive. One was the V&A museum lorry heading from the manor towards the chalk pits. The other was Bluebell, driven by Ashwariya, heading off to pick up the Jane Austen Appreciation Society for their trip to London. Ashwariya had told her they were going to stop at the fifteenth century Peahen pub in St Albans for lunch, and she had pre-ordered chicken and chips for twenty in the lounge to fortify everybody before attacking the London traffic and the, no doubt, chock-a-block roads around Wembley Stadium on World Cup Final day.

***

In the hangar, Charlie looked up as Cliff bounded into the office, brandishing four thick slabs of buttered bread, a jar of peanut butter and a bottle of Maxicola. Charlie could see that Cliff could barely contain himself. "Okay, Cliff, spit it out, what are you burning to tell me?"

"Charlie, this afternoon, after lunch, I have a date… with a woman! Will you help me? I am unsure what to do."

"Wow, Cliff, wonderful news. Who is it with? Where are you going to meet? And at what time?"

"Charlie, I feel like my heart is a washing machine on full spin. I think I feel like Aunt Elsie when she used to get all discombobulated. Poor Aunt Elsie, I do miss her. I miss Dad too, even though he was never here much and was always mad at me."

"Not only you, us. I know what you mean, Cliff. I miss them too. The loveliest thing is to remember them both at their best. We can always talk more about the good parts of the old days when we have time to reminisce. Right, back to today and this date of yours. Let's make our sandwiches and you can tell me all."

***

Loveday sat down on some flattened ferns on the top of the Hoo, thinking this was where Mrs Gascoyne may have stood to fire upon the plane. She could see the aerodrome and visualised Showgirl One's flightpath in GloGlo's skilful hands. The top of the loop must have been right above this spot. Loveday could only remember flashes of what she had glimpsed from the Tiger Moth before it corkscrewed towards the ground. She had been so focused on her role as the gunner, looking for the enemy biplane in her sights and getting into the spirit of the mock fight, that she had not taken in much of the scenery, especially once the dogfight began. She did remember looking straight down on, what must have been, the top of the Hoo but had not recognised it as such from above.

***

Cliff was so excited that he couldn't eat. "I don't know how it happened. I was in the drawing room organising the chairs for the match and ensuring the television could be seen by everyone. When I was done, I figured I'd go and see what the indoor film set looks like, being as it is their day off, so I sneaked into the ballroom. It was amazing.

They have turned both the main hall and ballroom into something that doesn't look familiar at all. A few crew members were touching up paintwork, ready for next week. Then, this lovely woman about our age came over and asked me if I was one of the Cuffley brothers and did I want to sit somewhere comfortably, so I could watch them work. So she found me a chair with a sign on the back which said, 'Director'. Then, she brought me a jam doughnut and explained to me what was going on.

"She told me the film's plot has Dynamite McQueen racing to find one of the lost seven wonders of the ancient world, the Hanging Gardens of Babylon, before the awful Hesketh Van Hydethorpe does. Dynamite wants to save the gardens for everyone to enjoy, whereas Hesketh wants to remove all the ancient artefacts, sell them to the highest bidder and turn the gardens into a theme park, like Wicksteed Park. You can imagine that is exactly what that horrible fountain man would do in real life if he wasn't an actor. Anyhow, the first part of the film is Dynamite finding the secret map, showing where the gardens are located. She flies to some place called Nineveh in Abyssinia, but on the plane Hesketh kidnaps her, steals the map, ties her up and hides her in the plane's front wheel well. Then he himself gets knocked on the head by another gang of thieves who steal the map from him. When he wakes up, he realises he has loved Dynamite all this time. He saves her from the wheel well just before the plane lands. Sharp-as-a-pin Dynamite had only given him half the map, and she had hidden the other half. While the other thieves are sleeping in the Nineveh Grand Hotel, Dynamite and Hesketh steal into their room to snatch the other half of the map back. The main hall has been turned into the Nineveh Grand Hotel."

Charlie was more interested in hearing about Cliff's upcoming date, but listened patiently as he carried on. "Sitting in the director's chair became boring after a while, as I was literally watching paint dry. When the crew were fiddling with the lighting, the woman with the doughnut brought me a cup of tea and showed me the clapperboard used to signal that filming is going to start. She was so nice and friendly and has such sparkling eyes. I had seen her before, on the first day when everyone arrived, but I had never been able to meet her in person. She was so easy to talk to, unlike other women. Well, except for the MacGuffins, but then they are like sisters. To me I mean. Of course they are sisters to themselves! Anyway, this lovely woman asked me about the manor and its history and if it would be possible to have a tour of the house, maybe this afternoon, as she wouldn't be needed on the set. I said yes right away, I didn't even think about it. So she said, 'Okay, it's a date,' just like that. I went red and dropped my doughnut, so she brought me another, and then I said I needed to get back here, and she said to meet her outside the manor at three o'clock. I said, 'Yes, it's a date' which made me go all hot again. And she said, 'Oh, I am glad you agree it's a date,' and kissed me on the cheek before I fled. Charlie, she kissed me! I don't know what to do. Should I change my clothes? How should I handle it? Is it really a date? What do you do on a date like this?"

Charlie grinned at his brother, his heart warming to

the possibility of Cliff having romance in his life. "It absolutely is a one hundred per cent, actual, authentic, *bona fide* date. Be yourself. Dates can be awful if you feel awkward and don't know what to say, but you already have a head start as she wants to see the house. So why don't you show her around and tell her what you know. Keep it casual. Consider starting with a drink in the kitchen, and I am sure there is some of Loveday's cake left in the tin on the counter. Ask her questions about herself. You know, where she was born, how she got into the film business, where she lives and what she thinks of Cuffley Manor, etcetera. Try to make the date last a couple of hours. If time flies by, it is a good sign. Once you have finished with the house, give her a tour of the gardens and bring her to the aerodrome. If you are enjoying her company, ask her if she might want to watch the World Cup Final tonight with us, especially as GloGlo is playing a key role in the flypast. And if it doesn't go well, consider telling her you have a few jobs to do at the aerodrome before the game starts and would it be all right to leave her at the house. Don't be nervous. She already likes you enough to bring you two doughnuts." laughed Charlie.

"But, what do I wear?" asked Cliff dejectedly looking down.

Charlie nodded in agreement. "I think we can find you something better than those oil-stained overalls. You still have a couple of hours before the date to get cleaned up so let's go back to the manor. When did you last have a bath? And by the way, most importantly, what is she called? Did you get her name?"

"Her name," said Cliff, "is Feeble."

"Crikey, are you sure? Did she say those exact words?" asked Charlie.

"Yes, I think so."

"Well, at some point during the 'date' you can ask her how she spells her name, as it is so unusual and ask where it came from. It boggles the mind, but hopefully there is a perfectly rational explanation. Feeble! Blimey. Before we go back to the house to get you cleaned up, I could use your help on something after we finish our sandwiches. It shouldn't take long, but I think we are the ones to do it. Yesterday, Constable Vanessa went through each room in the lodge to see if there is any explanation for Aunt Elsie's behaviour at the fête. She said the place looked untouched to her, neat as a pin, but she asked if we could take a look to see if we could find anything unusual. We should also take the opportunity to empty the fridge and food cupboards of perishable food. So how about once we finish lunch we go over there, walk around the place and return to the manor in enough time to get you sorted for your date? How does that sound?"

Cliff nodded. "I cannot believe Aunt Elsie is not here anymore. I miss seeing her about. I miss dropping in at the lodge for tea."

"I know," said Charlie, "At least it looks like she died quickly and, hopefully, painlessly. And the circumstances of it seem so strange. I cannot believe it. Did Aunt Elsie really shoot at Showgirl One? If the gunshot had hit one of the MacGuffin sisters it would have been tragic, and it would also have been murder which doesn't bear thinking about. Did her heart issue addle her brain somehow? She was over seventy after all. Such a shame she was alone, except for us. We were her family and she was ours. We will give her a good send-off when they release her body."

As the brothers walked through the forest and down the drive to the lodge, they shared their favourite memories of Aunt Elsie. Charlie opened the front door of the lodge with his master key and they went through the place, looking carefully for anything unusual. Everything looked exactly as they would have expected, very clean and tidy, everything had a place, and everything was in its place and so familiar to them after all these years. As they removed the perishable food from the fridge and cupboards, Charlie suddenly thought maybe they had better ask permission from Vanessa before they removed anything, even spoiled milk and a limp leek. He used Elsie's telephone to call the station and ask if the constable was there.

***

Mentally and physically exhausted from all the week's events and activities, Loveday drifted off to sleep, lying in the sun on top of the Hoo. She woke soon after, stood up blearily, and dusted herself off. Thank goodness she had eaten so well last night, otherwise her stomach would be rumbling by now. With the golf club, she poked through the undergrowth near where Mrs Gascoyne's body had been found, but to no avail. Looking out over the grounds, she could see the museum lorry in the distance, parked by what she assumed was the entrance to the chalk pits. She decided to head down there, find Dad and Tolly and see if she could help them with their search.

It took her a good hour to descend the Hoo and wend her way to the chalk pits through the woods behind the far end of the aerodrome. There she found the lorry, all locked up and sitting at the top of a snaking road which zigzagged down the side of a pit to a dark opening that must be a tunnel or a cave. Loveday shivered; she didn't like the idea of going in there alone so strengthened her grip on the golf club. She gingerly walked down to the tunnel opening and yelled, "Dad? Tolly?" but no one answered. Thinking it was a wasted journey, Loveday decided in no uncertain terms that she was not going into a dark tunnel on her own. As she was about to turn and head back up the side of the pit, she heard footsteps coming from deep inside the tunnel. She peered into the entrance and caught a flash of light reflecting off of a chrome bumper and silver bodywork. Recognizing the iconic gleaming radiator with its *Spirit of Ecstasy* statuette on top, Loveday knew she had found the missing Rolls-Royce in which Crêpes Suzette had escaped the Ravenwood Studios bomb blast. She entered the cave and walked around the car, examining it more closely. The footsteps behind her grew louder and faster. "Dad?" Suddenly she was pushed to the ground, hitting her head on the chrome bumper. Loveday moaned while her silent assailant tied her wrists behind her back and stuffed a gag into her mouth.

***

"Hello, Constable Otukile, it's Charlie Cuffley up at the manor. As you suggested, my brother and I have let ourselves into the lodge, you know where Mrs Gascoyne lived, and we have visited every room. Everything looks untouched and just as we remember it. I don't think anyone apart from yourself has been in here since the fête. We want to clear out the fridge and cupboards of perishable food, but we thought we had better ask you first."

Vanessa thanked them for calling, and approved their suggestion to remove any food which could go bad. "This certainly is a headscratcher, Mr Cuffley. I should also let you know, when an untimely, unexpected death occurs, the coroner always performs an autopsy, and the autopsy on Mrs Gascoyne was completed last night. This morning, the coroner confirmed Mrs Gascoyne's death was caused by a heart attack. We also received the results from our forensics laboratory which analysed the fingerprints on the gun and looked for gun residue on her clothes. The results confirmed Mrs Gascoyne was the last person to fire it. The coroner said there was a bruise on her body where her heart is. The bruise matches the gun stock, so it must have recoiled, hitting her in the chest, causing the heart attack. The coroner was also able to estimate the time of death as between four and six o'clock on Saturday afternoon which also fits. Based on when the Misses MacGuffin were shot at, we know the time of death was after five o'clock. The fingerprints also indicate she was left-handed. Can you confirm which hand she favoured?"

"Yes," said Charlie, "I remember she was left-handed like my father, my brother and me. My mum was the only one of us who was right-handed."

"Thank you, you have been so helpful. Have you or your brother had any further thoughts on Mrs Gascoyne's motivations for being on top of Cuffley Hoo in the middle of the fête and for shooting at the Misses MacGuffins and their biplane?"

"I am sorry, Constable, we are both at a complete loss."

"Mr Cuffley, the coroner has released Mrs Gascoyne's personal effects. I will bring them to you, along with the shotgun and your father's gun licence, which needs to be changed into your brother's name. I could cycle over to you right away."

"Yes, that would be fine. Was the gun cabinet key there? The shotgun was locked in the cabinet and she would have had to open it with the key."

"No, there was no key in her effects."

"That is odd. She must have taken the gun out, locked the cabinet and put the key back before she went up to the Hoo."

"I'd like to take a look at the gun cabinet if I may."

"Of course, I will show it to you when you come over. Can we start making arrangements for a funeral? I should also try to see if there is a will. She probably used one of the local solicitors in Hertford. I will start with Dad's old solicitor."

"That sounds like a good plan," said Vanessa. "I will be over within the hour. Shall I meet you at the lodge, the manor or the aerodrome?"

"Please come to the manor, Constable, to the door at

the back near the kitchen."

While waiting for Vanessa, Charlie helped Cliff pick out the clothes for his date. Charlie thought he must do the laundry more frequently as there were more clothes in Cliff's wicker basket than in his wardrobe. Luckily, he had a clean pair of jeans, his Clarks commandos were not too scuffed, and Charlie lent him one of his flower print shirts. "You look spiffy, Cliffy."

"And you're a poet and don't know it," retorted Cliff, using one of Aunt Elsie's favourite phrases.

Charlie looked at the clock. "You had better get going, Cliff. It always pays to be early. I will clean up here. Hopefully, the constable will arrive soon, and I can spirit her away so you and Miss Feeble have the kitchen to yourselves. I will go and put the kettle on to boil, lay out the tea things and rustle up some biscuits and cake so it is all ready when you come in. If the constable is late, I will wait outside and head her off at the pass."

Just as Charlie finished laying out the tea things for Cliff, Constable Otukile arrived on her bicycle, skidding to a stop on the gravel outside the kitchen window. Charlie opened the door to greet Vanessa and steer her away from the kitchen. "Good afternoon, Constable. Thank you for coming and bringing Aunt Elsie's belongings and Father's gun."

"Good afternoon, Mr Cuffley."

They both giggled at speaking so formally with an old school friend. "Cliff is just about to arrive with his first-ever date. I want to give them space, so can I quickly show you the gun cabinet and we can put Dad's Purdey back?

We will need to go to the library first, so we can get the key. Dad always kept the gun cabinet key in an old book, and we still keep it there to honour his memory."

"It all sounds most satisfactory, Mr Cuffley. Unfortunately, I haven't anything new to report. The mystery is now not what she did but why she did it," said Vanessa ruefully. "At the station, we have been racking our brains but have come up with nothing. While I was interviewing the fête attendees about what they saw, I also asked about what they knew about Mrs Gascoyne." She consulted her notebook. "You probably know all this. She was an only child, born Elsie Troake in 1895. Some of the older ones remembered her going to school in Maiden St Irene. She left there at fourteen, which was done back in those days. She started a job in service at Cuffley Manor in the 1920s and met her husband, who was the chauffeur here, and they had one son. Sadly, both father and son perished in the Second World War. After your mother died, Mrs Gascoyne moved into the manor to look after you and your brother, and once you were grown, she moved into the lodge. It seems she had always lived locally, and there was nothing remarkable about her life. Does that concur with what you know?"

"Yes, it does, she brought my brother and me up, and we loved her like a grandmother. She ruled us with a tough hand, but there was kindness too," said Charlie.

"As far as we can tell, it seems as if Mrs Gascoyne, entirely of her own volition, took your father's gun from a locked cabinet and, unseen on the afternoon of the fête when hundreds of people were milling about, clambered up Cuffley Hoo, shot at the Misses MacGuffin in their Tiger Moth biplane and then had a heart attack and died," said Vanessa.

"It seems so out of character. Where would she learn how to use a gun? And with such skill? I think she must have had a mental breakdown or something," said Charlie with a heavy heart.

"We interviewed all three of the Misses MacGuffin and none of them had any idea why Mrs Gascoyne would want to kill them. They had always gotten on with her, even Loveday who had only just met her. Do you think she knew anyone else in their family? They didn't think so, although they did say their father had come to Cuffley Manor in the 1940s while he was working for the Victoria and Albert Museum. It's possible Mrs Gascoyne might have met him at that time."

"Actually, Alfie, their father, Mr MacGuffin, is here at the moment. He still works for the V&A. Once we are done here, let's go and try to find him. The reason he visited Cuffley Manor in the 1940s was because the V&A was storing artefacts away from the London bombings and Cuffley Manor and its deep chalk pits was one of the places chosen for this. The reason for him being here now is to check whether any of the museum pieces were left behind, as there are several items which never made it back to London after the war. I think he and his assistant were planning to check out the old chalk pits today which is where the larger, heavier pieces were stored, the things which couldn't fit through the doors of the main house," said Charlie.

"Thanks for the tip, let's try to find Mr MacGuffin. It is always good to tie up these loose ends," said Vanessa thoughtfully as she processed this new information.

In the library, Charlie reached for Mark Twain's *The Prince and the Pauper*. An envelope had been stuck to the inside cover to hold the key, which was there. They descended the servant's stairs to the gun room in the basement, used the key to open the cabinet, and put the Purdey back in its place. "Is there anything else you would like to see before we try to find Mr MacGuffin?"

"No, thank you, I think the only thing left to do is head to the chalk pits." Vanessa paused. "Actually, on second thoughts, there is one thing sticking in my mind. It relates to the book you showed me, the one where you keep the key to the gun cabinet. There is a copy of the same book on Mrs Gascoyne's bookshelves in the lodge. Is it a coincidence? My intuition tells me it is not. I mean, it is a famous book by a famous author, but to have the same edition of the same book could be more than a coincidence. As one copy of the book was being used to hide a key, maybe there is something hidden in the other copy. I do have a strong feeling about this, so I think I need to examine the book at the lodge. How about if I check it out, and then we meet at the chalk pits in an hour. I can find my own way there. I remember the way through the woods from our childhood days playing near the pits. If I can borrow the lodge key, I can return it to you when we meet outside the chalk pit tunnels." Charlie concurred, and Vanessa left him to his own devices as she walked over to the lodge.

As Charlie walked back to the aerodrome, he could see the museum lorry chugging back from the chalk pits. He moved to the side of the road to wave the lorry down, and furrowed his brow as he could see there was only one person in the cab, and it wasn't Alfie.

Tolly stuck his head out of the window. "Hello, Mr Cuffley, how can I assist?"

"I am looking for Alfie," said Charlie. "Do you know where he is?"

"Well, I am looking for him myself," said Tolly. "We were both down in the tunnels exploring each one with the map you gave us. Then Alfie said he wanted me to get another torch as his was starting to flicker, so I went back to the lorry to get it and when I came back, he was nowhere to be found. I retraced my steps through all the tunnels but didn't find him. I was wondering if he had somehow come back to the manor."

"No, we haven't seen him at the house. Let's do a quick check of the aerodrome and head back to the chalk pits together, in case he has turned up," said Charlie. He climbed into the lorry's cab and drove with Tolly the five minutes to the aerodrome, where they found no one. *This is odd*, thought Charlie, *this place is completely quiet.* There was no activity around the Skyfreighter which, unusually, was sitting with its rear door open. A few of the other planes' owners had probably flown off for the afternoon, but no one was doing any maintenance or standing around chatting which was most unusual. *They can't be watching the football yet; the start of the game is hours away.*

Tolly and Charlie got back in the lorry and started on the return journey to the chalk pits. As the lorry left the aerodrome, the noise of a large plane flying over caused Charlie to ask Tolly to stop. "It does not sound like one of our regular planes, it is too large," said Charlie. They both looked up as a biplane much bigger than a Tiger Moth but smaller than the Skyfreighter flew over the treetops towards the hangars. Charlie said in wonderment, "Good gosh, it is the Brabazon Speedbird which brought the actors for their press call last week. I don't think the aerodrome was expecting them. I wonder if they are in trouble."

Tolly's voice dropped an octave, "Actually, they are not in trouble. You are."

***

Vanessa reached the lodge and let herself in. In each room, everything looked as she remembered. The two brothers had not disturbed anything. In the living room, she focused on the bookshelves, studying their contents. She saw the books had been organised in alphabetical order. There were no other books by Mark Twain on the shelves. In fact, Mark Twain stood out as being the only classic book on the shelves at all, which seemed to solely hold popular mysteries by Agatha Christie, John Dickson Carr and Dorothy L. Sayers. Vanessa reached for *The Prince and the Pauper* and pulled it out. It definitely looked like the same age and edition as the book up at the manor. She flicked through the pages which were pristine. It did not appear to have been a favourite read of Mrs Gascoyne's as it was in such perfect condition. There was no key or envelope inside the front cover. She held the book by the spine and shook it. Nothing. She ran her thumb over the pages like a flick book and shook it once again.

A small piece of stiff paper fell out on to the carpet. It was an old black and white photograph of three people, none of whom Vanessa recognised at first. There were two men, one on either side of a woman. On the back was a handwritten note: *To safeguard the family, if you ever see these two faces in person, kill them.* After a sharp intake of breath, Vanessa flipped the photograph over to study it. The clothes worn by the three people in the photograph dated it to being taken sometime in the late 1940s. The three people were sitting on grass with the edge of a checked tablecloth spread out in front of them. The camera had caught a corner of the tablecloth. The three faces looked happy and relaxed. There was something familiar about two of the faces, but it wouldn't come. However, if they were vaguely familiar to her, someone up at the manor should surely know more. She looked at her watch. It was time to meet Charlie.

The deafening roar of a plane flying low over the trees caused Vanessa to peer out of the lodge window up at the sky. Must be someone returning to the aerodrome after a Saturday sightseeing flight. How lovely to have the kind of life where you could take your plane out on a weekend afternoon in the same way you might go for a Sunday drive. The rich know how to live. Vanessa also rued needing to work on a Saturday while the rest of the Jane

Austen Appreciation Society were able to attend the World Cup Final. The things she sacrificed for her career, which had been going nowhere until there was an attempted murder at the fête. She could now show her true mettle as she was given the case and had just found a very important clue.

Vanessa's stomach rumbled loudly, a family trait, reminding her she had not had time for lunch and her mid-morning apple seemed many moons ago. She wondered if Loveday had dropped anything edible off at the aerodrome. How lovely to have your own cook like the Cuffleys, first Mrs Gascoyne and now Miss MacGuffin. And then it came to her in such a flash! Vanessa sat down on an armchair, flabbergasted and looked at the photograph again. The woman! It couldn't be, but she looked like Cuffley Manor's new cook, the one whom Mrs Gascoyne had shot at. The woman in the photograph was the spitting image of Loveday MacGuffin.

***

Charlie turned from looking up at the Speedbird to looking down at the barrel of a revolver with a silencer. Tolly ordered him to get out and turn around, expertly snapping handcuffs onto Charlie's wrists. He opened up the back of the lorry and pushed Charlie in. As Charlie fell forward, he could hear moaning coming from the shadows of the lorry's interior. His eyes adjusted to the darkness, enough to see it was both Alfie and Loveday lying there. They had each been handcuffed and gagged. Tolly stuffed a foul rag into Charlie's mouth, shut the doors and got into the cab. He drove back to the aerodrome and stopped, ready to greet the new arrival, which had landed and taxied up to the hangar, stopping next to the Skyfreighter. From inside the lorry, the three prisoners could hear no passengers, only a single voice, the pilot, who murmured familiarly with Tolly. The pilot was a woman.

***

As Vanessa walked briskly to the aerodrome, she racked her brains for insight into the photograph. Her gut told her it was significant, but what did it mean? How could Loveday MacGuffin be in a photograph taken in the 1940s? As she approached the edge of the forest, through the trees, she could see the newly arrived plane, which had 'Eighth Wonder Film Company' printed on the fuselage, parked in front of the hangars near the Skyfreighter and next to a lorry with 'Victoria and Albert Museum' painted on the side. Two people, a man and a woman, were talking in front of it. Vanessa stopped dead in her tracks. She could see the man, who she did not recognise, was pointing a gun at a woman who looked very similar to Loveday MacGuffin, but older. It was the woman in the photograph! Footsteps behind Vanessa alerted her to the nearing presence of two other people. She turned around to see Cliff and the film company's assistant approaching, hand in hand. Vanessa put her finger to her lips and waved her arms to get them to move to the side of the footpath under the trees. "Lord Cuffley," she whispered, as Cliff winced a little to hear his title, "I am here in my official capacity as a Constable of the Hertford Police. Something is going very wrong at the aerodrome. Do you recognise any of these people?" Vanessa whipped out the photograph for Cliff to look at.

"Oh, yes, my father is on the right as a young man. On the left is Alfie MacGuffin who is the father of Loveday, GloGlo and Reggie, though looking much younger in the photo than he looks today. The woman in the middle looks a lot like Loveday, doesn't she? But it can't be Loveday. She wasn't even born when this photograph was taken. Could it be Loveday's mother?"

Vanessa's mind whirred with the possibilities. "How about you, Miss *err*…"

"Currie," said Phoebe, "Phoebe Currie. I work with the Eighth Wonder Film Company. The plane that just landed is the company's passenger plane. I do not know why it is here. No arrival was scheduled for today."

"Miss Currie, do you recognise any of these faces?" asked Vanessa urgently, waving the photograph in front of her.

Phoebe took the photograph and studied it. "Looking at the clothing and the quality of the picture, this photograph must have been taken at least twenty-five years ago. Hmm, it's a much younger version but I know the woman in the photograph as Babette Kohlrabi, the head of the Eighth Wonder Film Company." Phoebe looked over to the plane again. "She is also the woman talking to the man with the gun over there. I heard Mr de Havilland threatening to complain to Miss Kohlrabi about having had to dance with Miss MacGuffin the other day, which he thought was a little beneath him as a star of the film. I guess he must have done so for her to arrive here today. My mother, who is the director of the film, will be absolutely livid."

Vanessa's mind raced. "I think we need reinforcements. I am going to radio back to Hertford Police Station to alert everyone available to come here as soon as possible. And we need to get ourselves armed. Lord Cuffley, do I have your permission to remove a shotgun from your gun cabinet?" Cliff nodded. The three of them ran back to the manor to get the key. Vanessa grabbed the Purdey which Aunt Elsie had used to fire at the MacGuffin sisters. She expertly loaded the ammunition and readied it for firing. Phoebe worried about the other actors and crew who were here in the manor and on the grounds and thought they ought to be warned somehow that there was a man with a gun at the aerodrome. Cliff told Vanessa about the way to send messages to every part of the rotunda and aerodrome using the tube mail system. Vanessa nodded. Cliff led them to the tube mail room where Phoebe and Vanessa wrote the messages and Cliff put them in the relevant canisters and sent them off. They then rushed stealthily back to the edge of the forest where it opened onto the aerodrome. Cliff told Phoebe she should stay inside the manor where she would be safe, but she insisted on coming with him and grabbed his hand with confidence.

***

In the manor, Joan and Blessing had spent the day changing bed sheets, dusting, carpet sweeping, checking the functionality of all the listening devices, listening to the previous day's tapes and examining personal items, all the while looking for clues. So far, nothing had turned up. This was not at all what they had expected. Surely the film company was linked to the *Fleur de Lys Crime Syndicate* and syndicate members were using the film company's presence at Cuffley Manor as a cover for sabotaging the World Cup Final.

Six syndicate inner circle agents had been killed when the bomb destroyed the Ravenwood Studios, leaving one agent at large who had an accomplice. But there had been only silence since, and the suspected WI-5 mole had not turned up either. While Joan and Blessing were in the attic listening to the taped conversations from all the bedrooms, they suddenly received a call from Morag on their compacts. Babette Kohlrabi, the head of the film company, had been kidnapped! Before Joan and Blessing had a chance to process this information, a buzz from the attic's tube post outlet alerted them to the arrival of another message, which further chilled them to the bone.

There is a gunman at the aerodrome. Stay hidden where you are. Police are on their way!

Joan looked alarmed at Blessing as she grabbed her handbag. Blessing looked wide-eyed at Joan and they ran downstairs, and out of the manor to the Hillman Minx.

Carefully removing a shopping bag on wheels from the boot, they sprinted along the footpath to the aerodrome, stopping when they found Vanessa, Phoebe and Cliff crouched down at the edge of the trees surveying the scene playing out on the other side of the landing strip. The two women joined them and both gasped as they recognised it was Tolly who had a revolver pointed at a woman they recognised as Babette Kohlrabi.

***

Hearing what sounded like a shopping trolley being dragged along the footpath, Vanessa looked behind her to see her mother and Mrs Spatchcock arriving. Crouching all together, they watched as Tolly took something large and gold from Babette Kohlrabi. Then he pushed her towards the museum lorry. To the observers, it looked like Babette would be put in the lorry, but instead, Tolly carried on talking. Using the binoculars she always kept in her shopping bag, Blessing groaned when she saw the expression of Tolly's face. Vanessa exhaled and swore under her breath. Babette Kohlrabi was one of the three people in the photograph and was being killed or kidnapped right in front of her eyes! When Joan removed a pistol from her handbag, and her mother removed a machine gun from her shopping bag, Vanessa's eyes widened.

***

Tolly smugly beamed, extremely confident in how well his plan was working. He had made use of two of the people bound up in the back of the lorry to lure Babette Kohlrabi to the aerodrome. "Ah, Miss Kohlrabi, or should I call you, Mrs Delice MacGuffin, or WI-5's most special agent, Dynamite McQueen? So glad all your identities could come."

"Ah, the new head of the *Fleur de Lys Crime Syndicate*, I presume, or maybe that is the role of Crêpes Suzette and you are just her accomplice, the pitiful underling marching to her drum?" A suppressed ripple of dismay travelled down Tolly's face.

"Oh, I see, I am right. So I am meeting the monkey, not the organ grinder, or should I say our mole? Well, that's a blow to my fragile ego." Delice held his attention while she assessed the situation and attempted to stall and unsettle him by gathering as much pertinent information as possible. "I received your message that you were holding hostage my husband and daughter, and here I am. You can stop pointing that gun at me, you unthinking flunky," said Delice with a cold glare, hoping to find some weakness in Tolly's relationship with Crêpes Suzette.

Tolly did not take his eyes off her face. "So much blather Mrs MacGuffin. I expected better from you. Don't worry about the gun. I think it will keep your mind on the task at hand. Crêpes Suzette is the genius who has helped me claim my birthright. I am the rightful heir to the Cuffley Estate."

"So, you think you are the illegitimate son of the deceased Lord Cuffley? A joke, surely. Will you answer me one question?" asked Delice.

Tolly nodded.

"I know you have been trying to find me since you realised that I had witnessed and escaped the explosion at the film studios. I also know you then tried to use my youngest daughter to get to me by posing as a disaffected groom hiring her catering services for his wedding. And then you watched my house while I gave you the slip and you ended up mistakenly following my daughters but they also gave you the slip at the train station. I realise now it was all you, wasn't it? So, my question is how did you discover my identity?"

Tolly steadied the revolver. "Well, your dimwit of a husband has a photo of you and your daughters in his office. At the film studio, when I was waiting to chauffeur Crêpes Suzette, I recognised you running out of the soundstage before the bomb went off. Once I made that connection, it became clear to us that Delice MacGuffin and Babette Kohlrabi were one and the same. Using Loveday, the daughter that most resembles you, as a decoy on the train was quite the merciless decision."

"Of course, I would never deliberately endanger my daughters. I had not put two and two together at that point."

"That is all by the bypass, Mrs MacGuffin. Are you going to show me the goods? If you show me yours, I will show you mine."

Delice opened her bag and handed him the World Cup Trophy.

"Thank you, chattel-of-dimwit Alfie. That wasn't too

hard, was it? I imagine you stole the trophy to ingratiate yourself with the syndicate," said Tolly, his narrowed eyes glinting.

"Actually, I stole the trophy as part of my ruse to join the syndicate's inner circle. Well, what are you going to do with me or are we going to stand here all day chatting?" asked Delice acidly.

"I think you will be interested in what I have in the back of the lorry. Go on, open it." Delice opened the rear door, and Tolly shone his torch over the gagged faces of Alfie, Loveday and Charlie who had wriggled their way into a sitting position.

"Well, I recognise two of them," said Delice icily, trying to keep control, "Who is the other one?"

"He is a nobody, one of my useless half-brothers. The other two are called insurance and collateral damage," said Tolly commandingly. "You shouldn't mess with Suzette. She was extremely angry WI-5 thwarted her plan to blow up the V&A. After today, the reputation of WI-5 will be in ashes. All it will take is your double-crossing WI-5 agent's face being splashed all over tomorrow's newspapers as the perpetrator of the biggest ever peacetime attack on British soil. And I get to claim my rightful place as Lord Cuffley. Not bad for a weekend's work, is it?"

Delice narrowed her eyes. "So, Suzette's lapdog yearns to be a member of the landed gentry! That's what this is all about."

Sirens could suddenly be heard in the distance, coming closer along the B-1000. Tolly looked momentarily surprised. "I think we need to be on our way.

Turn around and hold your hands out." Delice did so and Tolly snapped the handcuffs in place. "Get in the pilot seat, mother of all things MacGuffin. Alfie and Loveday, you two are coming with us. I wouldn't want any loved ones of Delice to miss the big match."

Tolly threw the bag containing the World Cup trophy into the Speedbird and lifted Loveday over his shoulder in a fireman's lift before pushing her through the plane's door. He did the same with Alfie, struggling a little with the older man's weight, before climbing inside himself and shutting the door. Charlie was left alone in the back of the lorry. The sirens' see-saw sound grew louder, and blue flashing lights could be seen through the trees along the driveway. With Tolly's revolver held to her temple, Delice used her cuffed hands to release the throttle and accelerate along the landing strip into the wind as a squadron of Morris Minor police cars appeared from the woods and chased the Speedbird.

***

Hearing the police sirens and with their trigger fingers at the ready, Joan and Blessing watched as Tolly forced Delice, Loveday and Alfie on to the plane at gunpoint. Vanessa swore again when she realised that not only was Babette Kohlrabi on the plane, but so was Alfie MacGuffin and his youngest daughter. And Alfie was the third person in the 1940s photograph.

As the Speedbird started taxiing along the landing strip, Vanessa flagged down one of the police cars, calling

Joan and Blessing to get in with her. The three women leaned their torsos out of the car's windows. Blessing aimed her machine gun at the plane's engines. Joan aimed her pistol at the undercarriage. Vanessa aimed her Purdey at the wings. Joan managed to hit a tyre, Blessing hit an engine and Vanessa pierced a wing. Despite their attempts to stop the plane, the Speedbird took off and cleared the trees before heading west. "Follow that plane!" yelled Joan.

Fever Pitch

At Duxford Airfield, the final rehearsals had gone smoothly. Although Reggie thought she looked ridiculous in the royal meringue and helmet with its huge tiara, it acted as another flying suit and in fact provided better insulation so she was quite warm. Beaver was quite happy his own helmet had been decorated with a gold crown to add a regal touch. Reggie could also see GloGlo was loving every minute, so she tried to relax into what was, without a doubt, going to be a unique experience, and, as Joan had said, it was an advantage to WI-5 to have an operative on the pitch of the big match.

In the late afternoon, the vintage planes took off in waves, heading for Wembley Stadium. Reggie found it quite difficult to clamber up on to Showgirl One's top wing in her stiff dress, but once she was up there and strapped in, she felt very safe. After helping Reggie and giving her a smack on the lips, declaring, "That is likely to be the closest I will ever get to kissing the queen of England," Beaver strapped himself in beside her.

Standing on Showgirl One's upper wing, Reggie tried to banish her awkwardness at being the centre of attention in her white frock and crown and to avoid reliving the circumstances the last time she was strapped to a Tiger Moth's wing. She calmed her nerves by focusing on this being a 'thank you' to GloGlo for saving her life at Ravenwood Studios and seeing Beaver being the belle of the ball in his naval wear. They looked at each other and held hands as they watched the rest of the Tiger Moth squadron take off, until it was only the Beatles' biplane and Showgirl One waiting for the signal to leave. After the Beatles trundled to the end of Duxford's runway, GloGlo followed and took off. It was going to take forty minutes for Showgirl One to reach the outskirts of North London.

***

Once the Speedbird had disappeared above the trees of the Cuffley Manor estate, Phoebe took charge, emboldened by Cliff's support, and rushed towards the museum lorry, where they discovered Charlie moaning in the back. They removed his gag and Cliff used bolt cutters from the aerodrome workshop to cut off Charlie's handcuffs. It did not take long to explain what little they all knew about the kidnapping. One of the policemen told them to make sure no one else touched the museum lorry as their forensic team would be giving it a good going over. They were instructed to go to the manor and sit tight by the telephone, in case the kidnappers contacted them.

***

Vesta, Fontaine, Yazmine and Nobby had been in Hertford all morning, missing all the action. Yazmine and Nobby were at Dr Otukile's surgery getting her ankle looked at.

Vesta and Fontaine were sitting in the bar of the Salisbury Arms going over the filming schedule. They all heard the cacophony of police sirens and wondered what was going on. Fontaine attempted to telephone Gaylord, his chauffeur, to get him to pick them all up, but there was no answer so, grumbling, they returned to Cuffley Manor by taxi to find police cars filling the drive. Filled in by Phoebe and Cliff, they were shocked at what had occurred but also sorry to have missed all the excitement.

A newly in-charge and confident Phoebe invited Vesta, Fontaine, Yazmine and Nobby to the manor's kitchen to sit with her and Cliff, while they helped Charlie recover from his ordeal and be near the telephone. Charlie was unable to add any clarity to the proceedings as, once he started to revive, he simply could not understand what had happened and why, only relieved it had been him and not Cliff who had been targeted. The fact that the formidable Babette Kohlrabi had turned out to be the mother of the MacGuffin sisters gobsmacked them all, although neither Vesta, Fontaine, Yazmine, Nobby nor Phoebe worried about Babette's fate, as she had a fearsome, imperious reputation well known by the cast and crew of the Eighth Wonder Film Company. Usually, Babette was the one doing the frogmarching, so no one could imagine why she had been kidnapped at gunpoint in the company plane with Mr MacGuffin and Loveday. However, they all agreed the kidnappers would have trouble on their hands if Babette was given any opportunity to escape. Charlie and Cliff worried about Loveday and Alfie, and how worried GloGlo, Reggie and

Beaver would be when they found out Alfie, Loveday and Mrs MacGuffin had been kidnapped.

At the mention of GloGlo, Reggie and Beaver, Cliff jumped up when he realised he had forgotten about the World Cup Final and their part in the pre-match ceremonies. Everyone moved into the drawing room where the television had been set up. Cliff had switched the set on in time for it to warm up enough to catch the start of the pre-match coverage and Showgirl One's starring role.

***

GloGlo waved at Reggie and Beaver from the cockpit, giving them the sign that Wembley Stadium was coming into view.

"I cannot believe we are doing this, Beaver!" yelled Reggie, as she clasped Beaver's hands.

"Once in a lifetime, Babycakes!" yelled Beaver, "once in a lifetime."

"For once, we are in complete agreement!" yelled Reggie as GloGlo banked over North London. Flying higher than the other planes, all the Tiger Moths flew in a large circle north of the Wembley Stadium, waiting for their cue. There was a sudden roar from below, and the Red Arrows sprinted underneath them, shooting across the sky and over the stadium, trailing red, white and blue smoke. Then, the squadron of Bombers flew across with a loud rumble. On cue, the Tiger Moths dropped down to a thousand feet and flew in a line towards the stadium. Even with all the wind noise, GloGlo, Reggie and Beaver could hear the crowd roaring.

Low over the stadium, the rest of the squadron of Tiger Moths flew in a circle above the stands, trailing more red, white and blue smoke. The roar of the crowd became noticeably louder as the Beatles were announced, and GloGlo dropped back to increase the drama of their entrance. The Beatles' biplane completed its circuit of the stadium and climbed into the sky to get high enough to enable 'John', 'Paul', 'George' and 'Ringo' to parachute safely down. At four thousand feet, the Beatles parachuted down together, holding hands, and landed safely in the centre of the pitch. They uncoupled their parachutes and ran under the stands waving to the ecstatic crowd.

With the announcement that the queen and Prince Philip were arriving, the crowd roared even louder. As GloGlo circled lower over the stadium, Beaver and Reggie did their best dignified royal waves. The temperature change from when they were high in the sky to being low over a hundred thousand people was quite marked. The crowd noise doubled in intensity when, halfway around, GloGlo flipped Showgirl One upside down. Reggie screamed the loudest and forgot to wave. GloGlo righted Showgirl One and climbed into the sky. At four thousand feet, she looked at Reggie and Beaver and gave them the signal. They released their clips and belts and jumped off the wing to skydive down for a thousand feet of royal freefall before opening their parachutes.

Suddenly, another plane came into GloGlo's sights and cut right across Showgirl One's flight path. GloGlo took evasive action to avoid a collision. Reggie and Beaver were holding hands during the freefall. As Reggie looked up to say a mental goodbye to GloGlo, she gasped seeing the Eighth Wonder Film Company Speedbird above them diving towards the stadium. She shook Beaver's arm to get his attention, and they both looked up to see a door open and two people wrestling in the doorway. One of them, a parachutist, kicked the other and, once freed, sidled along the wing and leapt into the air to skydive away from the impending crash, leaving a handcuffed Delice lying in the open doorway. Reggie could not believe her mother was aboard an aeroplane about to crash land into the World Cup Final crowd.

***

The Speedbird came swooping down towards them in a dive. When it was alongside them, Reggie and Beaver angled themselves and aimed towards the open door. Reggie and Beaver each managed to grab the doorframe while releasing each other's hands, and they fought to heave themselves inside. Reggie successfully revived her mother while Beaver wrestled to shut the door. Reggie, holding on to the seatbacks, followed Delice, who was making a beeline for the cockpit. She almost stopped in her tracks on passing Alfie and Loveday, bound and gagged and looking panicked. Through the cockpit window, the bright lights of Wembley Stadium drew nearer and nearer.

Delice's cuffed hands grabbed the yoke and pulled it

backwards with all her might in an effort to level the plane. Reggie removed the gag from Alfie and Loveday, while Beaver helped Delice regain control. Reggie grabbed a hairpin from Delice's librarian bun and used it to unlock her handcuffs. Then, she ran back to unlock Loveday and Alfie's handcuffs. On being freed, Loveday let out a sob. Alfie looked agog at Delice, sitting in the pilot's seat. Delice and Beaver had between them managed to regain control of the plane and pulled back on the flaps before skimming over the heads of the stadium crowd in the cheap seats.

Reggie gave her mother an order. "Mum, fly us up to three thousand feet to let Beaver and me jump out. Then, follow GloGlo in her magenta Tiger Moth back to Cuffley aerodrome. You should catch her up easily." Delice nodded at Reggie, as she sent the Speedbird into a steep climb, and yelled back to Loveday to grab the bag which Tolly had dropped in his haste to leave the plane. Barely holding herself together, Loveday mutely handed the bag to Reggie. Reggie opened it to reveal the World Cup trophy. She was able to tuck it into the big pocket on the front of her flying-suit-cum-dress.

At three thousand feet, Delice gave Beaver and Reggie the nod. Beaver opened the passenger door, and they both leapt off hand in hand, waiting until they were clear of the plane before opening their Union Jack parachutes in unison, and descending into the stadium, Reggie's dress billowing regally. They landed right in the centre circle of the pitch, holding hands, to the hugest roar they have ever heard. The roars became louder when

Reggie untucked her pocket and thrust the stolen trophy into the air. In a flash, half a dozen grounds crew ran over and helped them out of their parachutes. They were directed to leave through a tunnel under the stands, where the real Beatles and the England and Germany players were waiting and clapping. They were then taken to a room below the stands to remove their costumes.

***

Phoebe, Cliff, Vesta, Fontaine, Yazmine and Nobby were oddly relieved to be distracted by the World Cup's pre-match ceremonies. They watched the flypast and the Beatles parachuting, guessing correctly that Reggie and Beaver would be next. The stadium's cameras panned the sky to catch the royal lookalikes. Vesta yelled, Phoebe exclaimed and Fontaine and Nobby swore when they recognised the Eighth Wonder Speedbird flying into the camera shot and diving straight for the stadium past Showgirl One. Wide-eyed, they watched Reggie, who in her huge, gleaming, sparkly, white dress was extremely easy to spot, and Beaver skydive right into the diving plane! It seemed to take forever, but as soon as the Speedbird pulled out of the dive and righted itself above the stadium, they heaved a collective sigh of relief, knowing there was hope for its occupants. They were all in tears when Reggie and Beaver jumped out, parachuted down, landed safely and revealed the stolen trophy. "Now, that makes for very good television," said Vesta, impressed. "Who was the director? Does anyone know?"

***

In the changing room at Wembley Stadium, Reggie immediately began interrogating Beaver. "What just happened? Why were Mum, Dad and Loveday on an Eighth Wonder plane diving towards Wembley Stadium? They could have been killed! Thousands in the crowd would have died."

"I have no idea," said Beaver, "but I think we have saved ninety-eight thousand people from a fiery death, including the Royal Family, the Beatles, the national football teams of England and Germany and most of your family. Not bad for an evening's work!"

"But who was the parachutist who escaped from the Speedbird? Was it the kidnapper? Where did he or she go? We have to find him or her!"

As soon as they had changed out of their costumes, Reggie and Beaver hurriedly exited the stadium via the player's entrance and looked for the hire car GloGlo had organised. Suddenly, a Humber Super Snipe Hertfordshire Constabulary police car flashed its lights at them and opened its doors revealing Joan, Blessing and Vanessa, waving them to get inside. Reggie told the security guard to radio their hire car driver and tell her or him that she and Beaver had secured a ride and to head home and enjoy the game.

Once on the road, Joan filled in Reggie and Beaver on the events leading up to the Speedbird dive bombing Wembley Stadium with most of the MacGuffin family on board. As they pieced together the puzzle, the car fell silent for the first time when Vanessa, who had been listening intently to the conversation while negotiating London traffic, stopped them in their tracks with her words, "I have a theory as to why Mrs Gascoyne shot at your sisters at the fête."

Now that the conversation had suddenly jumped tracks, everyone listened as Vanessa filled them in on what she had surmised about Elsie Gascoyne, and the old photograph of Charlie's father with Alfie and Delice. "This is purely conjecture, but I think it is all to do with your sister Loveday looking so much like your mother in that photograph. When Loveday arrived last week, Mrs Gascoyne must have received an awful shock. Before Lord Cuffley died, he had given Mrs Gascoyne this ancient photograph with its cryptic and disturbing instruction to kill the two other people in the photograph if they turned up at Cuffley Manor. Once Mrs Gascoyne met Loveday, I think she immediately noticed the resemblance with the woman in the photograph. My guess is that she put a hastily conceived plan into action. She was devoted to the Cuffley family and would have done anything to protect them.

"She first attempted to kill Loveday in the kitchen before the fête, by putting rat poison in the pork pie your sister was going to eat, the pork pie that, unfortunately, Cliff ended up nabbing. I think that on realising she had poisoned one of her beloved Cuffley boys and could have killed him, she flew into some kind of panic. She must have learned the youngest of the Misses MacGuffin was replacing Cliff in Showgirl One and figured out that while the fête and flying display would have everyone's attention, all the noise of the planes and the crowd would cover any sound of a shot being fired from Cuffley Hoo. I also think she retrieved the shotgun without being seen by putting it in her trundle shopping bag on wheels, just like my mum apparently does, and walked through the woods to the Hoo, which was cordoned off to the public during the fête."

Vanessa gave her mum a steely look in the rear-view mirror. "I think the scramble up the Hoo, the heightened state she was in and the kickback of the Purdey into her chest must have collectively caused the heart attack which ultimately killed her."

As they listened, the cogs were turning in both Joan's and Reggie's minds and their eyes widened at the same time. "Of course!" they said in tandem. "Joan, you told me Elsie used to shoot rabbits and birds to feed the family if kitchen supplies were getting low, didn't you?"

"Yes, I knew she was a crack shot. Why didn't I put two and two together?"

Reggie yelped as puzzle pieces fell into place. "That must mean Mum and Dad knew Charlie and Cliff's Dad a long time ago. They kept that quiet. We knew Dad had been to Cuffley Manor with the museum during the war, but nothing more."

***

In the Speedbird, flying back to Cuffley aerodrome, with

a relieved GloGlo in the slower Tiger Moth flying ahead of them, Alfie and Loveday peppered Delice with questions. "I will answer every one of your questions, but first let me radio Morag to bring her up to date." Once she had briefed Morag, Delice glanced at Alfie and Loveday who were looking at her expectantly. "Well, I have been working for WI-5 undercover at the Eighth Wonder Film Company for many years. I couldn't tell anyone, not even you, my dear husband. Everything was going well until the explosion at Ravenwood Studios last month. Actually, let me start at the beginning."

Alfie and Loveday listened intently as Delice continued, "I have been a member of WI-5 for such a long time, involved in some pretty high-level missions. After I was injured in the train crash all those years ago, I suspected it had not been an accident, and the *Fleur de Lys Crime Syndicate* was behind it. I also suspected the syndicate was being financed by the box office receipts from the Dynamite McQueen films, so I volunteered to get a job with Eighth Wonder Film Company and work my way up. I felt I was the perfect person for the job as my experience working in film and photography for MI-4 and MI-7 during the War came in very useful. I am sorry I couldn't tell you Alfie. We had to keep it quiet, as leaks were starting to happen. Only Morag, Joan, Blessing and Madge, the head of WI-5, knew.

"Two years ago, I finally became head of the film company and gained a place, one step away from the syndicate's seven-member inner circle. I have now discovered one of those members was Crêpes Suzette, aided by the man you know as Tolly. Sorry, Alfie, he had you wrapped around his little finger.

"Now, the inner circle only ever met at Ravenwood Studios on the Dynamite McQueen soundstage, until it burnt down, which was Suzette's doing, as she attempted to, and succeeded in, killing all her competitors for the syndicate leadership in one fell swoop. If Reggie had not been on the roof that day, I could not have been alerted by Joan and would have also been killed. I am in Joan and Blessing's debt, doubly so because not only did they save my life but they also saved my daughter's. Since your dad's birthday, they also have been hiding me these past weeks in Joan's spare room."

"So, if that bastard Tolly is helping Suzette, how do we find Suzette?" asked Loveday. "You know I found her car in the chalk pits."

"Language, Loveday. Once I had escaped alive from Ravenwood Studios, my goal was to maintain my cover while acting like an ally of the syndicate. To that end, I stole the trophy as a bit of theatre to prevent everyone from being lulled into a false sense of security about the syndicate being decimated, and went to ground. I did suspect I was being followed but thought it might be a suspicious Scotland Yard, and I didn't want them putting two and two together. Hence, me slipping out the back of the house two weeks ago, while, Loveday, you left wearing my coat and beret, and with Reggie's quick thinking, you were able to give them the slip. If I suspected it had been Suzette and Tolly on my trail, I would never have put you in such danger!"

Loveday squeezed her mum's shoulders. "That's all right, Mum. When you gave me your coat, I thought you were being a bit weird about me going away. And I never was aware you could fly a plane. So impressive."

Alfie leaned in. "Your mum is amazing, Loveday. I am beginning to understand the list of things she has accomplished would fill several books."

Delice wiped a tear off her cheek. Alfie looked at her with sympathy. "I must apologise, as I think Tolly must have identified Mum from the photograph I have of all of us in my cubbyhole."

"Alfie, it is not your fault. As soon as I got the call from Morag telling me that my husband and daughter had been kidnapped, I knew the game was up. I followed Tolly's instructions to fly in the Speedbird to Cuffley aerodrome today, to give myself up in exchange for my family. It was when he had me at gunpoint at the aerodrome that he told me their aim was to destroy both the syndicate and WI-5 and claim the Cuffley title and estate as his own." Delice paused. "We should be at the aerodrome soon. I can see GloGlo starting her descent. If we find Tolly, he can lead us to Suzette. When we land, it will be clear to all and sundry that Delice MacGuffin and Babette Kohlrabi are one and the same. To some extent it will be a relief."

"Got it, Mum," said Loveday. "You can rely on us, although it will be you who is going to be bombarded with more questions."

Delice smiled at her daughter and husband. "Don't worry, if I can handle the Dynamite McQueen cast and crew, I can handle anything. Plus, I will have the support of my family and my team; that's Joan, Blessing and Morag. Those three have been running operations for me, keeping me hidden and sane and, today notwithstanding, almost completely out of trouble."

***

GloGlo's Tiger Moth flew low over Cuffley Manor. Cliff and Phoebe heard the engine and ran out of the rotunda to the aerodrome, running up to the plane before Showgirl One had even come to a complete halt. As they walked to the hangar, Phoebe filled GloGlo in on the kidnapping and hijacking of the film company's plane and that it was the young man from the museum who was the perpetrator. GloGlo sat down, right on the grass, in shock, as she realised three of her family members had been aboard the plane which had dived towards Wembley Stadium. Her trance of relief and horror was broken by the sound of propellers approaching the landing strip. It was the Speedbird. No one watching it had any idea who was on board.

On hearing and then seeing the Speedbird in the sky, GloGlo, Phoebe and Cliff ran to grab hammers and spanners, and whatever equipment could be used as weapons, from the aerodrome work benches. They hid behind the hangar doors as the Speedbird taxied towards them. As soon as they could see that Delice, Alfie and Loveday were the only people exiting the plane, they threw their weapons down and ran towards them. After hugs, cries and tears, they all ambled back to the manor as each filled the others in on what they had seen, what they knew and what they hadn't figured out. In the kitchen, Loveday put the kettle on and made tea. While it was steeping, a siren and the screech of tyres on gravel could be heard. It was Vanessa, Reggie, Beaver, Joan and Blessing returning in the Humber Super Snipe. After more explanations, hugs and tears, they gathered in front of the television to watch the rest of the big match.

***

Beaver and Reggie had found a corner of an enormous sofa and were sitting quietly next to Nobby, Yazmine, Loveday and GloGlo, who was still trying to process her mother being the head of Eighth Wonder Films. Cliff and Phoebe were sitting on chairs together at the back, holding hands and smiling. Vanessa had alerted her brother, Innocent, that Charlie needed some tender loving care, and she happily clocked him doting on Charlie on another sofa. Delice walked around the main hall with Alfie, talking quietly. Alfie was still limping from the physical rigours of being handcuffed, thrown in the back of the lorry and then on to the plane. Joan and Vesta were intently discussing Dynamite McQueen films, and Blessing and Vanessa were going over a plan to interview everyone while memories remained fresh. Even Fontaine sat there, although he just snorted and made catty comments about the footballers' shorts. Vanessa stood up and asked for no one to leave until they had been interviewed by her.

Vesta stood up suddenly. "Everybody, shush, the game is not over yet." The room became quiet until the final whistle blew. England had beaten Germany four goals to two! There was a great cheer. Loveday brought in champagne and corks were popped. Snack bowls were filled with crisps and everyone was temporarily jubilant.

"Right…" said Vanessa, "…before you get too sozzled on champagne, I need to ask my questions." Taking Delice first, Vanessa ushered each person into a side room and gradually pieced together the events of the day and the links between the syndicate, WI-5, the bus attack, the kidnapping, Delice's double life, Tolly's double life, the hijacking and the attempted attack on the World Cup Final. Once she was finished interviewing everyone, Vanessa stood in front of the television and welcomed questions from the group.

"What I still don't understand…" said Charlie, "… is why the focus on Cuffley Manor?"

"I think I have the answer," said Delice. "The syndicate grew out of the anonymous masked balls which were held at Cuffley Manor in the 1920s, where the fascist glitterati could have their fun while keeping their identities secret. I am sorry to tell you that it was all orchestrated by your grandparents. We also think the original head of the syndicate was one of your ancestors, and the previous head, until he died, was your father. My condolences to both you and Cliff for your loss at his recent death and for finding out this information at such an inopportune time."

"Oh my goodness, Dad was the head of an international crime group? As was his father before him?

And maybe his father before him? I knew we had been a bad lot in the past but not as so awful as is becoming apparent. Goodness, what a family! I know Dad always talked about his terrible upbringing, but he could never talk about the details. At least, we understand why," said Charlie ruefully.

"Do you think all this represents the end of the syndicate for once and for all?" asked Vanessa to Delice.

"Much as I would like to, I don't think we can assume the syndicate is toast. Crêpes Suzette will definitely have other plans. I do not think we have seen the last of her but she might need to pause to regroup. At least the new iteration of the syndicate clearly won't be led by the current Lord Cuffley," said Delice smiling at Cliff who blushed and nodded emphatically. "Don't forget that Tolly remains at large. I do think Suzette is pulling his strings with this mirage that he is the rightful heir to Cuffley Manor." Delice looked from Cliff to Charlie.

"Do you think those letters questioning our father's will came from Tolly and Suzette?"

"Yes, I do," said Delice gravely. "I think it was all part of the theatre of hate created by Suzette to keep Tolly focused unquestioningly on her insane plan. I think she has effectively brainwashed him. I imagine that she cooked up a warped story built on the proof his true father was Lord Cuffley and Tolly fell for it – hook, line and sinker. You know how the working class British male psyche works. What if the pauper was actually a prince?"

Charlie, Cliff and Vanessa looked at each other and gasped, "The book! *The Prince and the Pauper*."

"I am sorry if all this comes as such a shock," said Delice. "One piece of information that may make you all feel better is that I truly believe the main source of syndicate funding, the Eighth Wonder Film Company and the box office proceeds from the Dynamite McQueen films, will now be cut off. Although Suzette will want to continue the work of the syndicate for her own nefarious goals, she will not have access to any funds once we have closed all the relevant bank accounts which should happen Monday as soon as the bank opens."

"What do you mean?" asked Alfie. "No more Dynamite McQueen?" Fontaine looked shocked as the reality hit him that his career might be over.

"Don't you worry one bit, my darling," said Delice, patting Alfie's thigh. "I have learned a lot working at Eighth Wonder and have plans for the company to continue. We do need to keep the lucrative series running but for funding the force of good rather than evil. Anyway, can you imagine anyone telling Vesta that she is out of a job?" grinned Delice as she winked at Phoebe and Vesta, who magnanimously shrugged theatrically. The door slammed opened, grabbing everyone's attention. Ashwariya had returned and ran over to GloGlo for an embrace.

"I have a question," said Cliff as his arm shot up. "How was Aunt Elsie mixed up in it?"

Vanessa chimed in. "Our understanding is that Mrs Gascoyne was only on the periphery of all this. We think she might be the deceased Lord Cuffley's birth mother, and hence your paternal grandmother. I know that is quite a bombshell for you and your brother to hear, but Mrs MacGuffin tells me that WI-5 has been following this lead for some time apparently. Your father gave Mrs Gascoyne a photograph for safekeeping which featured Mr and Mrs MacGuffin in their younger days and a message to kill them, should they ever turn up at Cuffley Manor. I think it had something to do with Lord Cuffley thinking that if Mr and Mrs MacGuffin came to Cuffley Manor, it must be because he was about to be unmasked as head of the syndicate. When Miss Loveday MacGuffin turned up here almost two weeks ago, Mrs Gascoyne saw the likeness to her mother in the photo and flew into action without thinking it through. First by ham-fistedly contaminating Loveday's pork pie with rat poison…" At this, Cliff turned pale. "… and shooting at the Misses MacGuffin in their biplane."

Delice and Alfie exchanged knowing glances, realising that although Vanessa was correct, there was also another reason why Lord Cuffley would fear being unmasked.

Vanessa noticed their wordless exchange. "Actually, Mr and Mrs MacGuffin, perhaps you can clarify some questions about the photograph. Why were you photographed with the former Lord Cuffley? When exactly was the photo taken? And where?" Alfie looked at Delice and Delice looked at Alfie.

Delice answered slowly, "It is a long story, and it is getting late. Everyone is exhausted. Would it be possible to talk tomorrow? Then everyone will know everything."

Vanessa understood and agreed it was way past

everyone's bedtime. She did not think Alfie and Delice were much of a flight risk, especially with their daughters in attendance. "My superiors would prefer it if I could take you both down to Hertford police station to spend the night in the cells. However, can I receive your daughters' collective assurance that you will not leave the vicinity? Good. Tomorrow we can all meet back here at nine in the morning. Agreed? Is the time acceptable to Your Lordship?" Vanessa smiled at Cliff who nodded, stunned at all the information swirling around him.

Reggie, GloGlo, Loveday and Charlie also nodded as Cliff raised his hand and said, "Actually, I have another question, but it's for Phoebe," said Cliff as immediately he fell to one knee and said in a clear voice, "Will you be my proper girlfriend, Phoebe?" while handing her a cheese and onion hula hoop purloined from the bowl.

"Of course, I will, Clifford," said Phoebe who held out her hand so Cliff could put the hula hoop on her little finger, the only one it would fit. As a stunned Cliff had forgotten to get to his feet, she got down on her knees and gave him a big, long kiss.

"My goodness, he's a quick worker," said Reggie, nudging Beaver in the chest, "so much faster than you!"

Trapped in the Sky

A bleary Loveday was in the manor kitchen early to prepare Sunday breakfast for everyone under orders to attend Vanessa's meeting. With the shock of yesterday's near-death experience and the revelations about her mother still reverberating throughout her mind, her head swam with all the moving parts. Cooking was comforting.

At the aerodrome control tower, GloGlo and Ashwariya discussed what happened well into the night and continued over tea in the morning. The Sunday newspapers were full of rave reviews of the World Cup Final, England's historic win and the amazing stunts that occurred during the pre-game ceremonies. Everyone agreed that the opening ceremony's final stunt of the queen and Prince Philip arriving via parachute with the *supposedly* stolen trophy and saving all the Stadium's occupants from a plane crash was a denouement without parallel. A big celebratory, televised parade was occurring later that morning with the England football team travelling by open-top bus along The Mall to Buckingham Palace to be greeted by the queen.

Looking at the headlines from her maisonette, Reggie, who was also feeling pretty knocked out, commiserated to Beaver, "The poor queen, she must be exhausted. She hates football."

***

Everyone was starting to gather in the kitchen to help Loveday with the breakfast preparations, feeling a burgeoning sense of camaraderie after the events of the day before. Delice was refreshing the teapots. Yazmine was making coffee and Nobby was filling a jug with orange juice. Beaver was wrangling cutlery and crockery. Vesta was overseeing a big frying pan full of Braughing sausages, bacon and mushrooms. Fontaine was overseeing the toaster in a rare display of fellowship. He was hoping to get some of Loveday's homemade bread, nicely toasted and slathered in marmalade, before his driver arrived to whisk him away from all this tiresome drama which he was not at the centre of. Loveday was checking on the status of two huge trays of individual cheesy, breakfast Yorkshire puddings which were rising in the oven to Alfie's satisfaction. Even Tansy had made a surprise appearance and was wiping down the buffet table in the dining room, inexplicably wearing a fur coat. Phoebe was showing Cliff how a clapperboard worked.

The Dynamite McQueen cast and crew members made furtive, sidelong glances at Delice, still agog their fearsome boss, Babette Kohlrabi, was the mother of the MacGuffin sisters and was here pouring tea for them all in the kitchen. As he circled the breakfast trays, it dawned on Fontaine that this might be the end of his career with the Dynamite McQueen films, unless he could butter up Delice. Delice intuitively understood Fontaine's constant thinking about himself and his career. She came over and faced him, putting both hands on his shoulders, quietly saying, "I know all this news is shocking, Fonty. Do take a bit of time and collect yourself. And by the way, be a little nicer to my daughters; otherwise, I will see to it that you will never walk again, let alone work again." Fontaine blanched. He kept his eyes on the toaster, but nodded slowly without a sound.

***

Vanessa appeared in full police uniform while breakfast was underway. "*Ooh,* something smells good. No tea for me yet, thanks. I want to start by saying thanks to you all for being here bright and early this morning, and particularly to Mr and Mrs MacGuffin for keeping to your part of the bargain."

"You know," said Vesta, "this is like an Agatha Christie novel where all the suspects are gathered in one room for the final scene, where Poirot explains what happened and who did it."

"Except that here," said Vanessa with conviction, "it will be Mr and Mrs MacGuffin who will explain. By the way, what happened yesterday has everyone flustered all the way to the top of Scotland Yard. Expect a mass of police cars to arrive soon. I am the advance party so prepare yourselves to be here all day. Yes, even you Mrs Currie, Miss Navarra, Mr de Havilland, and Mr *errr…* what is your name?"

"Mr Abdelmahmoud. Everyone calls me Nobby."

"And Mr Abdelmahmoud. The police will want to interview everyone, again, and seal off that Speedbird plane before a forensic team can go over it. If I could get my questions answered before they all get here and sideline me, I would be most grateful. I would like to start with Babette Kohlrabi or whatever name you are going by today."

"My name is Mrs Alfie MacGuffin," said Delice with a wink at her husband.'

"If I may ask you to come over here, Mrs MacGuffin. Next up will be your husband."

***

As Vanessa and Delice moved towards a quiet corner of the room where two chairs were set up opposite each other and Vanessa set up her notepad and pen on a side table, Cliff and Charlie came in to tell everyone the television was on and warmed up to watch the World Cup winner's parade along The Mall towards Buckingham Palace. As everyone wandered in with their breakfasts, Charlie and Cliff waggled the aerial and twiddled the knobs before a hazy picture emerged of crowds at The Mall. As the image grew sharper, the commentator could be heard filling in time, as it was another hour before the parade would start. "And on this beautiful British summer's morn, a sunrise worthy of Wordsworth, Keats, Milton, Byron and Samuel Taylor Coleridge, we wait for the players to arrive for this historic occasion. Watch for their bus to arrive through the Admiralty Arch like a Roman army arriving after a victorious conquest. The crowds that have gathered are more numerous than were in Wembley Stadium yesterday evening. Last night was the biggest win for England since the Second World War, completing a long journey of patriotic revival this country has been waiting for. London is the new Xanadu and Wembley Stadium will forever be its stately pleasure-dome. Oh, it makes you proud. Proud to be British!"

A collective groan travelled around the room. Cliff turned the volume down to zero while the faint ringing of sirens off in the distance was getting louder. Scotland Yard was on its way to Cuffley Manor. Suddenly, a lorry was heard screeching to a halt on the gravel outside. A moment later, the main door to the manor burst open and Gaylord Cadwallader, Fontaine's driver, wearing his full glittery chauffeur regalia and fur collar, strode into the drawing room brandishing a gun. "Everyone sit down, hands behind your backs!"

"Tolly!" mouthed Loveday at Reggie, recognising his voice.

Alfie yelled out, "Tolliver, what the blazes!" Tolly grabbed a surprised Cliff and pulled him in front, placing the barrel of his gun to Cliff's temple with one hand and stuffing a gag into his mouth with the other. He threw a pile of handcuffs and rags on to the floor.

"Everyone, do as I say, otherwise Lord Cuffley gets it." Tolly fired the gun into the ceiling and a shower of plaster rained down.

"Oh no, you don't," said Phoebe, as she leapt forward brandishing her clapperboard. She brought the clapper down with a crash on Tolly's hand, knocking his gun to the ground, and grabbed Cliff. "Get your paws off my boyfriend, you vermin in ermine."

"Actually, it's oh no, YOU, don't," said Tansy, removing a gun from her voluminous coat and pointing it at Phoebe. Tolly picked up his gun, got back to his feet, pulled Cliff towards him and rested the gun's barrel against Cliff's temple.

Delice looked at Joan and Blessing before narrowing her eyes at Tansy. "Crêpes Suzette! We guessed you would be a part of all this. Your signature is all over the Ravenwood Studios explosion and your sad attempt at the Victoria and Albert Museum."

Everyone else in the room looked completely blank. Tansy fired a shot at Delice's feet.

"Shut up, you witch. You will soon be dead. This country will be brought to its knees in front of the world's media, and my boyfriend is going to end up being the lord and master of this aristocratic pile."

"Don't be ridiculous, there are too many people here witnessing your depravity."

"Don't worry yourself too much, no one is going to live to tell tales."

A collective gasp filled the room.

"You cannot claim a hereditary title and this estate without irrefutable evidence," said Delice playing for time, hoping Scotland Yard would arrive. "Suzette, late last year, did you murder Lord Cuffley?"

Suzette glared at Delice. "Once I discovered that my future father-in-law was the head of the syndicate, I needed him to die so I could take his place and Tolly could inherit. However, I did not murder Lord Cuffley. When I pulled my gun on him in that horrifically decorated Baltic Bedroom, he had a fatal heart attack, just like his sad sack mother, Elsie. It must have run in the family."

Tolly tried to maintain his composure while looking shocked at the revelation that Tansy had a hand in his father's death and that heart attacks run in the family. "We do have proof that I am the eldest son of Lord Cuffley," he continued through gritted teeth.

Tansy plucked a small bundle of envelopes from Tolly's breast pocket. "Here is the proof. Love letters written in Lord Cuffley's own hand to Tolly's mother, dated before and after Tolly was conceived."

"But that handwriting is not my dad's," moaned Cliff whose face was very close to the letters.

Reggie, who was sitting closest to Tansy, narrowed her eyes and spoke up. "That looks like my dad's writing!"

Tansy looked momentarily wrong-footed and confusion swept across Tolly's face.

"I think you had better tell them, Alfie," said Delice.

Alfie, recognising his own writing, turned pale and slowly said, "Tolly, I think I must be your father, as at the time of writing those letters, I was Lord Cuffley – before swapping identities with Cliff and Charlie's father during the war. I am so sorry, I never realised until now I had a son."

The MacGuffin sisters gasped as the sirens of Scotland Yard sounded more loudly.

"Mr MacGuffin," said Tolly, exchanging a perturbed

glance with Tansy, "I don't believe you. Before you annoy Suzette any more, would you be so kind as to handcuff everybody and stuff a rag in each of their mouths, and make it quick?" With Tansy's gun trained on him, Alfie did as he was told. Tansy handcuffed Alfie's wrists, and Tolly viciously stuffed a rag into his mouth. "Everyone outside and into the museum lorry."

With an imperceptible nod between Vanessa, Delice, Joan and Blessing, everyone marched in a line, out the door and up the ramp into the museum lorry. Reggie, GloGlo and Loveday looked at each other in confusion. What did their dad mean? The blast radius of his bombshell announcement meant they barely registered the guns being waved in their faces, and they followed the others distractedly. Delice and Fontaine were the last ones to get into the lorry. As Fontaine marched up the ramp, Tolly knocked him to the ground with the butt of his gun. "I've been wanting to do that for many months, you pathetic narcissist." Tansy forcefully pushed Delice into the lorry, who tripped over Fontaine and fell against everyone else, sending them into a heap on the floor. Tolly locked and bolted the rear door and the lorry's engine started up. With a squeal of tyres on gravel, Tolly floored the accelerator and headed into the woods, away from the main road and the advancing police cars, making for the aerodrome. The whole group imprisoned in the lorry fell against the rear doors as the vehicle accelerated up a steep sharp incline and came to an abrupt stop, sending everyone flying forwards. The all-encompassing sound of aeroplane engines starting up alerted them to being imprisoned in the loudly vibrating cargo hold of an aeroplane. GloGlo recognised the engine sound as being the film company's Skyfreighter cargo plane. The vibration and the noise intensified in the lorry, before suddenly, everything and everyone in the back was thrown around against the rear doors as if in a washing machine. The Skyfreighter was taking off.

***

What seemed like hours but was only five minutes later, Loveday groaned. Being one of the first forced into the lorry, she had banged her head when everyone fell on top of her and was knocked unconscious. The sound of the wind and engines was intense. Starting to come to, she realised her gag had caught on something sharp when she fell and had been almost ripped off, so at least she could breathe easily. Her hands were handcuffed in front of her, and she was lying on her back on top of a most uncomfortable sack of, what felt like, potatoes. Loveday became aware her nose must be bleeding, as she had a metallic taste in her mouth, dripping down her throat. Opening her eyes, she saw nothing but the darkness of the inside of the lorry. Her head throbbed with the most excruciating pain, and it was intensely cold. As her eyes adjusted to the gloom, she saw a sliver of light coming from the air vent in the roof, from the gaps between the lorry's rear door and its frame and via the peephole window behind the driver's head. She remembered she was back in familiar territory, tied up in the museum lorry.

Was it only yesterday? How had she gotten Tolly so wrong? She spat out the rest of the rag and attempted to speak. A muffled noise nearby alerted her to Joan. Loveday lent forward, and with her teeth, removed Joan's rag from her mouth. She did the same with whoever else was near enough to bite, who in turn then helped his or her neighbours.

Reggie took command and yelled as much as she could over the noise of the aircraft, which was at least somewhat muffled by being inside the lorry. "Situation report. We are locked in the museum lorry in the cargo hold of Eighth Wonder's Brabazon Skyfreighter, flying goodness knows where. Vanessa, does Scotland Yard know enough to follow this plane?"

"Well," said Vanessa loudly, "they know everything we discussed last night. I wrote my report and gave it in first thing this morning on my way to meet you all. It is highly likely that someone at Scotland Yard has read it, so they know about the syndicate, the bus attack, the fête attack and the foiled attempt to blow up the headquarters of WI-5 and sabotage the World Cup Final. On arrival at Cuffley aerodrome and finding no one there, they will see this huge plane taking off and put two and two together. But apart from following us by car and radar, they will be none the wiser as to where we are going or why. Just like we are none the wiser."

"Actually," chimed in Delice, "we are somewhat wiser. Gaylord or Tolly, as some of us know him, is the *Fleur de Lys Crime Syndicate* agent who hijacked the other plane yesterday. Masquerading as Tansy Brockett-Storrs,

Crêpes Suzette, the renowned Marquise of Disguise and Queen of Kaboom, has been using him to keep an eye on WI-5 and the film company."

Reggie had been biting her tongue. "That is all well and good, but our first priority should be getting out of here. We need to free ourselves from these handcuffs, escape from the lorry, overpower our captors and safely land this plane."

"Yes, you are right, Reg, absolutely," said Blessing. "Alfie, what do we know about the lorry? Is there anything we can use to escape?"

"There should be a toolbox in the back which might contain something sharp," said Alfie, "Unless Tolly has removed anything that might be useful. As our eyes adjust to the gloom, we may be able to find something."

Delice made a suggestion. "Reggie, can you use your teeth to take out one of my hairpins? We need to get one set of handcuffs off and then all the others will get done in a jiffy." Though they were still being shaken around like a fairground ride, Reggie was able to remove a pin from Delice's bun and pass it to her mother, who was able to shimmy into position and unlock Reggie's and Blessing's cuffs who then unlocked everyone else's.

Now that his hands were free, Fontaine suddenly came alive and stood up. "That bloody bastard hit me in the face. Nobody damages the de Havilland visage and lives to tell the tale. Just wait until I get my hands on him."

Once they were all free, Alfie staggered forward to the toolbox he could see at the bottom of the wall behind the cab and found a tin of WD-40, a pair of pliers, a Stanley knife, an adjustable spanner, a mallet, a set of screwdrivers, a torch and a shovel – the means of a possible escape.

"As long as the plane remains level, it is a good sign." said GloGlo standing up. "Now, as I am the tallest one here, let me peek at what can be seen through the peephole window behind the cab."

GloGlo moved forward. "Okay, I have a good view of the lorry's cab and most of the front half of the cargo compartment. The cab is empty. In front of us is the Brabazon Thunderbolt nose-to-nose with the lorry. It looks empty as well. There are also some boxes and equipment stacked against the fuselage."

Suddenly they all fell forward in a heap. "We have started descending. This angle feels far too steep to be a controlled landing!" yelled GloGlo as she continued to describe what could be seen through the peephole. "The door to the cockpit is opening. Tolly and Tansy are coming out. They have changed into flying suits. Tansy is putting on a parachute and arguing with Tolly. Tolly is walking towards us with a pile of parachutes. Good grief, Tansy just walloped Tolly in the back of the head and he has slumped onto the parachutes. Stay quiet, everyone. Get ready to leap on Tansy if she opens the back of the lorry."

Everyone held their breath as Tansy walked round to the back and checked the lorry's rear door to make sure it was secure. She could be heard moving to the back of the plane when the noise level inside the lorry became suddenly louder. A big whoosh of wind rattled the lorry's rear doors, and GloGlo could see boxes and pieces of equipment starting to move about in the front. "Tansy has opened the rear cargo door," said GloGlo, "Anything not tied down is in danger of being sucked out, including the heap of parachutes. She has just jumped out! Tolly is still lying comatose on the floor."

Due to the steep downward angle of the Skyfreighter, all the cargo was pressed against the front of the compartment, and the lorry was starting to roll forward against the nose cone of the Thunderbolt. The cockpit door was still open and no one was flying the plane.

"We need to get out of here," said Reggie urgently. "Tansy must have set the autopilot. GloGlo, if we can break you out of the lorry, you can try to gain control of this plane. We could force the door, go through the air vent in the roof, or break through the cab. Grab a tool and get working on it! The strongest to the door, the smallest to the vent and the rest of us to the cab."

Beaver, Charlie, Cliff and Alfie went at the door. Vesta was the smallest person so GloGlo hoisted her up to the roof with Vesta's legs supported by Delice and Loveday in a human pyramid. Nobby led the rest to attack the peephole window in the cab, which was not big enough for a body to get through but was big enough for an arm. The peephole window snapped first, after much pummelling with a hammer. Vesta was using the screwdriver to remove the air vent in the roof. The rear door had not budged an inch, even though the men had used all the brute force they could muster. Blessing surveyed the back door hinges and identified screws for Vanessa to undo.

GloGlo went to help the peephole team with her long arms. She was able reach through and touch the driver's seat but could not quite reach the dashboard. Feeling about on the seat, she found the keys and pulled them back through the peephole. Joan snatched them out of her hand and looked for a key to the back doors but to no avail. Vesta finally removed the air vent. "I think I can wriggle through," she said. "No upstart chauffeur is going get the better of me, my daughter nor her future husband, let alone my leading lady and man! Give me the keys."

Vesta removed the vent and was able to get both arms through the hole. Her shoulders were next and lastly her whole body. She was free.

The wind hit Vesta with full force, and she was able to stop herself from being blown off the lorry roof and out of the cargo door only by hanging on to the edge of the hole in the roof. "I need you to hold on to me, otherwise I will get blown out. Create a human chain, starting with the next smallest!" yelled Vesta.

Nobby, Beaver, Charlie and GloGlo created a cradle with their arms and hands. Next smallest was Reggie so she was hoisted up to the roof and grabbed Vesta's foot. Vesta, whilst lying flat on the roof, buffeted by the wind, shimmied towards the top of the cab with Reggie firmly holding on to her ankles. Phoebe was next, then Joan, then Alfie, then Vanessa, then Yazmine. Vesta hung down the side of the cab, grabbed the driver's door handle and opened the door. The human chain held firm. Suddenly, Vesta was inside the cab. She put the keys in the ignition, found the rear door release button and unlocked it. "Hang on tight!" she yelled.

The rear door flew up and the wind knocked everyone over. As it was too windy for anyone to climb out, they grabbed at each other to hold on. Delice yelled, "The cargo door button is on the fuselage over there. Make a human chain to reach it. The strongest should go first!" A second human chain, led by Beaver, emerged out of the rear of the lorry and crawled towards the open cargo door. Near the door, the wind was so strong it was difficult to get him close, but suddenly the wind dropped and the din abated as the cargo door began to close.

The lorry-roof-chain gang carefully helped each other down. Before the cargo door was completely closed, GloGlo ran towards the cockpit, grabbing handholds along the side of the fuselage for safety. Close to the cockpit door, she crawled over a large pile of boxes, sacks and crates that had gathered between the Thunderbolt and the bulkhead, and a groaning Tolly. From the cockpit doorway, central London stretched out below her, getting closer by the second.

Delice and Joan made it into the cockpit next as London's skyline was filling the windows at an alarming rate. GloGlo sat in the pilot seat and pulled back on the throttle to raise the Skyfreighter's nose up. Delice sat in the co-pilot seat and Joan leaned forward between the two. Beaver, Reggie, Vesta and Vanessa crammed in the space behind them, and the rest clustered around the doorway, holding on to whatever or whoever they could to remain upright.

GloGlo found the button marked autopilot and

toggled it to disengage. She and Delice both pulled back on the yoke as hard as they could. The cargo plane levelled off. Everyone let out a cheer and hugged whoever was closest. Yazmine laughed out loud. Fontaine wept uncontrollably. "Now, to find somewhere to land," said GloGlo.

"Let's head west and follow the Thames towards London Airport," suggested Joan, as Delice tried to get the radio to work. GloGlo was about to agree when the empty fuel light flashed and the fuel alert klaxon sounded. They could see the Tower of London approaching off to their right. GloGlo yelled, "Tansy has smashed the radio and we're running out of fuel. I don't think we are going to reach London Airport! We are going to have to land immediately. Where can we safely land a plane in central London?"

"Bollocks! Tansy ripped my radio off when I was handcuffed," cried Vanessa.

"And she removed all our compacts," said Joan. "Damn and blast."

Alfie had an idea. "The museum lorry has a small radio in the glove compartment for communicating with Morag." He dashed off to see if it was still there.

Reggie turned and called out after him. "Is there an A-Z in there as well? It might help us find somewhere long enough and wide enough to land this crate." A sudden blast of air sent Alfie tumbling forwards and the noise level rose. Reggie screamed, as she could see the cargo door was opening again. "GloGlo!"

Everyone looked back to see what was causing the

noise and the screaming. Delice realised she had hit the cargo door button when she was fiddling with the adjacent radio button. Immediately, she toggled the cargo door button back to its original position and the door closed. Alfie clambered over Tolly who grabbed his ankle causing him to fall forward.

"I am so sorry, Alfie," said Tolly before Reggie kicked him in the head and grabbed his gun from his pocket. Pointing it at Tolly, Reggie screamed at Alfie to head to the lorry.

Alfie grabbed an A-Z from the glove compartment, throwing it to Phoebe, who threw it Cliff, who threw it to Nobby, who threw it to Vanessa, who threw it to Reggie, who handed it to Delice. Alfie felt around the back of the glove compartment, and his hands closed on the radio. It crackled into life as he headed back to the cockpit.

"Mayday, mayday, Morag, are you there?"

Silence.

"Come on, Morag, you work every bleeding weekend, why not this one?"

And suddenly, a sound and a voice. "Oh hiya, Alfie petal flower! Morag here, having a wee break with a cuppa. I had nodded off on my Agatha Christie while listening to the radio. I've got the World Cup winners' parade on, and the commentator is doing such an awful job of filling in while waiting for the bus to arrive with the players. It's fearfully behind schedule. His droning voice put me to sleep, and I was dreaming about Andy Stewart."

"MAYDAY! MAYDAY!"

Wait. What? Mayday? What do you mean Mayday?"

"Morag, listen, there is not enough time to give you a detailed blow by blow but there is a crowd of us imprisoned in a Brabazon Skyfreighter cargo plane about to crash into London's West End. We are about to run out of fuel and need to know where to land."

"It is so obvious, Alfie. Use the landing strip built by the military to evacuate the Royal Family in an emergency." said Morag briskly.

"What, what do you mean, Morag? I don't understand," said Alfie.

"The Mall, my little cullen skink. It is probably a bit short, but it is your best bet. Hold on to your sporran, Alfie, and I'll measure it on the map."

"Morag, we don't have a lot of time," cried Alfie urgently.

"I estimate The Mall is two and half thousand feet long and one hundred and twenty-five feet wide, tree to tree. My Observer's Book of Aircraft will give me the Skyfreighter's specifications. I don't suppose you know if it is a Skyfreighter 1, 2, 3 or 4?"

"Morag!"

"It's a Skyfreighter 1!" yelled GloGlo.

"Here it is. The Brabazon Skyfreighter 1 has a wingspan of one hundred and fifteen feet, so you are all right there. You have five feet of clearance on either side. Loads of space. It looks like the Skyfreighter 1 needs eight thousand feet of road to land safely and you only have a third of that at best and… oh no that's taking off, just a second, let me figure it out. My little square sausage, the weight has to be… yes, okay, right. You will need three thousand feet of landing strip, so The Mall is your best bet"

At the controls, Delice and GloGlo were already descending in the direction of The Mall knowing there was likely no alternative. Delice realised the roadway had been cleared in anticipation for the World Cup parade of champions, and Morag confirmed the parade had not yet started. "No traffic or pedestrians." A lucky break.

Morag continued, "I have alerted the palace, which will get in touch with Her Majesty and call in reinforcements. The parade will not start for ten minutes, so the road will be clear. Can you get rid of any weight? Not you, Alfie pet, I mean the plane! Can you see Buck House?"

Delice tried to sound calm to help GloGlo keep her focus. "GloGlo, keep the new Post Office Tower hard on our right. The green patch up ahead must be St James Park on the left and Green Park on the right. Look, you can see the Palace and there's The Mall. Oh goodness, it doesn't look very wide, does it?"

"Morag says you have five feet clearance on either side of each wing but the length is five hundred feet short of perfection. Will you be able to reduce landing speed, GloGlo!" shouted Alfie who was starting to panic.

GloGlo gritted her teeth and ordered everyone to sit on the floor with their heads down, in crash position. "Mum, let's line up with the absolute centre of The Mall and I will bring the airspeed down to one hundred and fifty knots. Then full-on flaps as we pass over Admiralty Arch and undercarriage down."

The low fuel klaxon was tooting alarmingly louder

and louder. On approaching Admiralty Arch, GloGlo toggled the undercarriage button, and suddenly, there was a huge explosion. The plane juddered violently and dipped.

"What was that? Pull up... pull up!" yelled Joan. Looking down, they could see the road near Admiralty Arch littered with aeroplane wheel flotsam and undercarriage jetsam.

"Suzette must have installed incendiary devices in the undercarriage to stop any hope of a safe landing," said Delice.

GloGlo looked out the side windows. "And we have fires on both wings. Oh my goodness, here comes the palace, help me to pull up, Mum. Mum!"

They could see the royal family standing on the palace balcony, awaiting the parade and the changing of the guard, wide-eyed as they watched the aircraft aiming straight for them. The crowds lining The Mall screamed, running into the adjoining parks. GloGlo and Delice pulled on the yoke enough to pull the Skyfreighter up, so it missed the flagpole on the top of the palace. All the royal family members dove for cover except Princess Anne and Queen Elizabeth, who looked GloGlo straight in the eye and twirled her right hand, giving the universal sign for 'go around and try again'. Princess Anne made an emphatic V sign with both arms.

"Her Majesty just told us to circle round and try again," said Reggie with authority, "so we had better do it. GloGlo, you are doing brilliantly. We are with you all the way."

"Morag must have managed to get through to Madge," said Alfie.

Loveday looked at Reggie and Alfie with confusion. Even GloGlo gave her mother a quick glance before wheeling round.

"Queen Elizabeth is Madge – the head of WI-5," said Delice matter of factly. "Madge stands for Majesty."

"Okay, everyone, hang on. We just need enough fumes for one last attempt," said GloGlo.

All the television cameras, as well as the attention of the crowds along The Mall and those watching at home, were fixed on the Eighth Wonder Film Company Skyfreighter. Gasping and pointing, they saw the plane's wings on fire, as it turned to make another approach. And over the din, another collective gasp could be heard when a squadron of almost thirty double-decker buses charged through Admiralty Arch heading towards Buckingham Palace.

"Oh cripes, what are they doing?" moaned GloGlo who could see them in the distance. "The Mall is meant to be clear for another five minutes. Don't say the parade got going early! Dad, radio Morag."

"Wilco squadron leader," said Alfie. "Come in Morag, are you there?"

"I sure am, Alfie, my little Heart of Midlothian, I am sitting on my wee botty waiting for instructions. The radio and television commentators are having kittens at what you are doing, so stick with it."

"Madge gave us the signal to try again, so we are approaching a second time. However, we have no undercarriage, are out of fuel and all these buses have appeared. Has the parade started?" shouted Alfie gravely.

"Not to worry, Alfie dear, no, it has not. We know about your undercarriage. Twenty-nine buses of the WI-5 Routemaster Omnibus Formation Driving Team are coming to your rescue! Those buses are WI-5 engineered to perfection, and you are going to belly flop the Skyfreighter on to them. Risky, I know, but needs must. Fragrance can see you quite clearly. She is driving Drusilla, the lead bus. They are going to be your undercarriage by forming an arrow formation which matches your wingspan and fuselage," said Morag with glee. "All will be well if you match your speed to theirs, and they match their speed to yours so mind you do. Easy as pie!"

"Oh goodness," said Alfie, "I think Princess Anne signalled to GloGlo what you have just said."

"Oh yes, Anne is another WI-5 member, in training, of course. Equestrian division. I am in touch with Madge through the radio transmitter in her handbag. Why else do you think she lugs it around? She has to be in touch with WI-5 twenty-four seven, three six five," said Morag flatly as if it were patently obvious.

The colour drained from GloGlo's face as she lined up the Skyfreighter with The Mall. The cockpit klaxons were blaring furiously, and all the lights were blinking. "Here we go again. This is it. Come on, my beauty. Crash positions, everyone!" shouted GloGlo. They had one more shot. Suddenly, GloGlo felt strangely calm as her nerves fell away, and she focused on the task at hand.

Morag's voice came loudly through the radio. "GloGlo, the buses are almost at eighty miles per hour. Once you are directly over the top of them, reduce your speed to seventy knots and your altitude to fifteen feet four and half inches, exactly one foot above the height of a Routemaster."

"Cripes!" exclaimed Loveday. "Won't we squash the buses into red metal crêpes?"

Joan dismissed her concerns. "Don't be silly Loveday, these are not your regular buses, they are the WI-5 fleet, totally reinforced and modified. Their top floors can revolve as well as be released."

"Well, I'll be blowed," said Vesta. "Usually, you can't find a bus for love nor money when you want one and here there are twenty-nine, all coming along at once."

"Will everyone else please be quiet!" said GloGlo.

"What is our speed?" asked Delice.

"One hundred and thirty knots, and we need to slow to seventy in less than fifteen seconds," said GloGlo, swallowing her words as she gripped the yoke. She focused on the rear buses which could be seen in front of them, as the plane flew over Admiralty Arch. "Flaps are on maximum already, we are going to overshoot. Hold on, everyone, brace yourselves."

"Use the trees," said Delice.

"Pardon?" asked GloGlo.

"She is right, it is a brilliant idea," said Reggie. "Use the upper branches to slow us down, the wings should hold, it's British engineering after all! The trees along The Mall are seventy feet high. Drop down to thirty feet, and any branches longer than five feet will touch our wingtips."

And that was when GloGlo noticed that speed was the least of their troubles. "Look at all the lampposts and flagpoles all along The Mall, in front of the trees. They are going to slice our wings off and we will crash!"

Morag's voice was heard over the radio. "Don't worry GloGlo, Madge is on it." As Morag finished talking, the queen pulled a big red lever behind the balcony balustrade, and all the flagpoles along both sides of The Mall telescoped into the ground, and each set of lampposts hinged away from the road.

GloGlo shook her head at what she had just witnessed, pushed the control stick forward, dipped the Skyfreighter down to thirty feet and aimed at the rearmost bus. The airspeed indicator fell from one hundred and twenty to one hundred and ten to one hundred, as the flames from the plane's wings set the trees along The Mall on fire. GloGlo dropped the altitude down to twenty feet as the back of the buses filled the cockpit windows. "Still too fast… too fast. We are going to overshoot," roared GloGlo

"Open the rear cargo door and use the ramp as a drag," said Reggie. "It will hang down behind the last bus and drag along the ground. We can evacuate everyone down the ramp."

"Okay. Get ready, it is going to be a bumpy ride!" yelled Delice. "Ash, get ready to reverse the lorry out and down the ramp. Take Joan, Blessing, Vanessa, Charlie, Cliff and Phoebe with you. Drag Tolly into the back, if you can. Yazmine, you must have been in the Thunderbolt a thousand times, can you get it going? You can squeeze in four more people. Take Fontaine, Nobby, Vesta and Beaver.

"The MacGuffin family is staying to safely land the plane. We got everyone into this mess, and we will get ourselves out of it. The rest of you make your escape. It is your best chance."

As the cockpit emptied, GloGlo opened the rear cargo door and wind filled the inside of the plane. GloGlo could feel the cargo ramp starting to drag on the road surface. "100... 90... 80 knots. We're slowing down," said Reggie. "Dad, tell them to go immediately."

Ashwariya could see in the lorry's wing mirrors that the dragging ramp was causing sparks on the road. Putting the lorry into reverse, she gunned it expertly down the ramp through the sparks and smoke. Yazmine turned the Thunderbolt's ignition key and pressed her foot to the floor. Wincing, she yelled "Hold on to your hats, everybody!" as the Thunderbolt shot down the ramp and on to The Mall, narrowly avoiding the lorry which had skidded to one side. Both vehicles then turned and chased after the buses and the Skyfreighter.

"Both vehicles made it out safely, we can see them!" yelled Reggie who, with Loveday, had looked back to check through the open cargo door.

"Now we are getting too slow," groaned GloGlo.

"No problem," said Delice as she pushed the button to raise the ramp. The immediate reduction in drag caused the Skyfreighter to speed forward and cast a huge shadow over the buses' arrow formation. Twelve buses formed the arrowhead under the wings and seventeen formed the spine, two abreast, from nose to tail, with Fragrance and Drusilla in the lead.

"Come on, come on," urged GloGlo to the Skyfreighter, "74 knots… 73… 72…"

"The buses are under us. Down, down, NOW, GloGlo." GloGlo pushed the yoke forward and the Skyfreighter belly flopped onto the buses. "We're down, off engines!"

"Skyfreighter clear!" yelled Alfie to Morag.

"The Skyfreighter has landed!" declared Reggie. With the Palace fast approaching, the buses braked and started to skid with the weight of the plane, causing their top decks to start to buckle into the bottom decks. Two front tyres exploded. The MacGuffins assumed crash positions. Reggie sneaked a peek out of the cockpit window and wished she hadn't. Buckingham Palace with the gold Victoria Memorial in front was looming.

"We are not going to stop in time! Oh gosh, what's that?" asked Loveday looking right. She saw a Routemaster bus with blackened windows careening through Green Park straight towards them.

"Morag, enemy attack, three o'clock," shouted Delice into the radio.

***

In the Thunderbolt, Yazmine and Fontaine nodded at each other, having acted out this scene before at the denouement of *Dynamite McQueen and the Buckingham Palace*

Brouhaha. They had seen the enemy bus fast approaching on the right, and Yazmine had lined it up in the windscreen's gunsight. She pressed a big pink button on the Thunderbolt's dashboard, and a missile shot out from under the bonnet into the side of the bus. It exploded, and the bus skidded out of control. Fragrance veered to avoid the worst of the crash, with the enemy bus bouncing off Drusilla's backside. Beaver could see an ejector seat launch, sending the enemy driver high into the sky.

Fragrance spotted another enemy bus sprinting towards Drusilla, this time from St James Park. A gunsight appeared on her windscreen with a big white dot moving into the centre. Pressing a green button, Drusilla's radiator slid apart to reveal a missile. With her hands on the wheel, Fragrance stood and head-butted the big pink button on Drusilla's dashboard. The enemy bus took a direct hit and careened into the wreckage of the other bus. In the Thunderbolt, Dynamite McQueen raced around the phalanx of buses, bouncing up over curbs and dodging lampposts, to get ahead of the Skyfreighter and act as a barrier if needed.

Watching from the Skyfreighter, the MacGuffin sisters exchanged glances before looking ahead at the rapidly approaching Buckingham Palace. "We are not going to stop in time, heads down, hold on, everyone," roared Reggie.

The crowds roared as they realised the fleet of buses supporting the Skyfreighter, brakes screaming, were running out of road. Fragrance radioed the bus squadron. "On three, everyone make a 360-degree handbrake turn."

"Wilco, squadron leader."

"One-two-three, now!"

Waving and tossing flags into the air with excitement, thinking this must be part of the show, the throng of people watched incredulously as twenty-nine buses started to pirouette beneath the Skyfreighter's fuselage and wings like a Busby Berkeley omnibus ballet. Their rotating roofs allowed them to turn while keeping the Skyfreighter moving forward. In what appeared to be slow motion, the Skyfreighter's nose pushed the Victoria Memorial statue off its base, as the entire assembly smashed through Buckingham Palace's gates. The Skyfreighter finally came to rest, its nose gently touching the royal family's balcony.

***

Reggie yelled suddenly, pointing up. An armed parachutist was falling from the sky aiming straight for the palace balcony where the queen still stood stoically. It was Tansy.

In the Thunderbolt, which had reached the Palace, Yazmine and Fontaine put on helmets, tracked the parachuting Tansy into the centre of the Thunderbolt's crosshairs and hit the pink button on the dashboard. The Thunderbolt's roof slid back and both she and Fontaine shot up and out like human cannon balls, aiming for and smashing into Tansy right before she landed on the balcony, where all three rolled onto the floor tangled in a heap. Princess Anne leapt forward and struck Tansy in the face with her cherished, hardback copy of *Black Beauty*. Tansy struggled to get up and pushed past Princess Anne, knocking Fontaine to the ground and turning to face the queen. Suddenly, a high kick from Dynamite McQueen made contact with Tansy's chin and knocked her backwards. The queen smiled a little, as she removed a copy of Burke's Peerage from her handbag and smashed it over Tansy's head. "Noblesse oblige."

Delice opened the Skyfreighter's cockpit window and looked right into the face of the queen.

"We apologise, Your Majesty, for the unorthodox nature of our arrival and all the mess."

"It is all right, Delice, Morag filled me in. I suggest you come and have a strong cup of tea before the footballers arrive, guzzle the milk and hog the scones. And it looks like you have brought the family. How lovely."

Reggie managed to open the cockpit door, but the steep fifteen-foot drop to the palace courtyard gave her pause. Madge signalled to the guards below to remove their busbies and create a thick pile of black furry hats for the MacGuffin family to jump into. Reggie went first, followed by Loveday, Alfie, Delice and GloGlo, who, as captain of the Skyfreighter, thought she should be the last to disembark. Delice emerged from the cushioning pile, pulled Alfie up and kissed him. Ashwariya and Beaver ran up and dived into the mass of fur to grab GloGlo and Reggie respectively and plant big smackers on their lips. Loveday, not to be left out, grabbed one of the hatless guards and kissed him while an errant Union Jack flag floated down on top of them.

***

Later in the afternoon, after the queen had left to greet and congratulate England's winning football team, and Tolly and Tansy had been patched up and marched off to the cells, the MacGuffin family sat in the palace's west garden, drinking tea from Limoges cups. At last, Loveday, GloGlo and Reggie were able to grill Delice and Alfie.

"So, spill the beans, Mum and Dad. Dad, what was that story you told about being Lord Cuffley? Were you just trying to distract Tolly and Tansy, I mean Suzette? Everything seems to come back to the photograph found at Cuffley Manor with its note to murder you both should you ever appear. Tell us everything."

"It is a very long tale, my little knickerbocker glories," said Alfie sheepishly. "I think your mother is the best person to tell it. Delice?"

"Well," said Delice, "over thirty years ago, the first actress to play Dynamite McQueen was me." Delice paused, letting the information sink in. "And that really kick-started everything that led to you all being born and what happened today. If you think the events of the past few weeks have been exciting, in my humble opinion, they pale in comparison to how everything kicked off in the 1930s. So, if you're sitting comfortably, I shall begin the story of the original Queens of Kaboom."